Swimsuit

A complete list of books by James Patterson
is on pages 406–407. For previews of upcoming
books by James Patterson and more
information about the author, visit
www.JamesPatterson.com.

Swimsuit

A NOVEL

James Patterson

AND

Maxine Paetro

LITTLE, BROWN AND COMPANY

NEW YORK   BOSTON   LONDON

7/09

Little, Brown and Company
Hachette Book Group
237 Park Avenue, New York, NY 10017
Visit our Web site at www.HachetteBookGroup.com

First Edition: June 2009

Little, Brown and Company is a division of Hachette Book Group, Inc. The Little, Brown name and logo are trademarks of Hachette Book Group, Inc.

The characters and events in this book are fictitious. Any similarity to real persons, living or dead, is coincidental and not intended by the author.

Library of Congress Cataloging-in-Publication Data
Patterson, James.
  Swimsuit : a novel / by James Patterson & Maxine Paetro. — 1st ed.
    p. cm.
  ISBN 978-0-316-01877-7
 1. Models (Persons) — Crimes against — Fiction.   2. Kidnapping —
Investigation — Hawaii — Fiction.   3. Parent and child — Fiction.
4. Reporters and reporting — Fiction.   5. Hawaii — Fiction.
6. Psychological fiction.   I. Paetro, Maxine.   II. Title.
  PS3566.A822S87 2009
  813'.54 — dc22   2009006617

10 9 8 7 6 5 4 3 2 1

RRD-IN

Printed in the United States of America

To the home team:
Suzie and John, Brendan and Jack

Prologue

JUST THE FACTS

I KNOW THINGS I don't want to know.

A true psychopathic killer is nothing like your everyday garden-variety murderer. Not like a holdup guy who panics and unloads his gun into a hapless liquor store clerk, or a man who bursts into his stockbroker's office and blows his head off, and he's not like a husband who strangles his wife over a real or imagined affair.

Psychopaths aren't motivated by love or fear or rage or hatred. They don't feel those emotions.

They don't feel anything at all. Trust me on that one.

Gacy, Bundy, Dahmer, BTK, and the other all-stars in the twisted-killer league were detached, driven by sexual pleasure and the thrill of the kill. If you thought you saw remorse in Ted Bundy's eyes after he'd confessed to killing thirty young women, it was in your own mind, because what distinguishes psychopaths from all other killers is that they don't care at all. Not about their victims' lives. Not about their deaths.

But psychopaths can *pretend* to care. They mimic human emotion to pass among us and to lure their prey. Closer and closer. And after they've killed, it's on to the next new and better thrill, with no boundaries, no taboos, no holds barred.

I've been told that it's "distracting" to be so consumed by appetite, and so psychopaths screw up.

Sometimes they make a mistake.

You may remember back to the spring of 2008 when the swimsuit model Kim McDaniels was abducted from a sandy beach in Hawaii. No ransom demand was ever made. The local cops were slow, arrogant, and clueless, and there were no witnesses or informants who had any idea who had kidnapped that beautiful and talented young woman.

At that time, I was an ex-cop turned mystery writer, but since my last book had gone almost straight from the shipping carton to the remainder racks, I was a third-strike novelist doing the next best thing to writing pulp fiction.

I was reporting crime for the *L.A. Times,* which, on the upside, was how the highly successful novelist Michael Connelly got his start.

I was at my desk twenty-four hours after Kim went missing. I was filing yet another routinely tragic story of a drive-by fatality when my editor, Daniel Aronstein, leaned into my cube, said "Catch," and tossed me a ticket to Maui.

I was almost forty then, going numb from crime scene

fatigue, still telling myself that I was perfectly positioned to hook a book idea that would turn my life around one more time. It was a lie I *believed* because it anchored my fraying hope for a better future.

The weird thing is, when the big idea called me out—I never saw it coming.

Aronstein's ticket to Hawaii gave me a much-needed hit. I sensed a five-star boondoggle, featuring oceanfront bars and half-naked girls. And I saw myself jousting with the competition—all that, and the *L.A. Times* was picking up the tab.

I grabbed that airline ticket and flew off to the biggest story of my career.

Kim McDaniels's abduction was a flash fire, a white-hot tale with an unknown shelf life. Every news outlet on the planet was already on the story when I joined the gaggle of reporters at the police cordon outside the Wailea Princess.

At first, I thought what all the journos thought, that Kim had probably been drinking, got picked up by some bad boys, that they'd raped her, silenced her, dumped her. That the "Missing Beauty" would be top o' the news for a week, or a month, until some celebrity bigot or the Department of Homeland Security grabbed back the front page.

But, still, I had my self-delusion to support and an expense account to justify, so I bulled my way into the black heart of a vile and compelling crime spree.

In so doing, and not by my own devising, I became *part* of the story, selected by a profoundly psychotic killer with a cherished self-delusion of his own.

The book you hold in your hands is the true story of a skillful, elusive, and, most would say, first-rate monster who called himself Henri Benoit. As Henri told me himself, *"Jack the Ripper never dreamed of killing like this."*

For months now, I've been living in a remote location getting "Henri's" story down. There are frequent electrical brownouts in this place, so I've gotten handy with a manual typewriter.

Turns out I didn't need Google because what isn't in my tapes and notes and clippings is permanently imprinted on my brain.

Swimsuit is about an unprecedented pattern killer who upped the ante to new heights, an assassin like no other before or since. I've taken some literary license in telling his story because I can't know what Henri or his victims were thinking in a given moment.

Don't worry about that, not even for a second, because what Henri told me in his own words was proven by the facts.

And the facts tell the truth.

And the truth will blow your mind, as it did mine.

—Benjamin L. Hawkins
May 2009

Part One

THE CAMERA LOVES HER

Chapter 1

KIM McDANIELS WAS BAREFOOT and wearing a blue-and-white-striped Juicy Couture minidress when she was awoken by a thump against her hip, a *bruising* thump. She opened her eyes in the blackness, as questions broke the surface of her mind.

Where was she? What the hell was going on?

She wrestled with the blanket draped over her head, finally got her face free, realized a couple of new things. Her hands and feet were *bound*. And she was in some kind of cramped compartment.

Another thump jolted her, and Kim yelled this time, *"Hey!"*

Her shout went nowhere, muffled by the confined space, the vibration of an engine. She realized she was inside the trunk of a *car*. But that made no freaking sense! She told herself to *wake up!*

But she *was* awake, feeling the bumps for real, and so she fought, twisting her wrists against a knotted nylon rope that didn't give. She rolled onto her back, tucking her knees to her chest, then *bam!* She kicked up at the lid of the trunk, not budging it a fraction of an inch.

She did it again, again, *again,* and now pain was shooting from her soles to her hips, but she was still locked up, and now she was hurting. Panic seized her and shook her hard.

She was *caught.* She was *trapped.* She didn't know how this had happened or why, but she wasn't dead and she wasn't injured. She *would* get away.

Using her bound hands as a claw, Kim felt around for a toolbox, a jack or a crowbar, but she found nothing, and the air was getting thin and foul as she panted alone in the dark.

Why was she here?

Kim searched for her last memory, but her mind was sluggish, as if a blanket had been thrown over her brain, too. She could only guess that she'd been drugged. Someone had slipped her a roofie, but who? When?

"Hellllllllpppp! Let me out!" she yelled, kicking out at the trunk lid, banging her head against a hard metal ridge. Her eyes were filling with tears and she was getting mad now on top of being scared out of her mind.

Through her tears, Kim felt a five-inch-long bar just above her. It had to be the interior trunk release lever, and she whispered, *"Thank you, God."*

Chapter 2

KIM'S CLAW-HANDS TREMBLED as she reached up, hooked her fingertips over the lever, and pulled down. The bar moved—too easily—and it didn't pop the lid.

She tried again, pulling repeatedly, frantically working against her certain knowledge that the release bar had been disabled, that the cable had been cut—when Kim felt the car wheels leave the asphalt. The ride smoothed out, and that made her think the car might be rolling over sand.

Was it going into the ocean?

Was she going to drown in this trunk?

She screamed again, a loud, wordless shriek of terror that turned into a gibbering prayer, *Dear God, let me out of this alive, and I promise you*—and when her scream ran out, she heard music coming from behind her head. It was a female vocalist, something bluesy, a song she didn't know.

Who was driving the car? Who had done this to her? For what possible reason?

And now her mind was clearing, running back, flipping through the images of the past hours. She started to remember. She'd been up at three. Makeup at four. On the beach at five. She and Julia and Darla and Monique and that other gorgeous but weird girl, Ayla. Gils, the photographer, had been drinking coffee with the crew, and men had been hanging around the edges, towel boys and early morning joggers agog at the girls in their little bikinis, at the wonder of stumbling onto a *Sporting Life* swimsuit shoot right *there*.

Kim pictured the moments, posing with Julia, Gils saying, *"Less smile, Julia. That's great. Beautiful, Kim, beautiful, that's the girl. Eyes to me. That's perfect."*

She remembered that the phone calls had come after that, during breakfast and throughout the whole day.

Ten freaking calls until she turned off her phone.

Douglas had been calling her, paging her, stalking her, driving her crazy. It was Doug!

And she thought about earlier that night, after dinner, how she'd been in the hotel bar with the art director, Del Swann. It was his job to oversee the shoot and be her chaperone afterward. But Del had gone to the men's room, and somehow he and Gils, both of them as gay as birds, disappeared.

And she remembered that Julia was talking with a guy at the bar, and she'd *tried* to get Julia's attention but Julia wouldn't make eye contact...so Kim had gone for a walk on the beach....*And that was all she remembered.*

Her cell phone had been clipped to her belt but switched off. And now she was thinking that Doug had flipped out, rage-aholic that he was—stalker that he'd become. Maybe he'd paid someone to put something into her drink.

She was getting it together now. Brain working fine.

She shouted, *"Douglas? Dougie?"*

And then, as though God Himself had finally heard her calling, *a cell phone rang inside the trunk.*

Chapter 3

KIM HELD her breath and listened.

A phone rang, *but it wasn't her ring tone.* This was a low-pitched burr, not four bars of Weezer's "Beverly Hills," but if it was like most phones, it was programmed to send calls to voice mail after three rings.

She couldn't let that happen!

Where was the damned phone?

She fumbled with the blanket, ropes chafing her wrists. She reached down, pawed at the flooring, felt the lump under a flap of carpet near the edge, bumped it farther away with her clumsy...*oh no!*

The second ring ended, the third ring was starting, and her frenzy was sending her heart rate out of control when she grasped the phone, a thick, old-fashioned thing, clutched it with her shaking fingers, sweat slicking her wrists.

She saw the illuminated caller ID number, but there was no name, and she didn't recognize the number.

But it didn't matter *who* it was. Anyone would do.

Kim pushed the Send button, pressed the phone to her ear, called out hoarsely, "Hello? *Hello? Who's there?*"

But instead of an answer, Kim heard singing, this time Whitney Houston, "I'll al-ways love you-ou-ou" coming from the car stereo only louder and more clearly.

He was calling her from the front seat of the car! She shouted over Whitney's voice, "Dougie? Dougie, what the hell? *Answer me.*"

But he didn't answer, and Kim was quaking in the cramped trunk, tied up like a chicken, sweating like a pig, Whitney's voice seeming to taunt her.

"Doug! What do you think you're doing?"

And then she knew. He was showing her what it was like to be ignored, teaching her a lesson, but *he wouldn't win.* They were on an island, right? How far could they go?

So Kim used her anger to fuel the brain that had gotten her into Columbia premed, thinking now about how to turn Doug around. She'd have to play him, say how sorry she was, and explain sweetly that he had to understand *it wasn't her fault.* She tried it out in her mind.

See, Dougie, I'm not allowed to take calls. My contract strictly forbids me to tell anyone where we're shooting. I could get fired. You understand, don't you?

She'd make him see that even though they'd broken up, that even though he was *crazy* for what he was doing to her, *criminal* for God's sake, he was still her darling.

15

But—and this was her plan—once he gave her an opportunity, she'd knee him in the balls or kick in his kneecaps. She knew enough judo to disable him—as big as he was. Then she'd run for her life. And then the cops would bury him!

"Dougie?" she yelled into the phone. "Will you please answer me? Please. This really isn't funny."

Suddenly the music volume went down.

Once again, she held her breath in the dark and listened over the pulse booming in her ears. And this time, a voice spoke to her, a *man's voice*, and it was warm, almost loving.

"Actually, Kim, it *is* kind of funny, and it's kind of wonderfully romantic, too."

Kim didn't recognize the voice.

Because it wasn't Doug's.

Chapter 4

A NEW KIND of fear swept through Kim like a cold fire, and she started to pass out. But she got a grip on herself, squeezed her knees together hard, bit her hand, and kept herself awake. And she replayed the voice in her head again.

"*It is kind of funny, and it's kind of wonderfully romantic, too.*"

She didn't know that voice, didn't know it at all.

Everything she'd envisioned a moment ago, Doug's *face*, his *weakness* for her, her learning how to win him over when he got out of control—that was all *gone*.

Here was the new truth.

A complete stranger had tied her up and thrown her into the trunk of his car. She'd been *kidnapped*—but why? Her parents weren't rich! What was he going to do to her? How was she going to escape? She was—but how?

Kim listened in silence before asking, "Who is this?"

The voice was mellow and calm when he spoke again.

"Sorry to be so rude, Kim. I'll introduce myself in a minute or two. It won't be very long now. And don't worry. Everything's going to be fine."

The line went dead.

Kim blanked when the phone call cut off. It was as if her mind had been disconnected, too. Then the thoughts tumbled in. She found hope in the stranger's reassurance. So she clung to it. He was acting…nice. He'd said, *"Everything's going to be fine."*

The car took a hard left, and Kim rolled against the side of the trunk, braced her feet against the wall of the compartment. And she realized that she was still gripping the phone!

She held the keypad close to her face. She could barely read the numbers by the pale light of the faceplate, but she still managed to punch in 911.

She listened to the three rings, then four, and then the operator's voice. "Nine-one-one. What's your emergency?"

"My name is Kim McDaniels. I've been—"

"I didn't get that. Please spell your name."

Kim rolled forward as the car come to a stop. Then the driver's side door slammed—and she heard the key turning in the trunk lock.

Kim gripped the phone tighter, scared that the operator's voice would be loud enough to give her away, but more scared that if she hung up she'd lose the GPS connection between herself and the police, her best hope of rescue.

The phone call could be traced. That was correct, wasn't it?

"I've been kidnapped," she spat.

The key was turned, left and right, the lock not quite unlatching, and in that fraction of a minute Kim desperately revisited her plan. It was still good. Say her kidnapper wanted to have sex with her. She could survive that, obviously, but she had to be smart, make him her friend, remember everything so she could tell the police.

The trunk lid lifted, and moonlight spilled over her feet.

And Kim's plan to seduce her abductor flew out of her mind. She hauled back her knees and kicked hard at the man's thighs. He jumped back, avoiding her feet, and before she could see his face, the blanket was thrown over hers, the cell phone ripped from her hands.

Then — there was the prick of a needle in her thigh.

Kim heard his voice as her head rolled back and the light faded.

"Fighting me is pointless, Kim. This isn't about you and me. It's a whole lot bigger than that, trust me. But, then, why should you trust me?"

Chapter 5

KIM CAME to consciousness.

She was lying faceup on a bed inside a glowing, yellow-painted room. Her arms were tied and anchored behind her head. Her legs, a long way away, were roped to the metal frame of a bed. A white satin sheet was tucked under her chin, draped between her legs. She couldn't be a hundred percent sure, but she thought she was naked under the sheet.

She pulled at the rope holding her arms behind her, and she got terrifying glimmers of what might happen to her next, nothing that matched the man's promise that "everything's going to be fine." Then she heard grunts and squeals coming from her throat, sounds she'd never made before.

She got nowhere with the ropes, so she lifted her head

and as best she could, looked around the room. It seemed unreal, like a stage set.

To the right side of the bed were two closed windows, hung with gauzy curtains. There was a table beneath the windows loaded with lit candles of all heights and colors, and there were tropical flowers.

Birds of paradise and ginger—very masculine to her eyes, sexual really—stood erect in a vase beside the bed.

Another look around, and she took in cameras, two of them. Professional grade, mounted on tripods on either side of her.

She saw lights on stands and a sound boom she hadn't noticed at first, positioned above her head.

She became aware of the roar of surf, loud, as if the waves were crashing against the walls. And there she was, pinned like a butterfly at the center of it all.

Kim took in a deep breath, and screamed, "HELP MEEEEEE."

When her scream faded, a man's voice came from behind her head. "Hey, hey. Kim. No one can *hear* you."

Kim turned her head harder to the left, stretched her neck with tremendous effort, and saw a man sitting in a chair. He was wearing earphones, and he pulled them down from his head so that they were resting on his collarbones.

Her first look at the man who'd taken her.

She didn't know him.

He had medium-length hair, was maybe in his late thirties. He had regular features that could almost be called handsome. He was muscular, wearing form-fitting, expensive-looking clothes, a gold watch she'd seen in *Vanity Fair*. Patek Philippe. The man in the chair looked to her like the actor who played the lead in the latest James Bond movie, Daniel Craig.

He put the earphones back on and closed his eyes as he listened. He was *ignoring* her.

"Hey! Mister! *I'm talking to you!*" Kim shouted.

"You should hear this," the man said. He named the music, told her that he knew the artist, that this was a first studio cut.

He stood, brought the headphones over to her, and put one of the earpieces against her ear.

"Isn't that great?"

Kim's escape plan evaporated. She'd missed her big chance at seduction. She thought, *Whatever he wants to do, he's going to do.* But she could still beg for her life. Tell him it will be more fun if she participated — but her mind was scrambled from the injection he gave her and she felt woozy, too weak to move.

She looked into the man's light gray eyes, and he looked back as though he felt affection for her. Maybe she could use that. She said, "Listen to me. People know I'm missing. Important people. Life Incorporated. You've heard of them? I have a curfew. All the models do. The police are already looking for me…"

"James Blond," as she suddenly thought of him, said to her, "I wouldn't worry about the police, Kim. I was very careful." He sat beside her on the bed, placed his hand on her cheek admiringly. Then he put on blue latex gloves.

He lifted something from a nail in the wall, a mask of some sort, and when he put it on, his features became distorted. And *very* scary.

"What are you doing? What are you doing?"

Kim's screams ricocheted around the small room. The man said, "That was *great*. Could you do that again? Are you ready, Kim?"

He walked around to each of the cameras, checked the angle through the lenses, turned them on. The bright lights blazed.

Kim followed the blue gloves as they whisked the satin sheet away from her body. It was cool in the room, but the sweat immediately beaded up on her skin. She knew.

He was going to rape her.

"You don't have to do this," she said.

"I *do*."

Kim started keening, a whimper that rose to a cry. She turned her face away, stared toward the closed windows, heard the nameless stranger's belt buckle hit the floor. She began sobbing without reservation as she felt the drag of latex running over her breasts, the feeling in her groin as he opened her with his mouth, the blunt feel of him pushing his way in, her muscles tightening to stop him from entering her.

His breath was soft against her face as he spoke into her ear.

"Just go along with this, Kim. Just go along. I'm sorry, but it's a job I'm doing for a lot of money. These people watching are big fans of yours. Try to understand."

"I want you to *die*," she said. She bit down on his wrist, drawing blood, and then he hit her, slapped her hard on each of her cheeks. Tears made her skin sting.

She wanted to pass out, but she was still conscious, very much under the blond stranger's body, hearing him grunting, feeling—too much. So she did her best to block out everything but the sound of the waves and thoughts about what she would do to him when she got away.

Chapter 6

WHEN KIM WOKE UP she was sitting in a bathtub of warm water, leaning with her back against the sloping rim, her hands tied under the suds.

The blond stranger was on a stool beside her, washing her with a sea sponge as naturally as though he'd bathed her many times before.

Kim's stomach heaved, and she vomited bile into the tub. The stranger stood her up in one powerful swoop, saying "Alley Oops," and she noticed again how strong he was. This time she heard a hint of an accent but couldn't place it. Maybe Russian. Or Czech. Or German. Then he pulled the bathtub plug and turned on the shower.

Kim swayed under the spray, and he held her up, supported her body as she cried out and hit at him, trying to kick but losing her footing. She started to go down, and he caught her again, laughing, saying, "You're a little something special, aren't you?"

Then he wrapped her in very plush white towels, swaddled her like a baby. When he settled her on the closed toilet seat, he held out a glass of something for her to drink.

"Take this," he said. "It will help you. Honestly it will."

Kim shook her head, said, "Who are you? Why are you doing this to me?"

"Do you want to remember this evening, Kim?"

"You've got to be kidding, you effing pervert."

"This drink will help you forget. And I want you to be asleep when I take you home."

"When are you taking me home?"

"It's almost over," he said.

Kim raised her hands toward him, noticing that the rope binding her wrists together was different now. It was dark blue, possibly silk, and the pattern of knots was intricate, almost beautiful. She took the glass from him and emptied it down.

Next the stranger asked her to bend her head forward. She did, and he towel-dried her hair. Then he brushed it, making tendrils and curls with his fingers, and he brought bottles and brushes out of the long drawer of the vanity surrounding the sink.

He applied makeup to her cheeks and lips and eyes with a deft hand, dabbing a little concealer at a raw place near her left eye, wetting the brush with his tongue, blending the foundation in, saying, "I'm very good at this, don't worry."

He finished his work, then reached his arms around and

under her, lifted her towel-wrapped body, and carried her into the other room.

Kim's head lolled back as he placed her on the bed. She was aware that he was dressing her, but she didn't assist him at all as he pulled a bikini bottom up her thighs. Then he tied the strap of the swimsuit top behind her back.

The suit looked to Kim a lot like the Perry Ellis she'd been wearing toward the end of the shoot. Red with a silver sheen. She must have mumbled, "Perry Ellis," because James Blond said, "It's even better. I picked this out myself when I was in Saint-Tropez. I got it just for you."

"You don't know me," she said, the words pouring sideways out of her mouth.

"Everyone knows you, honey. Kimberly McDaniels. What a beautiful name, too." He moved her hair to one side and knotted a second swimsuit tie behind her neck, tied a bow, apologized if he'd pulled at her hair.

Kim wanted to make a remark, but she forgot what she was going to say. She couldn't move. She couldn't scream. She could barely keep her eyes open. She looked into the pale gray eyes that caressed her.

He said, "Stunning. You look so beautiful for your close-up."

She tried to say, "Screw you," but the words blended together and came out as a long, tired sigh. "Scoooooooo."

Chapter 7

INSIDE A PRIVATE LIBRARY on the other side of the world, a man named Horst sat back in his leather-upholstered armchair and watched the large HD screen beside the fireplace.

"I like the blue hands," he said to his friend Jan, who was swirling his drink in a chunky glass. Horst turned up the volume with the remote.

"It's a nice touch," Jan agreed. "With the swimsuit, and the skin, she is as American as apple pie. Are you quite sure you *saved* the video?"

"Of course I did. Look now," said Horst. "Watch now how he quiets his animal."

Kim was lying on her stomach. She was perfectly hogtied, her hands behind her back and tethered to her legs, which were bent up at the knees. Along with the red swimsuit, she was wearing shiny black patent leather shoes with five-inch heels and slick red soles. They were top designer shoes, Christian Louboutin, the very best, and Horst thought they looked more like toys than shoes.

Kim was pleading with the man his audience knew as "Henri." She was sobbing softly. "Please, please untie me. I'll play my role. It will be even better for you, and I'll never tell *anyone.*"

Horst laughed, said, "That is the truth. She will never tell anyone."

Jan put down his glass, then said with edgy impatience, "Horst, please roll back the video."

On screen, Kim said again between sobs, "I'll never tell *anyone.*"

"That's good, Kim. Our secret, eh?"

Henri's face was transformed by the plastic mask and his digitally altered voice, but his performance was strong and his audience was avid. Both men leaned forward in their chairs, watched as Henri stroked Kim, rubbed her back, and murmured to her until she stopped whimpering.

And then, as she seemed to go to sleep, he straddled her body, wrapping his hand in the young woman's long, damp, yellow hair.

He lifted her head from the flat of the bed, pulling hard enough that Kim's back arched, and the force of the pull made her cry out. Possibly she saw that he'd picked up a serrated knife with his right hand.

"Kim," he said. "You'll wake up soon. And if you ever remember this, it will seem like a bad dream."

The beautiful young woman was surprisingly quiet as

Henri made the first deep cut across the back of her neck. Then, as the pain caught up with her—hauled her violently out of her stupor—her eyelids flew open and a curdled scream erupted from her painted mouth. She wrenched her body as Henri sawed and cross-sawed through her muscles, *and then the scream cut out,* leaving an echo as Henri completely severed Kim's head from her body in three long strokes.

Arterial blood spurted against the yellow walls, emptied onto the satin bedsheets, ran down the arm and loins of the naked man kneeling over the dead girl.

Henri's smile was quite visible through the plastic mask as he held Kim's head by her hair so that it swung gently as it faced the camera. A look of pure despair was still fixed on her beautiful face.

The killer's digitized voice was eerie and mechanical, but Horst found it extremely satisfying.

"I hope everybody's happy," Henri said.

The camera held on Kim's face for another long moment and then, although the audience wanted more, the screen went black.

Part Two

FLY BY NIGHT

Chapter 8

A MAN STOOD at the edge of a lava-rock seawall staring out at the dark water and at the clouds turning pink as dawn stormed Maui's eastern shore.

His name was Henri Benoit, not his real name, but the name he was using now. He was in his thirties with medium-length blondish hair and light gray eyes, and he stood at about six feet tall in his bare feet. He was shoeless now, his toes half-buried in the sand.

His white linen shirt hung loosely over his gray cotton pants, and he watched the seabirds calling out as they skimmed the waves.

Henri thought those birdcalls could have been the opening notes of another flawless day in paradise. But before the day had even begun, it was down the crapper.

Henri turned away from the ocean and jammed his PDA

into a trouser pocket. Then, as the wind at his back blew his shirt into a kind of spinnaker, he strode up the sloping lawn to his private bungalow.

He swung open the screened door, crossed the lanai and the pale hardwood floors to the kitchen, poured himself a cup of Kona java. Then out again to the lanai, where he sank down into the chaise beside the hot tub and settled in to think.

This place, the Hana Beach Hotel, was at the top of his A-list: exclusive, comfortable, no TV or even a telephone. Surrounded by a few thousand acres of rain forest, perched on the coast of the island, the unobtrusive cluster of buildings made a perfect haven for the very rich.

Being here gave a man a chance to relax fully, to be whoever he truly was, to realize his essence as a human.

The cell phone call from Europe had shot his relaxation all to hell. The conversation had been brief and essentially one-way. Horst had delivered both the good and bad news in a tone of voice that attacked Henri's sense of free agency with the finesse of a shiv through a vital organ.

Horst had told Henri that the job he had done had been well received, but there were *issues*.

Had he chosen the right victim? Why was Kim McDaniels's death the sound of one hand clapping? Where was the press? Had they really gotten all they'd paid for?

"I delivered a brilliant piece of work," Henri had snapped. "How can you deny it?"

"Watch the attitude, Henri. We're all friends, yes?"

Yes. Friends in a strictly commercial enterprise in which

34

one set of amigos controlled the money. And now Horst was telling him that his buddies weren't quite happy enough. They wanted *more*. More twists. More action. More clapping at the end of the movie.

"Use your imagination, Henri. Surprise us."

They would pay more, of course, for additional contracted services, and after a while the prospect of more *money* softened the edges of Henri's bad mood without touching the core of his contempt for the *Peepers*.

They wanted more?

So be it.

By the time his second cup of coffee was finished, he had mapped out a new plan. He dug a wireless phone out of his pocket and began making calls.

Chapter 9

THAT NIGHT SNOW FELL LIGHTLY on Levon and Barbara McDaniels's house in Cascade Township, a wooded suburb of Grand Rapids, Michigan. Inside their efficient but cozy three-bedroom brick home, the two boys slept deeply under their quilts.

Down the hall, Levon and Barbara lay back-to-back, soles touching across the invisible divide of their Sleep Number bed, their twenty-five-year connection seemingly unbroken even in sleep.

Barbara's night table was stacked with magazines and half-read paperbacks, folders of tests and memos, a crowd of vitamin supplements around her bottle of green tea. *Don't worry about it, Levon, and please don't touch anything. I know where everything is.*

Levon's nightstand favored his left brain to Barb's right:

his neat stack of annual reports, annotated copy of *Against All Reason,* pen and notepad, and a platoon of electronics—phones, laptop, weather clock—all lined up four inches from the table's edge, plugged into a power strip behind the lamp.

The snowfall had wrapped the house in a white silence—and then a ringing phone jarred Levon awake. His heartbeat boomed, and his mind reeled in instant panic. *What was happening?*

Again the phone rang, and this time Levon made a grab for the landline.

He glanced at the clock, which read 3:14 a.m., and wondered who the hell would be calling at this hour. And then he knew. It was Kim. She was five hours behind them. He figured she'd gotten that mixed up somehow.

"Kim? Honey?" Levon said into the mouthpiece.

"Kim is gone," said the male voice in Levon's ear.

Levon's chest tightened, and he couldn't catch his breath. Was he having a heart attack? "Sorry? What did you say?"

Barb sat up in bed, turned on the light.

"Levon?" she said. "What is it?"

Levon held up a hand. *Give me a second.* "Who is this?" he asked, rubbing his chest to ease the pain.

"I only have a minute, so listen carefully. I'm calling from Hawaii. Kim's disappeared. She's fallen into bad hands."

Levon's fear filled him from scalp to toes with a cold terror. He clung to the phone, hearing the echo of the man's voice: *"She's fallen into bad hands."*

It made no sense.

"I don't get you. Is she hurt?"

No answer.

"Hello?"

"Are you listening to what I'm saying, Mr. McDaniels?"

"Yes. Who is this speaking, please?"

"I can only tell you once."

Levon pulled at the neck of his T-shirt, trying to decide what to think. Was the man a liar, or telling the truth? He knew his name, phone number, that Kim was in Hawaii. How did he know all that?

Barb was asking him, *"What's happening? Levon, is this about Kim?"*

"Kim didn't show up at the shoot yesterday morning," said the caller. "The magazine is keeping it quiet. Crossing their fingers. Hoping she'll come back."

"Have the police been called? Has someone called the police?"

"I'm hanging up now," said the caller. "But if I were you, I'd get on the next plane to Maui. You and Barbara."

"Wait! Please, wait. How do you know she's missing?"

"Because I did it, sir. I saw her. I liked her. I took her. Have a nice day."

Chapter 10

"WHAT DO YOU *WANT?* Tell me what you *want!*"

There was a *click* in Levon's ear followed by a dial tone. He toggled the directory button, read "Unknown" where there should have been a caller ID.

Barb was pulling at his arm. "Levon! *Tell me! What's happened?*"

Barb liked to say that she was the flamethrower in the family and that he was the fireman—and those roles had become fixed over time. So Levon began to tell Barb what the caller had said, strained the fear out of his voice, kept to the facts.

Barb's face reflected the terror leaping inside his own mind like a bonfire. Her voice came through to him as if from a far distance. "Did you *believe* him? Did he say where she *was?* Did he say what happened? My God, what are we talking about?"

"All he said is she's gone..."

"She never goes anywhere without her cell," Barb said, starting now to gasp for breath, her asthma kicking in.

Levon bolted out of bed, knocked things off Barb's night table, spilling pills and papers all over the carpet. He picked the inhaler out of the jumble, handed it to Barb, watched her take in a long pull.

Tears ran down her face.

He reached out his arms for her, and she went to him, cried into his chest, "Please...just call her."

Levon snatched the phone off the blanket, punched in Kim's number, counted out the interminable rings, two, then three, looking at the clock, doing the math. It was just after ten at night in Hawaii.

Then Kim's voice was in his ear.

"Kim!" he shouted.

Barb clapped her hands over her face in relief—but Levon realized his mistake.

"It's only a message," he said to Barb, hearing Kim's recorded voice. "Leave your name and number and I'll call you back. Byeeee."

"Kim, it's *Dad*. Are you okay? We'd like to hear from you. Don't worry about the time. Just call. Everybody here is fine. Love you, honey. Dad."

Barb was crying. "Oh, my God, Oh, my God," she repeated as she balled up the comforter, pressing it to her face.

"We don't know anything, Barb," he said. "He could be some moron with a sick sense of humor—"

"Oh, God, Levon. Try her hotel room."

Sitting at the edge of the bed, staring down at the nubby carpet between his feet, Levon called information. He jotted down the number, disconnected the line, then dialed the Wailea Princess in Maui.

When the operator came on, he asked for Kim McDaniels, got five distant rings in a room four thousand miles away, and then a machine answered. "Please leave a message for the occupant of Room Three-fourteen. Or press zero for the operator."

Levon's chest pains were back and he was short of breath. He said into the mouthpiece, "Kim, call Mom and Dad. It's important." He stabbed the 0 button until the lilting voice of the hotel operator came back on the line.

He asked the operator to ring Carol Sweeney's room, the booker from the modeling agency, who'd accompanied Kim to Hawaii and was supposed to be there as her chaperone.

There was no answer in Carol's room, either. Levon left a message: "Carol, this is Levon McDaniels, Kim's dad. Please call when you get this. Don't worry about the time. We're up. Here's my cell phone number..."

Then he got the operator again.

"We need help," he said. "Please connect me to the manager. This is an emergency."

Chapter 11

LEVON McDANIELS WAS SQUARE-JAWED, just over six feet, a muscular 165 pounds. He had always been known as a straight shooter, decisive, thoughtful, a good leader, but sitting in his red boxers, holding a dinky cordless phone that didn't connect to Kim — he felt nauseated and powerless.

As he waited for hotel security to go to Kim's room and report back to the manager, Levon's imagination fired off images of his daughter, hurt, or the captive of some freaking maniac who was planning God only knew what.

Time passed, probably only a few minutes, but Levon imagined himself rocketing across the Pacific Ocean, bounding up the stairs of the hotel, and kicking open Kim's door. Seeing her peacefully asleep, her phone switched off.

"Mr. McDaniels, Security is on the other line. The bed is

still made up. Your daughter's belongings look undisturbed. Would you like us to notify the police?"

"Yes. Right away. Thank you. Could you say and spell your name for me?"

Levon booked a room, then phoned United Airlines, kept pressing zeros until he got a human voice.

Beside him, Barb's breathing was wet, her cheeks shining with tears. Her graying braid was coming undone as she repeatedly pushed her fingers through it. Barb's suffering was right out in the open, and she didn't know any other way. You always knew how she felt and where you stood with Barb.

"The more I think about it," she said, her voice coming between jerky sobs, "the more I think it's a lie. If he took her... he'd want money, and he didn't ask for that, Levon. So... *why would he call us?*"

"I just don't know, Barb. It doesn't make sense to me either."

"What time is it there?"

"Ten thirty p.m."

"She probably went for a ride with some cute guy. Got a flat tire. Couldn't get a cell phone signal, something like that. She's probably all worked up about missing the shoot. You *know* how she is. She's probably stuck somewhere and *furious* with herself."

Levon had held back the truly terrifying part of the phone call. He hadn't told Barb that the caller had said that Kim had fallen into "bad hands." How would that help Barb? He couldn't bring himself to say it.

43

"We have to keep our heads on straight," he said.

Barb nodded. "Absolutely. Oh, we're going over there, Levon. But Kim is going to be as mad as *bees* that you told the hotel to call the police. Watch out when Kim's mad."

Levon smiled.

"I'll shower after you," Barb said.

Levon came out of the bathroom five minutes later, shaven, his damp brown hair standing up around the bald spot at the back. He tried to picture the Wailea Princess as he dressed, saw frozen postcard images of honeymooners walking the beach at sunset. He thought of never seeing Kim again, and a knifing terror cut through him.

Please, God, oh, please, don't let anything happen to Kim.

Barb showered quickly, dressed in a blue sweater, gray slacks, flat shoes. Her expression was wide-eyed shock, but she was past the hysteria, her excellent mind in gear.

"I packed underwear and toothbrushes and that's all, Levon. We'll get what we need in Maui."

It was 3:45 in Cascade Township. Less than an hour had passed since the anonymous phone call had cracked open the night and spilled the McDanielses out into a terrifying unknown.

"You call Cissy," Barb said. "I'll wake the kids."

Chapter 12

BARBARA SIGHED UNDER HER BREATH, then turned up the dimmer, gradually lighting the boys' room. Greg groaned, pulled the Spider-Man quilt over his head, but Johnny sat straight up, his fourteen-year-old face alert to something different, new, and maybe exciting.

Barb shook Greg's shoulder gently. "Sweetie, wake up now."

"Mommmmm, nooooo."

Barb peeled down her younger son's blanket, explained to both boys a version of the story that she halfway believed. That she and Dad were going to Hawaii to visit Kim.

Her sons became attentive immediately, bombarding Barb with questions until Levon walked in, his face taut, and Greg, seeing that, shouted, "Dad! What's goin' on?"

Barb swooped Greg into her arms, said that everything

was fine, that Aunt Cissy and Uncle Dave were waiting for them, that they could be asleep again in fifteen minutes. They could stay in their pj's but they had to put on shoes and coats.

Johnny pleaded to come with them to Hawaii, made a case involving jet skis and snorkeling, but Barb, holding back tears, said "not this time" and busied herself with socks and shoes and toothbrushes and Game Boys.

"You're not telling us something, Mom. It's still dark!"

"There's no time to go into it, Johnny. Everything's okay. We've just—gotta catch a plane."

Ten minutes later, five blocks away, Christine and David waited outside their front door as the arctic air sweeping across Lake Michigan put down a fine white powder over their lawn.

Levon watched Cissy run down the steps to meet their car as it turned in at the driveway. Cissy was two years younger than Barb, with the same heart-shaped face, and Levon saw Kim in her features, too.

Cissy reached out and enfolded the kids as they dashed toward her. She lifted her arms and took in Barb and Levon, as Barb said, "I forwarded our phone to yours, Cis. In case you get a *call*." Barb didn't want to spell it out in front of the boys. She wasn't sure Cis got it yet either.

"Call me between planes," Cis said.

Dave held out an envelope to Levon. "Here's some cash, about a thousand. No, no, take it. You could need it when you get there. Cabs and whatever. Levon, take it."

Fierce hugs were exchanged and wishes for a safe flight

and love-you's rang out loudly in the morning stillness. When Cissy and David's front door closed, Levon told Barb to strap in.

He backed the Suburban out of the drive, then turned onto Burkett Road, heading toward Gerald R. Ford International Airport, ramping the car up to ninety on the straightaway.

"Slow down, Levon."

"Okay."

But he kept his foot on the gas, driving fast into the star field of snow that somehow kept his mind balanced on the brink of terror rather than letting it topple into the abyss.

"I'll call the bank when we change planes in L.A.," Levon said. "Talk to Bill Macchio, get a loan started against the house in case we need cash."

He saw tears dropping from Barb's face into her lap, heard the click of her fingernails tapping on her BlackBerry, sending text messages to everyone in the family, to her friends, to her job. To Kim.

Barb called Kim's cell phone again as Levon parked the car, held up the phone so Levon could hear the mechanical voice saying, "The mailbox belonging to—*Kim McDaniels*—is full. No messages can be left at this time."

Chapter 13

THE McDANIELSES HOPSCOTCHED by air from Grand Rapids to Chicago and from there to their wait-listed flight to Los Angeles, which connected just in time to their flight to Honolulu. Once in Honolulu, they ran through the airport, tickets and IDs in their hands, making Island Air's turbo prop plane. They were the last people on, settling into their bulkhead seats before the doors to the puddle jumper closed with a startling bang.

They were now only forty minutes from Maui.

Only forty minutes from Kim.

Since leaving Grand Rapids, Barbara and Levon had slept in snatches. So much time had elapsed since the phone call that it was starting to feel unreal.

They now spun the idea that after Kim had given them hell for coming there, they'd be laughing about all of this, showing off a snapshot of Kim with that "oh, please" look on her face and standing between her parents, all of them wearing leis, typical happy tourists in Hawaii.

And then they'd swing back to their fear.

Where was Kim? Why couldn't they reach her? Why was there no return call from her on their home phone or Levon's cell?

As the airplane sailed above the clouds, Barb said, "I've been thinking about the bike."

Levon nodded, took her hand.

What they called "the bike" had started with another terrible phone call, seven years ago, this time from the police. Kim had been fourteen. She'd been riding her bike after school, wearing a muffler around her neck. The end of the scarf, whipping back behind her, got wrapped around the rear wheel, choking Kim, pulling her off the bike and hurling her onto the roadside.

A woman driving along saw the bike in the road, pulled up, and found Kim lying up against a tree, unconscious. That woman, Anne Clohessy, had called 911, and when the ambulance came, the EMTs couldn't get Kim to come back to consciousness.

Her brain had been deprived of oxygen, the doctors said. She was in a coma. The hospital's posturing told Barb that it might be irreversible.

By the time Levon had been reached at the office, Kim had been medevaced to a trauma unit in Chicago. He and Barb had driven three hours, got to the hospital, and found their daughter in intensive care, groggy but awake, a terrible bruise around her neck, as blue as the scarf that nearly killed her.

But she was alive. She wasn't back to a hundred percent yet, but she'd be fine.

"It was weird inside my head," Kimmy had said then. "It was like dreaming, only much more real. I heard Father Marty talking to me like he was sitting on the end of the bed."

"What did he say, sweetheart?" Barb had asked.

"He said, 'I'm glad you were baptized, Kim.'"

Now Levon took off his glasses, dried his eyes with the back of his hand. Barb passed him a tissue, saying, "I know, sweetie, I know."

This is how they wanted to find Kim now. *Fine.* Levon gave Barb a crooked smile, both of them thinking how the story in the *Chicago Trib* had called her "Miracle Girl," and sometimes they still called her that.

Miracle Girl who got onto the varsity basketball team as a freshman. Miracle Girl who was accepted into Columbia premed. Miracle Girl who'd been picked for the *Sporting Life* swimsuit shoot, the odds a million to one against her.

Levon thought, *What kind of miracle was that?*

Chapter 14

BARB TWISTED a tissue into a knot, and she said to Levon, "I should never have made such a fuss about that modeling agency."

"She wanted to do it, Barb. It's no one's fault. She's always been her own person."

Barb took Kimmy's picture from her purse, a five-by-seven headshot of eighteen-year-old Kim, taken for that agency in Chicago. Levon looked at the picture of Kim wearing a low-cut black sweater, her blond hair falling below her shoulders, the kind of radiant beauty that gave men ideas.

"No modeling after this," Levon said now.

"She's twenty-one, Levon."

"She's going to be a *doctor*. Barb, there's no good reason for her to be modeling anymore. This is the end of it. I'll make her understand."

The flight attendant announced that the plane would be landing momentarily.

Barb raised the shade and Levon looked out at the clouds flowing under the window, the peaks of them looking like they'd been hit with pink spotlights.

As the tiny houses and roads of Maui came into view, Levon turned to his wife, his best pal, his sweetheart.

"How're you doin', hon? Okay?"

"Never better," Barb chirped, attempting a joke. "And you?"

Levon smiled, brought Barb close, and pressed his cheek to hers, smelled the stuff she put in her hair. *What Barb smelled like.* He kissed her, squeezed her hand.

"Hang on," Levon said, as the airplane began its steep, sickening descent. And he sent out a thought to Kim. *We're coming for you, honey. Mom and Dad are coming.*

Chapter 15

THE McDANIELSES STEPPED from the plane's exit door to a wobbly staircase and from there down to the tarmac, the heat suffocating after the chilled air on the plane.

Levon looked around at the volcanic landscape, an astounding difference from Michigan in the black of night, with the snow falling down the back of his shirt collar as he'd hugged his sons good-bye.

He took off his jacket, patted the inside pocket to make sure that their return plane tickets were safe—including the ticket he'd bought for Kim.

The terminal was full of people, the waiting room in the same open-air section as the baggage claim. He and Barb turned cards over to an official in blue, swearing they were not bringing in any fruit, and then they looked for taxi signs.

Levon was walking fast, feeling a heightened need to get to the hotel and not watching his feet when he sidestepped a luggage trolley and just about stumbled over a young girl with yellow braids. She was clutching a fuzzy toy, standing in the middle of everything, just taking it all in. The child looked so self-assured that she reminded Levon again of Kim, and a wave of panic rose in him, making him feel dizzy and sick to his stomach.

Levon swept blindly forward, asking himself if Kim had used up her quota of miracles. Was her borrowed time up? Had the whole family made a tremendous mistake buying into a headline written by a reporter in Chicago, giving all of them a belief that Kim was so miraculous that nothing could ever hurt her?

Levon silently begged God again to please let Kim be safe at the hotel, make her be glad to see her parents, have her say, *I'm so sorry. I didn't mean to make you worry.*

With his arm around Barb, the two headed out of the terminal, but before they reached the taxi rank, they saw a man approaching—a driver holding up a sign with their name.

The driver was taller than Levon. He had dark hair streaked with gray, a mustache, and he wore a chauffeur's cap and livery jacket and alligator cowboy boots with three-inch heels.

He said, "Mr. and Mrs. McDaniels? I'm Marco. The hotel hired me to be your driver. Do you have claim tickets for your luggage?"

"We didn't bring any bags."

"Okay. The car's right outside."

Chapter 16

THE McDANIELSES WALKED behind Marco as Levon noted the driver's odd rolling gait in those cowboy boots and the man's accent, a trace of something—maybe New York or New Jersey.

They crossed the arrival lane to a traffic island where Levon saw a newspaper lying faceup on a bench.

In a heart-stopping double take, he realized that Kim was looking up at him from under the headline.

This was the *Maui News,* and the large black type spelled out, "Missing Beauty."

Levon's thoughts scattered, taking him a few stunned moments to understand that during the eleven or so hours he and Barb had been in transit, Kim had officially gone missing.

She wasn't waiting at the hotel.

Like the caller said, *she was gone.*

Levon grabbed the paper with a trembling hand, his heart bucking as he looked into Kim's smiling eyes, took in the swimsuit she was wearing in this picture, probably taken just a couple of days ago.

Levon folded the newspaper lengthwise, caught up to Marco and Barbara at the car, asked Marco, "Will it take long to get to the hotel?"

"About a half hour, and there's no charge, Mr. McDaniels. The Wailea Princess is paying for as long as you need me."

"Why are they doing that?"

Marco's voice turned soft. "Well, in light of the situation, sir."

He opened the car doors, and Levon and Barbara climbed in, Barb's face crumpling when she took the paper, crying while she read the story as the sedan slipped into the traffic stream.

The car sped onto the highway, and Marco spoke to them, his eyes in the rearview mirror, gently asking if they were comfortable, if they wanted more air or music. Levon thought ahead to checking in at the hotel, then going straight to the police, the whole time feeling as though he'd suffered a battlefield amputation, that a part of him had been brutally severed and that he might not survive.

Eventually, the sedan crawled down what looked like a private road, both sides massed in purple flowering vines. They drove by an artificial waterfall, slowed to a stop in front of the grand porte cochere entryway of the Wailea Princess Hotel.

Levon saw tiled fountains on both sides of the car, bronze statues of Polynesian warriors rising out of the water with spears in their hands on one side, outriggers filled with orchids on the other.

Bellhops in white shirts and short red pants hurried toward the car. Marco opened his door, and as Levon walked around the sedan to help Barb he heard his name coming at him from all directions.

People were running toward the hotel entrance — reporters with cameras and microphones.

Racing toward *them*.

Chapter 17

TEN MINUTES LATER, Barb was dazed and jet-lagged as she entered a suite that on another day, and in different circumstances, she would have thought "magnificent." If she had peeked at the rate card behind the door, she would have seen that the charge for the suite was over three thousand dollars a day.

She walked into the heart of the main room, as good as sleepwalking, seeing but not taking in the hand-knotted silk carpet, a pattern of orchids on a pale peach ground; the tapestry-upholstered furnishings; the huge flat-panel television.

She went to the window, looked out at the beauty without really seeing it, *just looking for Kim.*

There was a gorgeous swimming pool below, a complicated shape, like a square laid over a rectangle, with circular Jacuzzis at the shallow end. A fountain, like a champagne glass, in the middle spilled water over the children playing.

She scanned the rows of pure white cabanas around the pool, looking for a young woman in a chaise sipping a drink, Kim sitting at the poolside.

Barb saw several girls, some slimmer or heavier or older or shorter, but none of them Kim.

She looked out beyond the pool, saw a covered walk, wooden steps going down to the beach dotted with palm trees, fronted by the sapphire blue ocean, nothing but water between the edge of the beach and the coast of Japan.

Where was Kim?

Barb wanted to say to Levon, "I feel Kim's presence here," but when she turned, Levon wasn't there.

She noticed an ornate basket of fruit on the table near the window and went to it, heard the toilet flush as she lifted out the note that was in fact a business card with a message written on the back.

Levon, her poor dear husband, his eyes unblinking and pained behind his glasses, came toward her, asking, "What's that, Barb?"

She read out loud, "Dear Mr. and Mrs. McDaniels, please call me. We're here to help in any way we can."

The card was signed, "Susan Gruber, *SL*," and under her name was a room number.

Levon said, "Susan Gruber. She's the editor in chief. I'll call her now."

Barb felt hope. Gruber was in charge. She'd know something.

Fifteen, maybe twenty minutes later, the McDanielses' hotel room was full. Standing room only.

Chapter 18

BARB SAT ON one of the sofas, her hands clasped on her lap, waiting for Susan Gruber, this take-charge New York executive, with her bright white teeth and face as sharp as a blade, to tell them that Kim had had a fight with the photographer, or that she hadn't photographed well enough and so she'd been given the time off—or something, *anything* that would clear it all up, make it so that Kim was simply absent, not missing, not abducted, not in danger.

Gruber was wearing an aquamarine pantsuit and a lot of gold bracelets, and her fingers were cold when she reached out to shake hands with Barbara.

Del Swann, the art director, had dark skin, platinum hair, jewelry in one ear, and he was dressed in fashionably worn-out jeans and a tight black T-shirt. He looked like he was about to have a mental collapse, making Barbara think maybe he knew more than he was saying—or maybe he felt guilty because he was the last one to see Kim.

There were two other men. The senior one was forty-something, in a gray suit, had corporation written all over him. Barb had met men like this at Levon's Merrill Lynch conventions and business cocktail parties. She thought it was a pretty safe bet that he, and the junior clone standing to his right, were both New York lawyers who'd been over-nighted to Maui like a FedEx package in order to cover the magazine's ass.

And Barb looked at Carol Sweeney, a big woman wearing an expensive, if shapeless, black dress. As the booker from the modeling agency who'd landed this job for Kim and had gone on the shoot as Kim's chaperone, Carol looked like she'd swallowed a dog, that's how choked up she was.

Barb couldn't stand to be in the same room with Carol.

The senior suit, Barb forgot his name as soon as she heard it, told Levon, "We have a security team working to find out where Kim may have gone."

He didn't even look at Barb. Directed his attention to Levon. Pretty much, they *all* did. She knew she looked emotional, fragile. And who could say she didn't have good reason.

"What more can you tell us?" Barb asked the lawyer.

"There's no sign that anything happened to her. The police assume she's sightseeing."

Barb thought, *Levon, tell them,* but Levon had said to her before the magazine people arrived, "We'll take information in. We'll listen. But we've got to keep in mind that we don't know these people." Meaning, anyone attached to the magazine could have had something to do with Kim's disappearance.

Susan Gruber put her elbows on her knees and leaned forward, said to Levon, "Kim was inside the hotel bar with Del, and Del went to the men's room, and when he returned, Kim was gone. No one *took* Kim. She left on her own."

"So that's the story?" Levon asked. "Kim left the hotel bar on her own, and no one's heard from her, and she's been gone for a day and a half, and that means to you that Kim ditched the shoot and went sightseeing? Am I getting that right?"

"She's an adult, Mr. McDaniels," Gruber said. "It wouldn't be the first time a girl dumped a job. I remember this girl, Gretchen, took off in Cannes last year, showed up in Monte Carlo six days later."

Gruber was talking like this was her office, and she was patiently explaining her job to Levon. "We've got eight girls on this shoot." She went on to say how many people she had to supervise and all the things she had to cover, and how she had to be on the set every minute or looking at the day's shots...

Barbara felt the pressure building inside her head. All that gold on Susan Gruber, but no wedding ring. Did she have a child? Did she even know one? *Susan Gruber didn't get it.*

"We love Kim," Carol Sweeney blurted to Barb. "I...I felt that Kim was safe here. I was having dinner with one of the other models. I mean, Kim is such a good girl and so responsible, I never thought we had reason to worry."

"I only turned my back for a minute," said Del Swann. And then he started to cry.

It all became clear to Barb, why Gruber had brought her people to see them. Barbara had been raised to be nice, but now that she'd stopped denying the obvious, she had to say it.

"You're not *responsible*? Is that why you're all here? To tell us that you're *not responsible* for Kim?"

No one met her gaze.

"We've told the police everything we know," said Gruber.

Levon stood up, put his hand on Barb's shoulder, and said to the magazine people, "Please call if you learn anything. Right now, we'd like to be alone. Thanks."

Gruber stood, slung the strap of her handbag across her narrow chest, said, "Kim will be back. Don't worry."

"You mean, you *hope and pray with every miserable breath you take*," said Barbara.

Chapter 19

A MAN STOOD in the thick of the media gaggle outside the Wailea Princess main entrance, waiting for the press conference to start.

He blended in well, appeared to be a guy living out of a duffel bag, maybe sleeping on the beach. He had on sports sunglasses wrapped around his face like a windshield, even though the sun was going down. Dodgers cap over his rusty brown hair, vintage Adidas, rumpled cargo pants, and hanging down in front of his cheap Hawaiian shirt was a perfect replica of a press pass identifying him as a photographer, Charles Rollins of *Talk Weekly*, a publication that didn't exist.

His video camera was expensive, though, a state-of-the-art Panasonic, HD-compatible with a stereo microphone boom and a Leica lens, costing over six thousand bucks.

He pointed the lens at the grand front entrance of the Wailea Princess, where the McDanielses were taking up their positions behind a lectern.

As Levon adjusted the mic, Rollins whistled a few notes through his teeth. He was enjoying himself now, thinking that even Kim wouldn't recognize him if she were alive. He lifted his vid cam over his head and recorded Levon greeting the press, thinking he'd like the McDanielses if he got to know them. Well, fuck it anyway, he already liked them. What was not to like about the McDanielses?

Look at them.

Sweet, feisty Barbara. Levon, with the heart of a five-star general. Both of them, salt of the fucking earth.

They were grief-wracked and terrified, but still comporting themselves with dignity, answering insensitive questions, even the de rigueur "What would you say to Kim if she's listening to you now?"

"I'd say, 'We love you, darling. Please be *strong*,'" Barbara said with a quavering voice. "And to everyone hearing us, please, we're offering twenty-five thousand dollars for information leading to the return of our daughter. If we had a million, we'd offer that..."

And then Barbara's air seemed to run out. She turned, and Rollins saw her take a hit off an inhaler. And still, questions were fired at the supermodel's parents: *Levon, Levon! Have you gotten a ransom demand? What was the last thing Kim said to you?*

Levon leaned toward the microphones, answered the questions very patiently, finally saying, "The hotel management has set up a hotline number," and he read it to the crowd.

Rollins watched the journalists jumping up like flying fish, calling out more questions even as the McDanielses were stepping down, moving toward the embrace of the hotel lobby.

Rollins looked through his lens, zoomed in on the back of the McDanielses' heads, saw someone coming through the crowd, a semicelebrity he'd seen on C-Span hawking his books.

The subject of Rollins's interest was a good-looking guy of about forty, a journalist and best-selling detective novelist, dressed in Dockers and a pink button-down shirt, sleeves rolled up. Kind of reminded him of Brian Williams reporting from Baghdad. Maybe a little more rough-and-ready.

As Rollins watched, the writer reached out and touched Barbara McDaniels's arm, and Barbara stopped to speak with him.

Charlie Rollins saw an interview with the legitimate press in the making. He thought, *No kidding. The Peepers will love this. Kim McDaniels is going big-time. This is turning into a very big event, indeed.*

Chapter 20

THE JOURNALIST in the Dockers and pink shirt?

That was me.

I saw an opening as Levon and Barbara McDaniels stepped away from the lectern, the crowd closing in, circling them like a twister.

I lunged forward, touched Barbara McDaniels's arm, catching her attention before she disappeared into the lobby.

I wanted the interview, but no matter how many times you see parents of lost or abducted children begging for their son or daughter's safe return, you cannot fail to be moved.

Barbara and Levon McDaniels had gotten to me as soon as I saw their faces. It killed me to see them in such pain.

Now I had my hand gently on Barbara McDaniels's arm. She turned, and I introduced myself, handed her my card, and lucky for me, she knew my name. "Are you the Ben Hawkins who wrote *Red*?

"*Put It All on Red,* yes, that's mine."

She said she liked the book, her mouth smiling, although her face was rigid with anguish. Right then, hotel security made a cordon with their arms, a path through the crowd, and I walked into the lobby with Barbara, who introduced me to Levon.

"Ben's a best-selling author, Levon. You remember, we read him for our book club last fall."

"I'm covering Kim's story for the *L.A. Times,*" I told Mr. McDaniels.

Levon said, "If you want an interview, I'm sorry. We're out of steam, and it's probably best that we don't talk further until we meet with the police."

"You haven't spoken with them yet?"

Levon sighed, shook his head. "Ever talk to an answering machine?"

"I might be able to help," I said. "The *L.A. Times* has clout, even here. And I used to be a cop."

"Is that right?" Levon McDaniels's eyelids were sagging, his voice ragged and raw. He walked like a man who'd just run his feet off in a marathon, but he was suddenly interested in me. He stopped walking and asked me to tell him more.

"I was with the Portland PD. I was a detective, an investigator. Right now I cover the crime desk for the *Times.*"

McDaniels winced at the word "crime," said, "Okay, Ben. You think you can give us a hand with the police? We're going out of our minds."

I walked with the McDanielses through the cool marble lobby with its high ceilings and ocean views until we found a semisecluded spot overlooking the pool. Palm trees rustled in the island breeze. Wet kids in bathing suits ran past us, laughing, not a care in the world.

Levon said, "I called the police several times and got a menu. 'Parking tickets, press one. Night court, press two.' I had to leave a message. Can you believe that?

"Barb and I went over to the station for this district. Hours were posted on the door. Monday to Friday, eight to five, Saturday, ten to four. I didn't know police stations had closing hours. Did you?"

The look in Levon's eyes was heartbreaking. His daughter was missing. The police station was *closed* for business. How could this place look the way it did—vacation heaven—when they were slogging through seven kinds of hell?

"The police here mostly do traffic work, DWIs, stuff like that," I said. "Domestic violence, burglary."

I thought, but didn't say, that a few years ago a twenty-five-year-old female tourist was attacked on the Big Island by three local hoods who beat her and raped her and killed her.

She'd been tall, blond, sweet-looking, not unlike Kim.

There was another case, more famous, a cheerleader for the University of Illinois who'd fallen off the balcony of her hotel room and died instantly. She'd been partying with a couple of boys who were found not guilty of anything. And there was another girl, a local teenager, who called her friends after a concert on the island, and was never seen again.

"Your press conference was a good thing. The police will have to take Kim seriously," I said.

"If I don't get a call back, I'm going over there again in the morning," Levon McDaniels said. "Right now we want to go to the bar, see where Kim was hanging out before she vanished. You're welcome to join us."

Chapter 21

THE TYPHOON BAR was on the mezzanine floor, open to the trade winds, wonderfully scented by plumeria. Café tables and chairs were lined up at the balustrade, overlooking the pool and beyond, a queue of palm trees down to the sands. To my left was a grand piano, still covered, and there was a long bar behind us. A bartender was setting up, slicing lemon peel, putting out dishes of nuts.

Barbara spoke. "The night manager told us that Kim was sitting at this table, the one nearest the piano," Barbara said, tenderly patting the table's marble surface.

Then she pointed to an alcove fifteen yards away. "That would be the famous men's room over there. Where the art director went, to ah, just turn his back for a minute…"

I imagined the bar as it must have been that night. People

drinking. A lot of men. I had plenty of questions. Hundreds of them.

I was starting to look at this story as if I were still a cop. If this were *my* case, I'd start with the security tapes. I'd want to see who was in the bar when Kim was there. I'd want to know if anybody had been watching her when she'd gotten up from this table, and who might have paid the check after she left.

Had Kim departed with someone? Maybe gone to his room?

Or had she walked to the lobby, eyes following her as she made her way down the stairs, her blond hair swinging.

What then? Had she walked outside, past the pool and the cabanas? Had any of those cabanas been occupied late that night? Had someone followed her out to the beach?

Levon carefully polished his glasses, one lens, then the other, and held them out to see if he'd done a good job. When he put them back on, he saw me looking out at the covered walkway beyond the pool area that led to the beach.

"What do you think, Ben?"

"All of the beaches in Hawaii are public property, so there won't be any video surveillance out there."

I was wondering if the simplest explanation fit. Had Kim gone for a swim? Had she waded out into the water and gotten sucked under by a wave? Had someone found her shoes on the beach and taken them?

"What can we tell you about Kim?" Barbara asked me.

"I want to know everything," I said. "If you don't mind, I'd like to tape our conversation."

Barbara nodded, and Levon ordered G and Ts for them both. I was working, so I declined alcohol, asked for club soda instead.

I had already started shaping the Kim McDaniels story in my mind, thinking about this beautiful girl from the heartland, with brains and beauty, on the verge of national fame, and about how she had come to one of the most beautiful spots on earth and disappeared without trace or reason. An exclusive with the McDanielses was more than I'd hoped for, and while I still couldn't know if Kim's story was a book, it was definitely a journalistic whopper.

And more than that, I'd been won over by the McDanielses. They were nice people.

I wanted to help them, and I would.

Right now, they were exhausted, but they weren't leaving the table. The interview was on.

My tape recorder was new, the tape just unwrapped and the batteries fresh. I pushed Record, but, as the machine whirred softly on the table, Barbara McDaniels surprised me.

It was *she* who started asking questions.

Chapter 22

BARBARA RESTED her chin on her hands, and asked, "What happened with you and the Portland police department—and please don't tell me what it says in your book jacket bio. That's just PR, isn't it?"

Barbara let me know by her focus and determination that if I didn't answer her questions, she had no reason to answer mine. I wanted to cooperate because I thought she was right to check me out, and I wanted the McDanielses to trust me.

I smiled at Barbara's direct interrogatory style, but there was nothing amusing about the story she was asking me to tell. Once I sent my mind back to that place and time, the memories rolled in, unstoppable, none of them glorifying, none of them very pleasant, either.

As the still-vivid images flashed on the wide screen inside my head, I told the McDanielses about a fatal car wreck that had happened many years ago; that my partner, Dennis Carbone, and I had been nearby and had responded to the call.

"When we got to the scene, there was about a half hour left of daylight. It was gloomy with a drizzling rain, but there was enough light to see that a vehicle had skidded off the road. It had caromed off some trees like a two-ton eight ball, crashing out of control through the woods.

"I radioed for help," I said now. "Then I was the one who stayed behind to interview the witness who'd been driving the other car—while my partner went to the crashed vehicle to see if there were survivors."

I told the McDanielses that the witness had been driving the car coming from the opposite direction, that the other vehicle, a black Toyota pickup, had been in his lane, coming at him *fast*. He said that he'd swerved, and so had the Toyota. The witness was shaken as he described how the pickup had left the road at high speed, said that he'd braked—and I could see and smell the hundred yards of rubber he'd left on the asphalt.

"Response and rescue vehicles showed up," I said. "The paramedics pulled the body out of the pickup, told me that the driver had been killed on impact with a spruce tree and that he'd had no passengers.

"As the dead man was taken away, I looked for my partner. He was a few yards off the roadside, and I caught him sneaking a look in my direction. A little odd, like he was trying not to be seen doing something."

There was a sudden flurry of girlish laughter as a bride, surrounded by her maids of honor, passed through the bar to the lounge. The bride was a pretty blonde in her twenties. Happiest day of her life, right?

Barbara turned to see the bridal party, then turned back to look at me. Anyone with eyes could see what she was feeling. And what she was hoping.

"Go on, Ben," she said. "You were talking about your partner with the guilty look."

I nodded, told her that I turned away from my partner because someone called my name and that when I looked back again, he was closing the trunk of our car.

"I didn't ask Dennis what he was doing, because I was already thinking ahead. We had reports to write up, work to do. We had to start with identifying the deceased.

"I was doing all the right stuff, Barbara," I told her now. "I think it's pretty common to block out things we don't want to see. I should have confronted my partner right then and right there. But I didn't do it. Turns out that that sneaky, half-seen moment changed my life."

Chapter 23

A WAITRESS CAME OVER and asked if we wanted to refresh our drinks, and I was glad to see her. My throat was closing up and I needed to take a break. I'd told this story before, but it's never easy to get past disgrace.

Especially when you didn't earn it.

Levon said, "I know this is hard, Ben. But we appreciate your telling us about yourself. It's important to hear."

"This is where it gets *hard*," I told Levon.

He nodded, and even though Levon probably had only ten years on me, I felt his fatherly concern.

My second club soda arrived and I stirred at it with a straw. Then I went on.

"A few days passed. The accident victim turned out to be a small-time drug dealer, Robby Snow, and his blood came back positive for heroin. And now his girlfriend called on us. Carrie

Willis was her name. Carrie was crushed by Robby's death, but something else was bothering her. She asked me, 'What happened to Robby's backpack? It was red with silver reflecting tape on the back. There was a lot of money in there.'

"Well, we hadn't found any red backpack, and there were a lot of jokes about Carrie Willis having the nerve to report stolen drug money to the police.

"But Robby's girlfriend was convincing. Carrie didn't know that Robby was a dealer. She just knew that he was buying a piece of acreage by a creek and he was going to build a house there for the two of them. The bank papers and the full payment for the property—a hundred thousand dollars—were in that backpack because he was on his way to the closing. She put all that money in the backpack herself. Her story checked out."

"So you asked your partner about the backpack?" Barbara prompted.

"Sure. I asked him. And he said, 'Well, I sure as hell didn't see a backpack, red or green or sky blue pink.'

"So, at my insistence, we went to the impound, took the car apart, found nothing. Then we drove in broad daylight out to the woods where the accident happened and we searched the area. At least I did. I thought Denny was just rustling branches and kicking piles of leaves. That's when I remembered his face getting foxy the night of the accident.

"I had a long, hard talk with myself that night. The next day I went to my lieutenant for an off-the-record chat. I told him what I suspected, that a hundred thousand dollars in cash might have left the scene and was never reported."

Levon said, "Well, you had no choice."

"Denny Carbone was an old pit bull of a cop, and I knew if he learned about my conversation with the lieutenant he'd come at me. So I took a chance with my boss, and the next day Internal Affairs was in the locker room. Guess what they found in my locker?"

"A red backpack," said Levon.

I gave him a thumbs-up. "Red backpack, silver reflecting tape, bank papers, heroin, and ten thousand dollars in cash."

"Oh, my God," said Barbara.

"I was given a choice. Resign. Or there would be a trial. *My* trial. I knew that I wasn't going to win in court. It would be 'he said/he said,' and the evidence, some of it, anyway, had been found in my locker. Worse, I suspected that I was getting hung with this because my lieutenant was in on it with Denny Carbone.

"A very bad day, blew up a lot of illusions for me. I turned in my badge, my gun, and some of my self-respect. I could've fought, but I couldn't take a chance I'd go to jail for something I hadn't done."

"That's a sad story, Ben," said Levon.

"Yep. And you know how the story turns out. I moved to L.A. Got a job at the *Times*. And I wrote some books."

"You're being modest," Barbara said, and patted my arm.

"Writing is what I do, but it's not who I am."

"And who would you say you are?" she asked.

"Right now, I'm working at being the best reporter I can be. I came to Maui to tell your daughter's story, and, at the same time, I want you to have that happy ending. I want to see it, report it, be here for all the good feelings when Kim comes back safe. That's who I am."

Barbara said, "We believe you, Ben." And Levon nodded at her side.

Like I said, Nice people.

Chapter 24

AMSTERDAM. Five twenty in the afternoon. Jan Van der Heuvel was in his office on the fifth floor of the classic, neck-gabled house, gazing out over the treetops at the sightseeing boat on the canal, waiting for time to pass.

The door to his office opened, and Mieke, a pretty girl of twenty with short, dark hair, entered. She wore a small skirt and a fitted jacket, her long legs bare to her little lace-up boots. The girl lowered her eyes, said that if he didn't need her for anything she would leave for the day.

"Have a good evening," Van der Heuvel said.

He walked her to the office door and locked it behind her, returned to his seat at the long drawing table, and looked down at the street running along the Keizersgracht Canal until he saw Mieke get into her fiancé's Renault and speed away.

Only then did Van der Heuvel attend to his computer. The teleconference wasn't for another forty minutes, but he wanted to establish contact early so that he could record the proceedings. He tapped keys until he made the connection and his friend's face came on the screen.

"Horst," he said. "I am here."

At that same time, a brunette woman of forty was on the bridge of her 118-foot yacht anchored in the Mediterranean off the coast of Portofino. The yacht was custom-made, constructed of high-tensile aluminum with six cabins, a master suite, and a video conference center in the saloon, which easily converted to a cinema.

The woman left her young captain and took the stairs down to her suite, where she removed a Versace jacket from the closet and slipped it on over her halter top. Then she crossed the galleyway to the media room and booted up her computer. When the connection was made to the encrypted line, she smiled into the webcam.

"Gina Prazzi checking in, Horst. How are we today?"

Four time zones away, in Dubai, a tall bearded man wearing traditional Middle Eastern clothing passed a mosque and hurried to a hole-in-the-wall restaurant down the street. He greeted the proprietor and continued on through the kitchen, aromatic with garlic and rosemary.

Pushing aside a heavy curtain, he took the stairs down to the basement level and unlocked a heavy wooden door leading to a private room.

In Hong Kong's Victoria Peak section, a young chemist flicked on his computer. He was in his twenties with an IQ in the high 170s. As the software loaded, he looked through his curtains, down the long slope, past the tops of the cylindrical high-rises, and farther below to the brightly lit towers of Hong Kong. It was unusually clear for this time of year, and his gaze had drifted to Victoria Harbour and beyond, to the lights of Kowloon, when the computer signaled and he turned his attention to the emergency meeting of the Alliance.

In São Paulo, Raphael dos Santos, a man of fifty, drove to his home at just past three in his new Wiesmann GT MF5 sports coupe. The car cost 250,000 U.S. dollars and went from zero to sixty in under four seconds with a top speed of 193 miles per hour. Rafi, as he was called, loved this car.

He braked at the entrance to the underground garage, tossed the keys to Tomás, and took the elevator that opened inside his apartment.

There he crossed several thousand square feet of Jatoba hardwood floors, passed ultramodern furnishings, and entered his home office with its view of the gleaming facade of the Renaissance Hotel on Alameda Santos.

Rafi pressed a button on his desk, and a thin screen rose vertically up through the center. He wondered again at the purpose of this meeting. Something had gone wrong. But what? He touched the keyboard and pressed his thumb to the ID pad.

Rafi greeted the leader of the Alliance in Portuguese. "Horst, you old bastard. Make this good. You have our undivided attention!"

Chapter 25

IN THE SWISS ALPS, Horst Werner sat in the upholstered chair in his library. Flames leapt in the fireplace and pin lights illuminated the eight-foot-long scale model of the *Bismarck* he had made himself. There were bookshelves on every wall but no windows, and behind the cherrywood paneling was a three-inch-thick wall of lead-lined steel.

Horst's safe room was linked to the world by sophisticated Internet circuitry, giving him the feeling that this chamber was the very center of the universe.

The dozen members of the Alliance had all signed on to the encrypted network. They all spoke English to greater and lesser degrees, their live pictures on his screen. After greeting them, Horst moved quickly to the point of the meeting.

"An American friend has sent Jan a film as an amusement. I am very interested in your reaction."

A white light filled twelve linked computer screens and then clarified as the camera focused on a Jacuzzi-style tub. Inside the tub was a dark-skinned young girl, nude with long black hair, lying on her stomach in about four inches of water. She was tied up in the way that Americans quaintly call "hog-tied," her hands and feet behind her with a rope that also passed around her throat.

There was a man in the video, his back to the camera, and when he half turned, one of the Alliance members said, "Henri."

Henri was naked, sitting on the edge of the tub, the clear plastic mask obscuring his features. He spoke to the camera. "You see there is very little water, but enough. I don't know which is more lethal for Rosa. Whether she will choke or if she will drown. Let's watch and see."

Henri turned and spoke in Spanish to the sobbing child, then translated for the camera. "I told Rosa to keep her legs pulled back toward her head. I said if she could do that for another hour, I would let her live. Maybe."

Horst smiled at Henri's audacity, the way he stroked the back of the child's head, soothing her, but she cried out, clearly a great effort when she was so tired of trying to live.

"*Por favor. Déjame marchar. Eres malvado.*"

Henri spoke to the camera. "She says to let her go. That I am evil. Well. I love her anyway. Sweet child."

The girl continued to sob, gasping for air every time

her legs relaxed and the rope tightened around her throat. She wailed, "*Mama.*" Then her head dropped, her final exhalation causing bubbles to break the surface of the water.

Henri touched the side of her neck and shrugged. "It was the ropes," he said. "Anyway, she committed suicide. A beautiful tragedy. Just what I promised."

He was smiling when the video faded to black.

Gina spoke now, indignant. "Horst, this is in violation of his contract, yes?"

"Actually, Henri's contract only says he cannot take work that would prevent him from fulfilling his obligations to us."

"So. He is not technically in violation. He is just freelancing."

Jan's voice came over the speakers. "Yes. You see how Henri looks for ways to give us the finger? This is unacceptable."

Raphael broke in. "Okay, he is difficult, but let's admit, Henri has his genius. We should work with him. Give him a new contract."

"That says what, for example?"

"Henri has been making short films for us like the one we just saw. I suggest we have him make...a documentary."

Jan jumped in, excited. "Very good, Rafi. Wall-to-wall with Henri. A year in the life, *ja?* Salary and bonuses commensurate with the quality of the action."

"Exactly. And he's exclusive to us," said Raphael. "He starts now, on location with the parents of the swimsuit girl."

The Alliance discussed terms, and they put some teeth into the contract, penalties for failure to perform. That phrase provided a light moment, and then, after they had voted, Horst made the call to Hawaii.

Chapter 26

THE McDANIELSES AND I were still in the Typhoon Bar as dusk dropped over the island. For the past hour, Barbara had sweated me like a pro. When she was satisfied that I was an okay guy, she brought me into her family's lives with her passion and a natural gift for storytelling that I wouldn't have expected from a high school math and science teacher.

Levon could barely string two sentences together. He wasn't inarticulate. He just wasn't with us. I read him as choked up with fear and too anxious about his daughter to concentrate. But he expressed himself vividly with his body language, tightening his fists, turning away when tears welled up, frequently taking off his glasses and pressing his palms over his eyes.

I'd asked Barbara, "How did you learn that Kim was missing?"

At that, Levon's cell phone rang. He looked at the face-plate and walked away toward the elevator.

I heard him say, "Lieutenant Jackson? *Not tonight?* Why not?" After a pause, he said, "Okay. Eight a.m."

"Sounds like we have a date with the police in the morning. Come with us," Barbara said. She took my phone number, patted my hand. And then, she kissed my cheek.

I said good night to Barbara, then ordered another club soda, no lime, no ice. I sat in a comfortable chair overlooking the hundred-million-dollar view, and in the next fifteen minutes the atmosphere at the Typhoon Bar picked up considerably.

Handsome people in fresh suntans and translucent clothing in snow-cone colors dropped into chairs at the railing while singles took the high-backed stools at the long bar. Laughter rose and fell like the warm breeze that gusted through the wide-open space, riffling hairlines and skirt hems as it passed.

The piano player uncovered the Steinway, then turned sideways on the piano seat and broke into an old Peter Allen standard, delighting the crowd as he sang "I Go to Rio."

I noted the security cameras over the bar, dropped several bills on the table, and walked down the stairs and past the pool, lit now so that it looked like aqua-colored glass.

I continued past the cabanas, taking a walk that Kim might have taken two nights ago.

The beach was nearly empty of people, the sky still light enough to see the shoreline that ringed the whole of Maui like a halo around an eclipse of the moon.

I pictured walking behind Kim on Friday night. Her head might have been down, hair whipping around her face, the strong surf obliterating all other sound.

A man could have come up behind her with a rock, or a gun, or a simple choke hold.

I walked on the hard-packed sand, passing hotels on my right, empty chaises and cockeyed umbrellas as far as I could see.

After a quarter mile, I turned off the beach, walked up a path that skirted the Four Seasons, another five-star hotel where eight hundred bucks a night might buy a room with a view of the parking lot.

I continued on through the hotel's dazzling marble lobby and out to the street. Fifteen minutes later I was back sitting in my rented Chevy, parked in the leafy shadows surrounding the Wailea Princess, listening to the rush of waterfalls.

If I'd been a killer, I could've dumped my victim into the surf or slung her over my shoulder and carried her out to my car. I could've left the scene without anyone noticing.

Easy breezy.

Chapter 27

I STARTED my engine and followed the moon to Stella Blues, a cheerful café in Kihei. It has high, peaked ceilings and a wraparound bar, now buzzing with a weekend crowd of locals and cruise ship tourists enjoying their first night in port. I ordered a Jack Daniel's and mahimahi from the bar, took my drink outside to a table for two on the patio.

As the votive candle guttered in its glass, I called Amanda.

Amanda Diaz and I had been together for almost two years. She's five years younger than me, a pastry chef and a self-described biker chick, which means she takes her antique Harley for a run on the Pacific Coast Highway some weekends to blow off the steam she can't vent in the kitchen. Mandy is not only smart and gorgeous, but when I look at her, all those rock-and-roll songs about booming hearts and loving her till the day I die make total sense.

Right then I was aching to hear my sweetie's voice, and she didn't disappoint, answering the phone on the third ring. After some verbal high fives, and at my request, she told me about her day at Intermezzo.

"It was Groundhog Day, Benjy. Rémy fired Rocco, again," Amanda said, going into a French accent now. 'What I have to say to you to make you think like chef? This confit. It looks like pigeon *poop*.' He put about twelve *ooohs* in *poop*."

She laughed, said, "Hired him back ten minutes later. As usual. And then I scorched the crème brûlée. '*Merde, Ahmandah, mon Dieu*. You are making me *craaaaa-zy*.'" She laughed again. "And you, Benjy? Are you getting your story?"

"I met with the missing girl's folks. They're talking to me."

"Oh, boy. How grim was that?"

I caught Mandy up on the interview with Barbara, told her how much I liked the McDanielses and that they had two other kids, both boys adopted from Russian orphanages.

"Their oldest son was almost catatonic from neglect when the police in Saint Petersburg found him. The younger boy has fetal alcohol syndrome. Kim decided to become a pediatrician because of her brothers."

"Ben, honey?"

"Uh-huh. Am I breaking up?"

"No, I can hear you. Can you hear me?"

"Totally."

"Then listen. Be careful, will you?"

I felt a slight burr of irritation. Amanda was uncommonly intuitive, but I was in no danger.

"Careful of what?"

"Remember when you left your briefcase with all of your notes on the Donato story in a diner?"

"You're going to bring up the bus again, aren't you?"

"Since you mention it."

"I was under your spell, goofball. I was looking at you when I stepped off the curb. If you were *here* now, it could happen again—"

"What I'm saying is, you sound the same way *now* as you did then."

"I do, huh?"

"Yeah, you kinda do. So watch out, okay? Pay attention. Look both ways."

Ten feet away, a couple clinked glasses, held hands across a small table. Honeymooners, I thought.

"I miss you," I said.

"I miss you, too. I'm keeping the bed warm for you, so come home soon."

I sent a wireless kiss to my girl in L.A. and said good night.

Chapter 28

AT SEVEN FIFTEEN Monday morning, Levon watched the driver pull the black sedan up to the entrance of the Wailea Princess. Levon got into the front passenger seat as Hawkins and Barb got into the back, and when all the doors had slammed shut, Levon told Marco to please take them to the police station in Kihei.

During the ride, Levon half listened as Hawkins talked, telling him how to handle the police, saying to be *helpful,* to make the cops your friends and not to be belligerent because that would work against them.

Levon had nodded, grunted "uh-huh" a few times, but he was inside his head, wouldn't have been able to describe the route between the hotel and the police station, his mind fully focused on the upcoming meeting with Lieutenant James Jackson.

Levon came back to the present as Marco was parking at the mini–strip mall, and he jumped out before the car had fully stopped. He walked straight up to the shoebox-sized substation, a storefront wedged between a tattoo parlor and a pizzeria.

The glass door was locked, and so Levon jabbed the intercom button and spoke his name, saying to the female voice that he had an appointment at eight with Lieutenant Jackson. There was a buzz and the door opened and they were in.

The station looked to Levon like a small-town DMV. The walls were bureaucrat green; the floor, a buffed linoleum; the long hallway-width room lined with facing rows of plastic chairs.

At the end of the narrow room was a reception window, its metal shutter rolled down, and beside it was a closed door. Levon sat down next to Barbara, and Hawkins sat across from them with his notebook sticking out of his breast pocket, and they waited.

At a few minutes past eight, the shuttered window opened and people trickled in to pay parking tickets, register their cars, God knows what else. Guys with Rasta hair; girls with complicated tattoos; young moms with small, bawling kids.

Levon felt a stabbing pain behind his eyes, and he thought about Kim, wanting to know where she could be right now and if she was in any pain and why this had happened.

After a while, he stood up and paced along the gallery of Wanted posters, looked into the staring eyes of murderers and armed robbers, and then there were the missing-children posters, some of them digitally altered to age the kids to how they might look now, having disappeared so many years ago.

Behind him, Barbara said to Hawkins, "Can you believe it? We've been here two hours. Don't you just want to scream?"

And Levon did want to scream. *Where was his daughter?* He leaned down and spoke to the female officer behind the window. "Does Lieutenant Jackson know we're here?"

"Yes, sir, he sure does."

Levon sat down next to Barb, pinched the place between his eyes, wondered why Jackson was taking so long. And he thought about Hawkins, how he'd gotten in very tight with Barb. Levon trusted Barb's judgment, but, like a lot of women, she made friends fast. Sometimes too fast.

Levon watched Hawkins writing in his notebook and then some teenage girls joined the line at the front desk, talking in high-pitched chatter that just about took off the top of his head.

By ten fifteen, Levon's agitation was like the rumbling of the volcanoes that had raised this island out of the prehistoric sea. He felt ready to explode.

Chapter 29

I WAS SITTING in a hard plastic chair next to Barbara McDaniels when I heard the door open at the end of the long, narrow room. Levon leapt up from his seat and was practically in the cop's face before the door swung closed.

The cop was big, midthirties, with thick black hair and mocha-toned skin. He looked part Jimmy Smits, part Ben Affleck, and part island surfer god. Wore a jacket and tie, had a shield hooked into the waistband of his chinos, a gold one, which meant he was a detective.

Barbara and I joined Levon, who introduced us to Lieutenant Jackson. Jackson asked me, "What's your relationship to the McDanielses?"

"Friend of the family," Barbara said at the same time that I said, "I'm with the *L.A. Times*."

Jackson snorted a laugh, scrutinized me, then asked, "Do you know Kim?"

No.

"Have any information as to her whereabouts?"

No.

"Do you know these people? Or did you meet them, say, yesterday?"

"We just met."

"Interesting," Jackson said, smirking now. He said to the McDanielses. "You understand this man's job is to sell newspapers?"

"We know that," Levon said.

"Good. Just so you're clear, anything you say to Mr. Hawkins is going directly from your mouths to the front page of the *L.A. Times*. Speaking for myself," Jackson went on, "I don't want him here. Mr. Hawkins, have a seat, and if I need you, I'll call you."

Barbara spoke up. "Lieutenant, my husband and I talked it over last night, and it comes down to this. We trust Ben, and he has the power of the *L.A. Times* behind him. He might be able to do more for us than we can do alone."

Jackson exhaled his exasperation but seemed to concede the point. He said to me, "Anything out of *my* mouth has to be okayed by me before you run with it, understand?"

I said I did.

Jackson's office took up a corner at the back of the building, had one window and a noisy air conditioner; numbers were written on the blue plasterboard walls near the phone.

Jackson indicated chairs for the McDanielses, and I leaned against the doorframe as he flapped open a notepad, took down basic information.

Then he got down to business, working, I thought, off a notion that Kim was a party girl, questioning her late-night habits and asking about men in her life and drug use.

Barbara told Jackson that Kim was a straight-A student. That she had sponsored a Christian Children's Fund baby in Ecuador. That she was responsible to a fault and the fact that she hadn't returned their call was *way* out of character.

Jackson listened with a mostly bored look on his face before saying, "Yeah, I'm sure she's an angel. I'm waiting for the day someone comes in, says their kid is a meth head or a slut."

Levon sprang to his feet, and Jackson stood up a beat after that, but by then Levon had the advantage. He shoved his palms into Jackson's beefy shoulders, sending him backward into the wall, which shook with a loud crack. Plaques and photos crashed to the floor, which is what you'd expect when 180 pounds or so was used as a wrecking ball.

Jackson was the bigger and younger man, but Levon was mainlining adrenaline. Without pause, he reached down and grabbed Jackson up by his lapels and threw him against the wall again. There was another terrible crashing sound as Jackson's head bounced off the plasterboard. I watched him grab for the arm of his chair, which toppled, and sent him down a third time.

It was an ugly scene even *before* Levon crowned the moment.

He stared down at Jackson, and said, "Damn, that felt good. You son of a bitch."

Chapter 30

A HEAVYSET FEMALE OFFICER BARRELED toward the doorway as I stood there like a stump, trying to absorb that Levon had assaulted a *cop,* shoved him, thrown him down, cursed at him, and said it felt *good.*

Now Jackson was on his feet, and Levon was still panting. The woman cop yelled, *"Hey, what's going on?"*

Jackson said, "We're fine here, Millie. Lost my balance. Gonna need a new chair." And he waved her off. Then he turned back to Levon, who was shouting at him, "Don't you *get* it? I told you last *night.* We got a fricking *phone call* in Michigan. The man said he took my daughter, and you're trying to say Kim's a tramp?"

Jackson straightened his jacket, his tie, righted his chair. His face was red and he was scowling. He jerked the chair around, then shouted back at Levon, "You're *crazy,* McDaniels.

You realize what you just did, you stupid *fuck?* You want to be locked up? *Do you?* You think you're a tough guy? You want to find out just how tough *I am?* I could arrest your ass and have you put away for this, don't you know that?"

"Yeah, throw me in jail, damn you. Do that, because I want to tell the world how you treated us. What a yahoo you are."

"Levon, Levon," Barbara was up, begging her husband, pulling at his arm. "Stop, Levon. Control yourself. Apologize to the lieutenant, please."

Jackson sat down, rolled his chair up to his desk, said, "McDaniels, don't ever put a hand on me again. Due to the fact that you're out of your fucking mind, I'll minimize what just happened in my report. Now sit down before I change my mind and arrest you."

Levon was still blowing hard, but Jackson gestured to the chairs, and Levon and Barbara sat down.

Jackson touched the back of his head, rubbed his elbow, then said, "Half the time, a kid goes missing, one of the parents knows what happened. Sometimes both of them. I had to see where you were coming from."

Levon and Barbara stared. And we all got it. Jackson had provoked them to see how they'd react.

It had been a test. They'd passed. In a manner of speaking.

"We've been investigating this case since yesterday morning. Like I told you when I called," Jackson said, glaring at Levon. "We've met with the *Sporting Life* people, also the desk and bar staff at the Princess. So far, we got nothing from that."

104

Jackson opened his desk drawer, took out a cell phone, one of those thin, half-human devices that takes pictures, sends mail, and tells you when you're low on oil.

"This is Kim's phone," Jackson said. "We found it on the beach behind the Princess. We've dumped the data and found a number of phone calls to Kim from a man named Doug Cahill."

"Cahill?" Levon said. "Doug Cahill used to date Kim. He lives in Chicago."

Jackson shook his head. "He was calling Kim from *Maui*. Called her every hour until her mailbox filled up and stopped taking incoming calls."

"You're saying Doug is *here*?" Barbara asked. "He's in Maui now?"

"We located Cahill in Makena, worked on him for two hours last night before he lawyered up. He said he hadn't seen Kim. That she wouldn't talk to him. And we couldn't hold him, because we have nothing on him," Jackson said, putting Kim's cell phone back in the drawer.

"McDaniels, here's what we've got. You got a phone call saying Kim was in bad hands. And we have Kim's cell phone. We don't even know if a crime has been committed. If Cahill gets on a plane, there's nothing we can do to stop him from leaving."

I saw Barbara start, shock coming over her face again.

"Doug's not your guy," Levon said.

Jackson's eyebrows shot up. "Why do you say that?"

"I know Doug's voice. The man who called us wasn't Doug."

Chapter 31

WE WERE BACK in the black sedan. This time I was in front, beside the driver. Marco adjusted his rearview mirror, and we exchanged nods, but there was nothing to say. It was all going on in the backseat between Barbara and Levon.

Levon was explaining to his wife, "Barb. I didn't tell you what that bastard said *verbatim* because there was nothing to be gained from it. I'm sorry."

"I'm your wife. You had no right to hold back what he said."

"'She's fallen into bad hands,' okay? That's the only thing I didn't tell you, and I still wouldn't tell you, but I had to tell Jackson. I tried to spare you, sweetheart, I wanted to spare you."

Barb cried, "Spare me? You lied to me, Levon. You lied." And then Levon was crying too, and I realized that this was what had been binding Levon up, why he'd been so glassy-eyed and removed. A man had said that he was going to hurt his daughter and Levon hadn't told his wife. And now he couldn't pretend anymore that it wasn't true.

I wanted to give them some privacy, so I lowered the window, stared out at the beachfront whizzing by, at the families picnicking by the ocean, as Kim's parents suffered terribly. The contrast between the campers and the weeping couple behind me was excruciating.

I made a note, then swiveled in my seat and, trying for something comforting, I said to Levon, "Jackson isn't subtle, but he's on the case. He might be a pretty good cop."

Kim's father leveled hard eyes on me.

"I think you're right about Jackson. He nailed you in five seconds. Look at you. You parasite. Writing your story. Selling newspapers on our pain."

I felt the accusation like a gut punch—but there was some truth in it, I guess. I swallowed the hurt and found my compassion for Levon.

I said, "You've got a point, Levon. But even if I'm exactly what you say, Kim's story could get out of control and eat you alive.

"Think of JonBenet Ramsey. Natalee Holloway. Chandra Levy. I hope Kim is safe and that she's found fast. But whatever happens, you're going to want me with you. Because I'm not going to fan the flames and I'm not going to make anything up. *I'm going to tell the story right.*"

Chapter 32

MARCO WATCHED UNTIL Hawkins and the McDanielses passed between the koi ponds and entered the hotel before he put the car in gear, eased out onto Wailea Alanui Drive, and headed south.

As he drove, he felt under the seat, pulled out a nylon duffel bag, and put it beside him. Then he reached behind the rearview mirror where he'd parked the cutting-edge, wireless, high-resolution, micro–video camera. He ejected the media card and dropped it into his shirt pocket.

He had a thought that maybe the camera had slipped during the drive back from the police station and the angle might have been off, but even if he just got the crying, he had his sound track for another scene. Levon talking about bad hands? Priceless.

Sneaky Marco.

Imagine their surprise when they figure it all out. If they ever do.

He felt a rush as he added up the cash potential of his new contract, the thick stack of euros with the possibility of doubling his take, depending on the vote of the Alliance on the project as a whole.

He would thrill them to the roots of their short hairs, that's how good this film would be, and all he had to do was what he did best. How could a job possibly be better than this?

Marco saw his turn coming up, signaled, got into the right lane, then entered the parking lot of the Shops at Wailea. He parked the Caddy in the southernmost section of the lot, far from the mall's surveillance cameras and next to his nondescript rented Taurus.

Hidden behind the Caddy's tinted glass, the killer stripped himself of all things Marco: the chauffeur's cap and wig, fake mustache, livery jacket, cowboy boots. Then he took "Charlie Rollins" out of the bag. The baseball cap, beat-up Adidas, wraparound shades, press pass, and both cameras.

He changed quickly, bagged the Marco artifacts, then made the return trip to the Wailea Princess in the Taurus. He tipped the bellman three bucks, then checked in at the front desk, lucking out, getting a king-size bed, ocean view.

Leaving the desk, heading for the stairway at the far end of the marble acreage of the lobby, Henri as "Charlie Rollins" saw the McDanielses and Ben Hawkins sitting together around a low glass table, coffee cups in front of them.

Rollins felt his heart kick into overdrive as Hawkins

turned, looked at him, pausing for a nanosecond—maybe his reptilian brain was making a match?—before his "rational" brain, fooled by the Rollins getup, steered his gaze past him.

The game could have been over in that one look, but *Hawkins hadn't recognized him*—and he'd been sitting right beside him in the car for hours. This was the real thrill, skating along the razor's edge and getting away with it.

So Charlie Rollins, photographer from the nonexistent *Talk Weekly,* jacked it up a notch. He raised his Sony—*say cheese, mousies*—and snapped off three shots of the McDanielses.

Gotcha, Mom and Dad.

His heart was still pounding as Levon scowled and leaned forward, blocking his camera's-eye view of Barbara.

Ecstatic, the killer took the stairs to his room, thinking now about Ben Hawkins, a man who interested him even more than the McDanielses did. Hawkins was a great crime writer, every one of his books as good as *The Silence of the Lambs*. But Hawkins hadn't quite made it to the big time. Why not?

Rollins slipped the card key into the slot and got the green light. His door opened onto a scene of casual magnificence that he barely noticed. He was busy turning ideas over in his mind, thinking about how to make Ben Hawkins an integral part of his project.

It was just a question of how best to use him.

Chapter 33

LEVON PUT DOWN HIS COFFEE CUP, the porcelain chattering against the saucer, knowing that Barb and Hawkins and probably the entire gang of Japanese tourists trooping by could see that his hands were shaking. But he couldn't do a thing about it.

That damned bloodsucking paparazzo pointing the camera at him and Barb! Plus he was reeling from the aftershocks of his out-of-control fight with Lieutenant Jackson. He still felt the shove in the balls of his hands, still felt a flush of mortification at the idea that he could be in a jail cell right now, but hell, he'd done it, and that was that.

The bright side: maybe he'd motivated Jackson to bust his ass on Kim's behalf. If not, too bad. They weren't going to be relying entirely on Jackson anymore.

Levon felt someone coming up behind him, and Hawkins was getting out of his chair, saying, "There he is now."

Levon looked up, saw a thirtyish man coming across the lobby in slacks and a blue sports jacket over a bold Hawaiian-print shirt, his bleached-blond hair parted in the middle. Hawkins was saying, "Levon, Barbara, meet Eddie Keola, the best private detective in Maui."

"The *only* private detective in Maui," Keola said, his smile showing braces on his teeth. God, Levon thought, he's not much older than Kim. *This* was the detective who found the Reese girl?

Keola shook hands with the McDanielses, sat down in one of the richly upholstered rattan-backed chairs, and said, "Good to meet you. And forgive me for jumping right in, but I've already got some feelers out."

"Already?" Barb asked.

"As soon as Ben called me, I reached out. I was born about fifteen minutes from here and I was on the force for a few years when I got out of school, University of Hawaii. I've got a good working relationship with the police," he said. He wasn't show-offy in Levon's opinion, was just stating his credentials.

"They've got a suspect," Keola added.

"We know him," Levon said, and he told Keola about Doug Cahill being Kim's ex-boyfriend, then went over the phone call back home in Michigan that had cracked open his universe like it was a raw egg.

Barb asked Keola to tell them about Carol Reese, the twenty-year-old track star from Ohio State who'd gone missing a couple of years before.

"I found her in San Francisco," Keola said. "She had a bad-news, violent boyfriend and so she kidnapped herself, changed her name and everything. She was powerfully mad at me for finding her," he said, nodding his head as he remembered.

Levon said, "Tell me how this would work."

Keola said he'd want to talk to the *Sporting Life* photographer, see if he might have filmed some bystanders at the shoot, and that he'd talk to hotel security, see the security tapes from the Typhoon Bar the night Kim disappeared.

"Let's hope Kim shows up on her own," Keola went on, "but if not, this is going to be basic, shoe-leather detective work. You'll be my only client. I'll pull in additional help as needed, and we'll work around the clock. It's over when you say it's over and not before. That's the right way to go."

Levon discussed rates with Keola, but it really didn't matter. He thought about the hours posted on the door at the police station in Kihei. Monday through Friday, eight to five. Saturday, ten to four. Kim, in a dungeon or a ditch, helpless.

Levon said, "You're hired. You've got the job."

Chapter 34

MY PHONE RANG as soon as I opened the door to my room.

I said hello to a woman who said, "Ben-ah Haw-keens?" Strong accent.

I said, "Yes, this is Hawkins," and I waited for her to tell me who she was, but she didn't identify herself. "There's a man, staying in the Princess hotel."

"Go on."

"His name is Nils Bjorn, and you should talk to him."

"And why's that?"

My caller said that Bjorn was a European businessman who should be investigated. "He was in the hotel when Kim McDaniels went missing. He could be...you should talk to him."

I pulled at the desk drawer, looking for stationery and a pen.

"What makes this Nils Bjorn suspicious?" I asked, finding the paper and pen, writing down the name.

"You talk to him. I have to hang up now," the woman said—and did.

I took a bottle of Perrier from the fridge and went out to my balcony. I was staying at the Marriott, a quarter mile up the beach from the much pricier Wailea Princess but with the same dazzling ocean view. I sipped my Perrier and thought about my tipster. For starters, how had she found me? Only the McDanielses and Amanda knew where I was staying.

I went back through the sliding doors, booted up my laptop, and when I got an Internet connection I Googled "Nils Bjorn."

The first hit was an article that had run in the London *Times* a year before, about a Nils Bjorn who had been arrested in London, held on suspicion of selling arms to Iran, released for lack of evidence.

I kept clicking and opening articles, all of which were similar if not identical to the first.

I opened another Perrier and kept poking, found another story on Bjorn going back to 2005, a charge of "aggravated assault on a woman," the legal term for rape. The woman's name wasn't mentioned, only that she was a model, age nineteen, and again, Bjorn wasn't indicted.

My last stop on Bjorn's Internet trail was *Skoal,* a glossy European society magazine. There was a photo that had been taken at a reception dinner for a Swedish industrialist who'd opened a munitions factory outside of Gothenburg.

I enlarged the photo, studied the man identified as Bjorn,

stared at his flashbulb-lit eyes. He had regular features, light brown hair, straight nose, looked to be in his thirties, and had not one remarkable or memorable feature.

I saved the photo to my hard drive and then I called the Wailea Princess and asked for Nils Bjorn. I was told he'd checked out the day before.

I asked to be put through to the McDanielses.

I told Levon about my phone call from the woman and what I knew about Nils Bjorn: He'd been charged with selling arms to a terrorist nation, and he'd been charged with raping a model. Neither charge had stuck. Two days ago he'd been staying at the Wailea Princess hotel.

I was trying to keep my excitement in check, but I could hear it in my voice.

"This could be a break," I said.

Chapter 35

LEVON WAS HOLDING for Jackson. After five minutes of Muzak, he was told the police lieutenant would call him back. He hung up the phone, turned on the television, a big plasma thing, took up half the wall, as the news was coming on.

First came the flashy graphic intro to *All-Island News at Noon* with Tracy Baker and Candy Ko'alani, and then Baker was talking about the "still-missing model, Kim McDaniels" and cutting to a picture of her in a bikini. Then Jackson's face was on the screen above the word "Live."

He was talking to the press in front of the police station.

Levon shouted, "Barb, come in here, *quick*," as he cranked up the volume. Barb sat next to him on the sofa just as Jackson was saying, "We're talking to a person of interest, and this investigation is ongoing. Anyone with information

117

about Kim McDaniels is asked to call us. Confidentiality will be respected. And that's all I can say at this time."

"They arrested someone or not?" Barb said, clutching his hand.

"A 'person of interest' is a suspect. But they don't have enough on him, or they'd be saying he was in custody." Levon cranked up the volume a little more.

A reporter asked, "Lieutenant, we understand you're talking to Doug Cahill."

"No comment. That's all I have for you. Thank you."

Jackson turned away and the reporters went nuts, and then Tracy Baker was back on the screen, saying "Doug Cahill, linebacker for the Chicago Bears, has been seen on Maui, and informed sources say he was Kim McDaniels's lover." A picture came on the screen of Doug in his uniform, helmet under his arm, huge grin, cropped blond hair, midwestern good looks.

"I could see him pestering her," Barb said, chewing on her lower lip, snatching the remote out of Levon's hand, dialing the volume down. "But hurt her? I do *not* believe that."

And then the phone rang. Levon grabbed it off the hook.

"Mr. McDaniels, this is Lieutenant Jackson."

"Are you arresting Doug Cahill? If you are, it's a mistake."

"A witness came forward an hour ago, a local who said he'd seen Cahill harassing Kim after the photo shoot."

"Didn't Doug tell you he hadn't seen Kim?" Levon asked.

"Right. So maybe he lied to us and so we're talking to him now. He's still denying any involvement."

"There's someone else you should know about," Levon said, and he told Jackson about Hawkins's recent phone call concerning a tip about an international businessman named Nils Bjorn.

"We know who Bjorn is," Jackson said. "There's no link between Bjorn and Kim. No witnesses. Nothing on the surveillance tapes."

"You talked with him?"

"Bjorn had checked out before anyone knew Kim was missing. McDaniels, I know you don't buy it, but Cahill is our guy. We just need time enough to break him."

Chapter 36

HENRI, in his Charlie Rollins gear, was having lunch at the Sand Bar, the hotel's exquisite beachside restaurant. Yellow market umbrellas glowed overhead, and teenagers ran up the steps from the beach, their tanned bodies glistening with water. Henri didn't know who was more beautiful, the boys or the girls.

Henri's waitress brought him liquid sugar for his iced tea and a basket of cheesy breadsticks and said his salad would be coming shortly. He nodded pleasantly, said he was enjoying the view and had no place he'd rather be than here.

A waiter pulled out a chair at the next table, and a pretty, young woman sat down. She wore her black hair in a short, boyish style, was dressed in a white bikini top and yellow shorts.

Henri knew who she was behind her Maui Jim shades.

When she put down her menu, he said, "Julia. Julia Winkler."

She looked up, said, "Sorry. Do I know you?"

"I know *you*," he said, held up his camera to say, I'm in the business. "Are you on a job?"

"I was," she said. "The shoot wrapped yesterday. I'm going back to L.A. tomorrow."

"Oh. The *Sporting Life* job?"

She nodded, her face getting sad. "I've been waiting around, hoping...I was rooming with Kim McDaniels."

"She'll be back," Henri said kindly.

"You think? Why?"

"I have a feeling she's taking a holiday. It happens."

"If you're so psychic, where is she?"

"She's out of my vibrational reach, but I can read you loud and clear."

"Sure. So what am I thinking?"

"That you're feeling sad and a little lonely and you wish you were having lunch with someone who would make you smile."

Julia laughed, and Henri signaled to the waiter, asked him to set Ms. Winkler up at his table, and the beautiful girl sat down next to him so that they were both looking out at the view.

"Charlie," he said, putting out his hand. "Rollins."

"Hi, Charlie Rollins. What am I having for lunch?"

"Grilled chicken salad and a Diet Coke. And here's what

else. You're thinking you'd like to stay over another day because a neighbor is taking care of your cat and it's so nice here, so what's the rush to go home?"

Julia laughed again. "Bruno. He's a Rottweiler."

"I knew that," Henri said, sitting back as the waitress brought his salad and asked Julia for her order, grilled chicken and a mai tai.

"Even if I were to stay over another night, I never date photographers," she said, eyeing the camera resting on the table facing her.

"Have I asked you out?"

"You will."

Their grins turned into laughter, and then Rollins said, "All right, I'll ask you out. And I'm taking your picture so the guys in Loxahatchee won't think I made this up."

"Okay, but take off your sunglasses, Charlie. I want to see your eyes."

"Show me yours, I'll show you mine."

Chapter 37

"WHOOOOOOO," Julia screamed as the chopper yawed into the coral-gold sky. The little island of Lanai grew huge, and then they were dropping softly to the tiny private heliport at the edge of the vast Island Breezes Hotel's greener-than-green golf course.

Charlie got out first and helped Julia to the ground as she held the collar of her windbreaker closed, her curly hair parting, her cheeks flushed. They ducked under the rotor blades and ran to a waiting car.

"You've got a great expense account, buddy," she said breathlessly.

"Our dream date's on me, Julia."

"Really?"

"What kind of person would expense a date with you?"

"Awww."

The driver opened the doors, and then the car rolled slowly over the carriage road to the hotel, Julia gasping as she entered the lobby, all velvety teal and gold and burgundy, dense Chinese carpets and ancient statuary. The sunset streamed through the open-air space, almost stealing the show.

Julia and Charlie had their twin massages in a bamboo hut open to the ocean's rhythmic pounding on the shore. The masseurs quartered the plumeria-scented sheets that covered them as their strong hands massaged in cocoa butter before proceeding to the long strokes of the traditional *lomi lomi* massage.

Julia, lying on her stomach, smiled lazily at the man she'd just met, saying, "This is too good. I don't want it to ever stop."

"It only gets better from here."

Dinner came hours later at the restaurant on the main floor. Pillars and soft lighting were the backdrop for their feast of shrimp and Kurubuta pork chops with mango chutney and an excellent French wine. And Julia was happy to let Charlie lead her in conversation about herself. She opened up to him, talking about her upbringing on an army base in Beirut, her move to Los Angeles, her lucky break.

Charlie ordered a dessert wine and the entire dessert menu: zuccotto, pralines and milk, chocolate mousse, Lanai bananas caramelized by the waiter at the table. The delicious fragrance of burnt sugar made him hungry all over again. He looked at the girl, and she was a girl now, sweet and vulnerable and available to him.

Four thousand dollars had been well spent, even if he stopped right now.

But he didn't.

They changed into their swimsuits in a cabana by the pool and took a long walk on the beach. Moonlight bathed the sand, turning the ocean into a magical meeting of rushing sound and frothing foam.

And then Julia laughed, and said, "Last one in the water is an old poop, and that will be you, Charlie."

She ran, screamed as the water lapped her thighs, and Charlie snapped off some quick shots before putting his camera back inside his duffel bag and setting it down.

"Let's see who's an old poop."

He sprinted toward her, dove into the waves, and surfaced with his arms around her.

Chapter 38

AFTER A QUICK DINNER out with Keola, I returned to my hotel room, checked for messages, had no new calls from the woman with the accent, or anyone else. I cranked up my computer, and after a while I sent a pretty fine seven-hundred-word story to Aronstein's in-box at the *L.A. Times.*

Work done for today, I turned on the TV and saw that Kim's story was headlining the ten o'clock news.

There was a banner, "Breaking News," and then the talking heads announced that Doug Cahill was a presumed suspect in the presumed abduction of Kim McDaniels. Cahill's picture came on the screen, fully uniformed for a Chicago Bears game, smiling at the camera like a movie star, all 6 feet, 3 inches, and 250 pounds of him.

Anyone would have been able to do the math. Cahill

could've easily picked up 110-pound Kim McDaniels and carried her under his arm like a football.

And then my eyes nearly jumped out of my head.

Cahill was shown in a video clip that had been shot two hours earlier. While I was having pizza with Eddie Keola, the action had taken place right outside the police station in Kihei.

Cahill was flanked by two lawyers, one of whom I recognized. Amos Brock was dapper in his pearl gray suit, a New York criminal defense attorney with a history of representing celebrities and sports stars who'd gone too far over to the dark side. Brock had turned into a star himself, and now he was defending Doug Cahill.

Station KITV had cameras trained on Cahill and Brock. Brock stepped to the microphone, said, "My client, Doug Cahill, hasn't been charged with anything. The accusations against him are preposterous. There's not a speck of evidence to support any of the allegations that have been going around, which is why my client hasn't been charged. Doug wants to speak publicly, this one and only time."

I grabbed the phone, woke Levon out of what sounded like a deep sleep. "Levon. It's Ben. Turn on the TV. Channel four. Hurry."

I stayed on with Levon as Cahill stood front and center. He was unshaven, wearing a blue cotton button-down shirt under a well-cut sports jacket. Without the pads and the uniform, he looked relatively tame, like a kid in a Wall Street management training program.

"I came to Maui to see Kim," Doug said, his voice shaking, thick with the tears that were also wetting his cheeks. "I saw her for about ten minutes three days ago and never saw her after that. I *didn't* hurt her. I love Kim, and I'm staying here until we find her."

Cahill handed the mic back to Brock: "To repeat, Doug had nothing to do with Kim's disappearance, and I will absolutely, unequivocally bring action against anyone who defames him. That's all we have to say for the moment. Thank you."

Levon said to me, "What do you make of that? The lawyer? Doug?"

"Doug was pretty convincing," I said. "Either he loves her. Or he's a very good liar."

I had another thought, one I didn't share with Levon. Those seven hundred words I'd just sent to Aronstein at the *Times*?

They were old news.

Chapter 39

I E-MAILED MY EDITOR, told him that Doug Cahill was going to be chum for the media feeding frenzy and why: that a mystery witness had seen him coming on strong with Kim, and that Cahill was being represented by Amos Brock, the current champion bully of defense attorneys.

"Here's an updated version of my article," I wrote Aronstein. "If nothing else, I'm fast."

And then I called our sports chief, Sam Paulson. He keeps odd hours, and I knew he'd be up.

Paulson likes me, but he doesn't trust anyone. I said, "Look, Sam, I need to know what kind of person Doug Cahill is. My story isn't going to mess with yours."

It was a wrestling match that went on for fifteen minutes, Sam Paulson protecting his position as the sports world's premiere "in" guy, while I tried to get something out of Paulson that would tell me if Cahill was dangerous *off* the playing field.

At last Sam gave me a tantalizing lead.

"There's a PR girl. I got her a job working for the Bears. Hawkins, I'm not kidding. This is off the record. This girl's a friend of mine."

"I understand."

"Cahill got this girl pregnant a couple months back. She's told her mother about the baby. She also told Cahill and me. She's giving Cahill a chance to do the right thing. *Whatever* the hell that might be."

"He was dating Kim when this happened with the other woman? You're certain?"

"Yep."

"Does he have any history of violence?"

"They all do. Sure. Bar fights. One zesty one when he played at Notre Dame. Crap like that."

"Thanks, Sam."

"Don't mention it," he said back. "I mean *really*. Don't mention it."

I sat on this bombshell for a few minutes, thinking through what this meant. If Kim knew Cahill had cheated on her, that was reason enough for her to dump him. If he wanted her back, if he was desperate, a confrontation could have led to something physical that might have gotten out of hand.

I called Levon. And I was startled by his reaction.

"Doug is a testosterone machine," he told me. "Kim said he was strong-willed, and we all know he was a killer on the field. How do we know what he's capable of doing? Barb still believes in him, but as for me, I'm starting to think maybe Jackson is right. Maybe they've got the right guy after all."

Chapter 40

JULIA FELT WEIGHTLESS in Charlie's arms, like an angel. Her long legs locked around his waist, and all he had to do was raise his knees, and she was sitting on his lap.

He did just that as they bobbed in the waves. She lifted her face to him, saying, "Charlie, this has been the most. The best."

"It gets better from here," he said again, his theme song for their date, and she grinned at him, kissed him softly, then deeply, a long salty kiss followed by another, electricity arcing like heat lightning around them.

He undid the string tie at her neck, jerked loose the tie behind her back, said, "You do a lot for a simple white bikini."

"What bikini?"

"Never mind," he said, and the swimsuit top drifted away,

a ribbon of white on the black waves, until it was gone, and she didn't seem to care.

Julia was too busy licking his ear, her nipples as hard as diamonds against his chest. She groaned as he shifted her so she was pressed even tighter to him, rubbing like an eager beaver against his dick.

He reached around and ran his fingers under the elastic of her bikini bottoms, touched the tender places, making her squeal and squirm like a kid.

She pushed down at the waistband of his swim shorts with the backs of her feet.

"Wait," he said. "Be good."

"I plan to be *great*," she said breathily, kissing him, pulling at his shorts again. "I'm dying for you." She sighed.

He unhooked her legs and pulled off the bottom half of her swimsuit. Carrying the naked girl in his arms, he walked out of the waves as water streamed off their bodies, silver in the moonlight.

Charlie said, "Hang on to me, monkey."

He brought her over to where he'd left his duffel bag next to a mound of black lava rock. He stooped and unzipped the bag, pulled out two enormous beach towels.

Still balancing the girl in his arms, he spread out one towel and laid Julia softly down, covered her with the second towel.

He turned away briefly, set the Panasonic camera on top of the duffel, and switched it on, angling it just so.

Then he faced Julia again, shucked his swim trunks, smiled when she said, "Oh my God, oh my *God*, Charlie."

He knelt between her legs, tonguing her until she cried out, "Please, I can't stand it, Charlie. I'm begging you, please," and he entered her.

Her screams were washed away by the ocean's roar, just as he had imagined they would be, and when they were done, he reached into the duffel bag and took out a knife with a serrated blade. Put the knife down on the towel beside them.

"What's that for?" Julia asked.

"Can't be too careful," Charlie said, shrugging off the question. "In case some bad guy is creeping around."

He raked back her short hair, kissed her closed eyes, put his arms around the naked girl, and warmed her up with his skin. "Go to sleep, Julia," he said. "You're safe with me."

"It gets better from here?" she teased.

"Piggy."

She laughed, snuggled against his chest. Charlie pulled the towel up over her eyes. Julia thought he was talking to her when he said into the camera lens, "Is everybody happy?"

"Totally, completely happy," she said with a sigh.

Chapter 41

ANOTHER WRENCHING TWENTY-FOUR hours passed for Levon and Barbara, and I felt helpless to ease their despair. The news shows were running the same old clips when I went to bed that night, and I was somewhere, deep in a troubling dream, when the phone rang.

Eddie Keola spoke to me, saying, "Ben, *don't* call the McDanielses on this. Just meet me in front of your hotel in ten minutes."

Keola's Jeep was running when I jogged out into the warm night, then quickly climbed up into the passenger seat.

"Where are we going?" I asked him.

"A beach called Makena Landing. The cops may have found something. Or somebody."

Ten minutes later, Eddie parked along the curving

roadside behind six police cruisers, vans from the Special Response Team and the coroner's office. Below us was a semicircle of beach, a cove that was bounded by fingers of lava rock before tapering out into the ocean.

A helicopter hovered noisily overhead, beaming its spotlight on the scramble of law enforcement people moving like stick figures along the shoreline.

Keola and I made our way down to the beach, and I saw that a fire department rescue vehicle had backed down to the water's edge. There were inflatable boats in the water, and a scuba team was going down.

I was sickened at the thought that Kim's body was submerged there and that she had disappeared to get away from an old boyfriend.

Keola interrupted my reverie to introduce me to a Detective Palikapu, a heavyset young cop in a Maui PD jacket.

"Those campers over there," Palikapu said, pointing to a cluster of children and adults on the far side of the lava-rock jetty. "They saw something floating during the day."

"A body, you mean," said Keola.

"They thought it was a log or garbage at first. Then they saw some shark activity and called it in. Since then, the tides took whatever it is under the bubble rock and left it there. That's where the divers are now."

Keola explained to me that the bubble rock was a shelf of lava with a concave undersurface. He said that sometimes people swam into caves like this one at low tide, didn't pay attention when the tide came in, and drowned.

Was that what had happened to Kim? Suddenly it seemed very possible.

TV vans were pulling up on the shoulder of the road, photographers and reporters clambering down to the beach, the cops stringing up yellow tape to keep the scene intact.

One of the photographers came up to me, introduced himself as Charlie Rollins. He said he was freelance and if I needed photos for the *L.A. Times* he could provide them.

I took his card, then turned in time to see the first divers coming out of the water. One of them had a bundle in his arms.

Keola said, *"You're with me,"* and we skirted the crime scene tape. We were standing on the lip of the shore when a boat came in.

The bright light from the chopper illuminated the body in the diver's arms. She was small, maybe a teenager or maybe a child. Her body was so bloated that I couldn't tell her age, but she was bound with ropes, hand and foot.

Lieutenant Jackson stepped forward and used a gloved hand to move the girl's long, dark hair away from her face.

I was relieved that the victim wasn't Kim McDaniels and that I didn't have to make a call to Levon and Barbara.

But my relief was swamped with an almost overwhelming sorrow. Clearly another girl, someone else's daughter, had been savagely murdered.

Chapter 42

A WOMAN'S HIGH-PITCHED scream cut through the chopper's roar. I turned, saw a dark-skinned woman, five feet two or so, maybe a hundred pounds, make a run toward the yellow tape, crying out, *"Rosa! Rosa! Madre de Dios, no!"*

A man running close behind her shouted, *"Isabel, don't go there. No, Isabel!"* He caught up and pulled the woman into his arms and she beat at him with her fists, trying to break free, the cords in her neck stretched out as she cried, *"No, no, no, mi bebé, mi bebé."*

Police surrounded the couple, the woman's frantic cries trailing behind as she was hustled away from the scene. The press, a pack of them, ran toward the parents of the dead child. You could almost see light glinting in their eyes. Pathetic.

Under other circumstances, I could've been part of that

pack, but right then I was behind Eddie Keola, scrambling up the rocky slope to where media setups dotted the upper ledge. Local TV correspondents fed the breaking news to the cameras as the small, twisted body was transferred by stretcher into the coroner's van. Doors slammed and the van sped away.

"Her name was Rosa Castro," Keola told me as we got into the Jeep. "She was twelve. Did you see those ligatures? Arms and legs tied back like that."

I said, "Yeah. I saw."

I'd seen and written about violence for nearly half my life, but this little girl's murder put such ugly pictures into my mind that I felt physically sick. I swallowed my bile and yanked the car door closed.

Keola started up the engine, headed north, saying, "See, this is why I didn't want to call the McDanielses. And if it *had* been Kim—"

His sentence was interrupted by the ringing of his cell phone. He patted his jacket pocket, put his phone to his ear, said, "Keola," then "Levon, *Levon*. It's not Kim. Yes. I saw the body. I'm *sure*. It's not your daughter." Eddie mouthed to me, "They're watching the news on TV."

He told the McDanielses we would stop by their hotel, and minutes later we pulled up to the main entrance to the Wailea Princess.

Barb and Levon were under the breezeway, zephyrs riffling their hair and their new Hawaiian garb. They were holding each other's white-knuckled hands, their faces pale with fatigue.

We walked with them into the lobby. Keola explained, without going into the unspeakable details.

Barbara asked if there could be a connection between Rosa's death and Kim's disappearance, her way of seeking assurances that no one could give her. But I tried to do it anyway. I said that pattern killers had preferences, and it would be rare for one of them to target both a child and a woman. *Rare, but not unheard of*, I neglected to add.

I wasn't just telling Barbara what she wanted to hear, I was also comforting myself. At that time, I didn't know that Rosa Castro's killer had a wide-ranging and boundless appetite for torture and murder.

And it never entered my mind that I'd already met and talked with him.

Chapter 43

HORST TASTED the Domaine de la Romanée-Conti, bought at Sotheby's for $24,000 per bottle in 2001. He told Jan to hold out his glass. It was a joke. Jan was hundreds of miles away, but their webcam connection almost made it seem as if they were in the same room.

The occasion of this meeting: Henri Benoit had written to Horst saying to expect a download at nine p.m., and Horst had invited Jan, his friend of many years, to preview the newest video before sending it out to the rest of the Alliance.

A ping sounded from Horst's computer, and he walked to his desk, told his friend he was downloading now, and then forwarded the e-mail to Jan in his office in Amsterdam.

The images appeared simultaneously on their screens.

The background was a moonlit beach. A pretty girl was

lying faceup on a large towel. She was nude, slim-hipped, small-breasted, and her short hair was finger-combed in a boyish fashion. The black-and-white images of form and shadow gave the film a moody quality, as though it had been shot in the 1940s.

"Beautiful composition," said Jan. "The man has an eye."

When Henri entered the frame, his face was digitally pixilated to a blur, and his voice had been electronically altered. Henri talked to the girl, his voice playful, calling her a monkey and sometimes saying her name.

Horst commented to Jan, "Interesting, yes? The girl isn't the least bit afraid. She doesn't even appear to be drugged."

Julia was smiling up at Henri, reaching out her arms, opening her legs to him. He stepped out of his shorts, his cock large and erect, and the girl covered her mouth as she stared up at him, saying, *Oh my God, Charlie.*

Henri told her she was greedy, but they could hear the teasing and the laughter in his voice. They watched him kneel between her thighs, lift her buttocks, and lower his face until the girl squirmed, grinding her hips, digging her toes into the sand, crying out, *"Please, I can't stand it, Charlie."*

Jan said to Horst, "I think Henri is making her fall in love. Maybe he is falling in love, too? Wouldn't that be something to watch."

"Oh, you think Henri can feel love?"

As the two men watched, Henri stroked, teased, plunged himself into the girl's body, telling her how beautiful she was and to give herself to him until her cries became sobs.

She reached her hands around his neck, and Henri took her in his arms and kissed her closed eyes, her cheeks and mouth. Then his hand became large in front of the camera, almost blocking the image of the girl, and reappeared again, holding a hunting knife. He placed the blade beside the girl on the towel.

Horst was leaning forward, watching the screen intently, thinking, *Yes, first the ceremony, now the ultimate sacrifice,* when Henri turned his digitally obscured face to the camera and said, "Is everybody happy?"

The girl answered, yes, she was completely happy, and then the picture went black.

"What is *this?*" Jan asked, jerked out of what was almost a trance state. Horst reversed the video, reviewed the last moments, and he realized it was over. At least for them.

"Jan," he said, "our boy is teasing us, too. Making us wait for the finished product. Smart. Very smart."

Jan sighed. "What a life he is having at our expense."

"Shall we make a wager? Just between you and me?"

"On what?"

"How long before Henri gets caught?"

Chapter 44

IT WAS ALMOST FOUR IN THE MORNING, and I hadn't slept, my mind still burning with the images of Rosa Castro's tortured body, thinking of what had been done to her before her life ended under a rock in the sea.

I thought about her parents and the McDanielses and that these good people were suffering a kind of hell that Hieronymus Bosch couldn't have imagined, not on his most inspired day or night. I wanted to call Amanda but didn't. I was afraid I might slip and tell her what I was thinking: *Thank God we don't have kids.*

I swung my legs over the bed, turned on the lights. I got a can of POG out of the fridge, a passion fruit, orange, and guava drink, and then I booted up my laptop.

My mailbox had filled with spam since I'd checked it last, and CNN had sent me a news alert on Rosa Castro. I scanned the story quickly, finding that Kim was mentioned in the last paragraph.

I quickly typed Kim's name into the search box to see if CNN had dragged any new tidbits into their net. They had not.

I opened a can of Pringles, ate just one, made coffee with the complimentary drip coffeemaker, then pecked away at the Internet some more.

I found Doug Cahill videos on YouTube: frat house clips and locker-room antics, and a video of Kim sitting in the stands at a football game, clapping and stomping. The camera went back and forth between her and shots of Cahill playing against the New York Giants, nearly decapitating Eli Manning.

I tried to imagine Cahill killing Kim, and I couldn't rule out that a guy who could slam into three hundred pounders was a guy who could get physical with a resistant girl and accidentally, or on purpose, break her neck.

But, in my heart, I believed that Cahill's tears were real, that he loved Kim, and, logically, if he *had* killed her he had the means to get lost anywhere in the world by now.

So I sent my browser out to search for the name the female tipster had whispered in my ear, the suspected arms trader, Nils—middle name, Ostertag—Bjorn. The search returned the same leads I'd gotten the day before, but this time I opened the articles that were written in Swedish.

Using an online dictionary, I translated the Swedish words for "munitions" and "body armor," and then I found another photo of Bjorn dated three years earlier.

It was a candid shot of the man with the regular, almost forgettable, features getting out of a Ferrari in Geneva. He was wearing a handsome chalk-striped suit under a well-cut topcoat, carrying a Gucci briefcase. Bjorn looked different in this photo from the way he looked at the industrialist's black-tie dinner, because Bjorn's hair was now blond. White blond.

I clicked on the last of the articles about Nils Ostertag Bjorn, and another photo filled my screen, this one of a man in a military uniform. He looked about twenty or so, had wide-spaced eyes and a boxy chin. But he looked nothing like the other photos of Nils Bjorn I'd seen.

I read the text beneath the photo and made out the Swedish words for "Persian Gulf" and "enemy fire," and then it hit me.

I was reading an obituary.

Nils Ostertag Bjorn had been dead for fifteen years.

I went to the shower, let the hot water beat down on my head as I tried to fit the pieces together. Was this simply a case of two men with the same unusual name? Or had someone using a dead man's identity checked into the Wailea Princess?

If so, had he abducted and possibly murdered Kim McDaniels?

Chapter 45

HENRI BENOIT WOKE UP between soft, white layers of bedding in an elegant four-poster bed in his room at the Island Breezes Hotel on Lanai.

Julia was snoring gently under his arm, her face warm against his chest. Late morning sunlight filtered through the filmy curtains, the whole wide Pacific only fifty yards away.

This girl. This setting. This inimitable light. It was a cinematographer's *dream*.

He brushed Julia's hair away from her eyes with his fingers. The sweet girl was under the spell of the kava kava, plus the generous lacing of Valium he'd put in her cup. She'd slept deeply, but now it was time to wake her for her close-up.

Henri shook Julia's arm gently, said, "Wakey, wakey, monkey face."

Julia cracked open her eyes, said, "Charlie? What? Is it time for my flight?"

"Not yet. Want another ten minutes?"

She nodded, then dropped off against his shoulder.

Henri eased out of bed and got busy, turning on lamps, replacing the media card in his video camera with a new one, setting the camera on the dresser, blocking out the scene. Satisfied, he removed the silk tassel tiebacks from the curtains, letting the heavy drapery fall closed.

Julia mumbled a complaint as he turned her onto her stomach. He said, "It's okay. It's just Charlie," as he tied her legs to the posts at the foot of the bed, making a clove hitch knot with the cords, and then he tied her arms to the headboard using an exotic Japanese chain knot that photographed beautifully.

Julia threw a sigh as she slipped into another dream.

Henri went to his duffel bag, sorted through the contents, put on the clear plastic mask and blue latex gloves, unsheathed the hunting knife.

Masked and gloved but otherwise naked, Henri placed the knife on the nightstand, then knelt behind Julia and stroked her back before lifting her hips and entering her from behind. She moaned in her sleep, never waking, as he pumped into her, his pleasure overtaking reason, and told her that he loved her.

Afterward, he collapsed beside her, his arm across the small of her back until his breathing slowed. Then he straddled the sleeping girl, twirled her short hair around the fingers of his left hand, and lifted her head a few inches off the pillow.

"Ow," Julia said, opening her eyes. "You hurt me, Charlie."

"I'm sorry. I'll be more careful."

He waited a moment before drawing the blade lightly across the back of Julia's neck, leaving a thin red line.

Julia only flinched, but with Henri's second cut, her eyelids flew open wide. She twisted her head, her eyes growing huge as she took in the mask, the knife, the blood. She sucked in her breath, shouted, *"Charlie! What are you doing?"*

Henri's mood shattered. He'd been filled with love for this girl, and now she was defying him, wrecking his shot, ruining everything.

"For God's sake, Julia. Show a little class."

Julia screamed, bucked violently against the restraints, her body having more range of motion than Henri expected. Her elbow collided with his hand, and as the knife danced away from him, Julia filled her lungs and let loose a long, undulating, horror-movie screech.

She'd left Henri no choice. It wasn't graceful, but it was ultimately the best means to the end. He closed his hands around Julia's throat and shook her. Julia gagged and thrashed against the ropes as he squeezed off her air, controlled every last second of her life. He released, then squeezed her neck again—and again—and then finally she was still. Because she was dead.

Henri was panting as he got off the bed and crossed the floor to the camera.

He leaned toward the lens, put his hands on his knees, said with a grin, "Better than I planned. Julia went off script and ended our time together with a real flourish. I just love her. Is everybody happy?"

Chapter 46

HENRI WAS STEPPING OUT of the shower when he heard a knock at the door. *Had someone heard Julia screaming?* A voice called out, "Housekeeping."

"Go away!" he shouted. "Do not *disturb*. Read the *sign*, huh?"

Henri tightened the sash of his robe, walked to the glass doors at the far end of the room, opened them, and stepped out onto the balcony.

The beauty of the grounds spread out before him like the Garden of Eden. Birds chirped their little hearts out in the trees, pineapples grew in the flower beds, children ran along the walks to the pool as hotel staff set up lounge chairs. Beyond the pool, the ocean was bright blue, the sun beat down on another perfect Hawaiian day.

There were no sirens. No men in black. No trouble on the horizon for him.

All was well.

Henri palmed his cell phone, called for the helicopter, then went to the bed and pulled the comforter over Julia's body. He wiped down the room, every knob and surface, and turned on the TV as he dressed in his Charlie Rollins gear. Rosa Castro's face grinned at him from the TV screen, a sweet little girl, and then there was the continuing story of Kim McDaniels. No news, but the search went on.

Where was Kim? Where, oh, where could she be?

Henri packed his gear, checked the room for anything he might have overlooked, and when he was satisfied he put on Charlie's wraparound sunglasses and ball cap, swung his large duffel onto his shoulder, and left the room.

He passed the housekeeper's cart on his way to the elevator, said to the stout brown woman vacuuming, "I'm in Four-twelve."

"I can clean now?" she asked.

"No, no. A few more hours, please."

He apologized for the inconvenience, said, "I've left something for you in the room."

"Thank you," she said. Henri winked at her, took the stairs down to the marvelous velvet jewel box of a lobby with birds flying through one side and out the other.

He settled his bill at the desk, then asked a groundskeeper for a lift out to the helipad. He was already thinking ahead as the hotel's oversize golf cart ran smoothly alongside the green, the wind picking up now, blowing clouds out to the sea.

He tipped the driver and, holding down his cap, ran toward the chopper.

After buckling in, he raised his hand to say hello to the pilot. He pulled on headphones and, as the chopper lifted, he snapped off shots of the island with his Sony, what any tourist would do. But it was all for show. Henri was well beyond the magnificence of Lanai.

When the helicopter touched down in Maui, he made an important call.

"Mr. McDaniels? You don't know me. My name is Peter Fisher," he said, brushing his speech with a bit of Aussie. "I have something to tell you about Kim. I also have her watch—a Rolex."

Chapter 47

THE KAMEHAMEHA HOSTEL on Oahu had been built in the early 1900s, and it looked to Levon like it had been a boardinghouse, with small bungalows surrounding the main building. The beach was right across the highway. Out on the horizon, surfers crouched above their boards, skimming the waves, waiting for the Big One.

Levon and Barbara stepped over backpackers in the dark lobby, which smelled musty, like mildew with a touch of marijuana.

The man behind the desk looked like he'd washed up on the beach a hundred years ago. He had bloodshot eyes, hair in a white braid even longer than Barb's, and a stained "Bullish on America" T-shirt with a name patch: "Gus."

Levon told Gus that he and Barb had a reservation for

one night, and Gus told Levon that he'd need to be paid in full before he handed over the keys, those were the rules.

Levon gave the man ninety bucks in cash.

"No refunds, checkout at noon, no exceptions."

"We're looking for a guest named Peter Fisher," Levon said. "He has an accent. Australian or South African maybe. 'Pee-ta Fish-a.' You have his room number?"

The clerk flipped pages of the guest book, saying, "Not everyone signs in. If they come in a gang, I only need the one signature of whoever's paying. I don't see any Peter Fleisher."

"Fisher."

"Either way, I don't see him. Most people eat in our dining room at dinner. Six dollars, three courses. Ask around later, and you might find your man."

Gus looked hard at Levon, said, "I know you. You're the parents of that model got killed over on Maui."

Levon felt his blood pressure rocket, wondered if today was the day he would be cut down by a fatal myocardial infarction. "Where'd you hear that?" he snapped.

"Whad'ya mean? It's on TV. In the newspapers."

"She's not dead," Levon said.

He took the keys. With Barb behind him, they climbed to the third floor, opened the door to an appalling room: two small beds, mattress springs poking at grimy sheets. The shower stall was black with mold, there were years of crud in the blinds, and the scatter rug looked damp to the touch.

The sign tacked over the sink read, *"Please clean up after yourselfs. There's no maid service here."*

Barbara looked helplessly at her husband.

"We'll go downstairs for dinner in a while and talk to people. We don't have to stay here. We could go back."

"After we find this Fisher person."

"Of course," Levon said. But what he was thinking was, *If Fisher hadn't checked out of this hellhole. If the whole thing wasn't a hoax like Lieutenant Jackson warned him from the day they met.*

Chapter 48

HENRI DIDN'T RELY on the costume, the cowboy boots or the cameras or the wraparound shades. The trappings were important, but the *art* of disguise was in the gestures and the voice, and then there was the X Factor. The element that truly distinguished Henri Benoit as a first-class chameleon was his talent for becoming the man he was pretending to be.

At half past six that evening, Henri strolled into the rustic dining room of the Kamehameha Hostel. He was wearing jeans, a summer-weight blue cashmere sweater, sleeves pushed up, Italian loafers, no socks, gold watch, wedding band. His hair, streaked gray, was combed straight back, and his rimless glasses framed the look of a man of sophistication and means.

He gazed around the rough-hewn room, at the rows of tables and folding chairs and at the steam table. He joined the line and took the slop that was offered before heading toward the corner where Barbara and Levon sat behind their untouched food.

"Mind if I join you?" he asked.

"We're about to leave," Levon said, "but if you're brave enough to eat that, you're welcome to sit down."

"What the heck do you think this is?" Henri asked, pulling out a chair next to Levon. "Animal, vegetable, or mineral?"

Levon laughed, "I was told it's beef stew, but don't take my word for it."

Henri put out his hand, said, "Andrew Hogan. From San Francisco."

Levon shook his hand, introduced Barb and himself, said, "We're the only ones here in the over-forty crowd. Did you know what this pit was like when you booked your room?"

"Actually, I'm not staying here. I'm looking for my daughter. Laurie just graduated from Berkeley," he said modestly. "I told my wife that Laur's having the time of her life camping out with a bunch of other kids, but she hasn't called home in a few days. A week, actually. So Mom is having fits because of that poor model who went missing, you know, on Maui."

Henri turned his stew over with his fork, looked up when Barbara said, "That's *our* daughter. Kim. The model who is missing."

"Oh, *Jesus*, I'm sorry. I'm so *sorry*. I don't know what to say. How're you holding up?"

"It's been awful," said Barb, shaking her head, eyes down. "You pray. You try to sleep. Try to keep your wits together."

Levon said, "You're willing to chase any scrap of hope. What we're doing here, we got a call from some guy named Peter Fisher. He said he had Kim's watch and if we met him here he'd give it to us and tell us about Kim. He knew that Kim wore a Rolex. You said your name is Andrew?"

Henri nodded his head.

"Cops told us the call was probably bull, that there are nut jobs who love to screw with people's heads. Anyway, we've talked to everyone here. No one's heard of Peter Fisher. He's not registered at the fabulous Kamehameha Hilton."

"You shouldn't stay here, either," said the man in blue. "Listen, I rented a place about ten minutes from here, three bedrooms, two baths, and it's *clean*. Why don't you two stay with me tonight? Keep me company."

Barbara said, "Nice of you to offer, Mr. Hogan, but we don't want to impose."

"It's Andrew. And you'd be doing me a *favor*. You like Thai food? I found a place not far from here. What do you say? Get out of this hole, and we'll go looking for our girls in the morning."

"Thanks, Andrew," said Barbara. "That's a nice offer. If you let us take you out to dinner, we'll talk about it."

Chapter 49

BARBARA WOKE UP in the dark, feeling sheer, naked terror.

Her arms were tied behind her back and they ached. Her legs were roped together at her knees and ankles. She was crammed into a fetal position against the corner of a shallow compartment that was moving!

Was she blind? Or was it just too dark to see? Dear God, what was happening? She screamed, *"Levon!"*

Behind her back, something stirred.

"Barb? *Baby?* Are you *okay?*"

"Oh, honey, thank God, thank *God* you're here. Are you all right?"

"I'm tied up. Shit. What is this?"

"I think we're in the trunk of a car."

"Christ! A trunk! It's Hogan. Hogan did this."

Muffled music came through the backseat to where the couple lay trussed like hens in a crate.

Barbara said, "I'm going crazy. I don't understand any of this. What does he want?"

Levon kicked at the trunk's lid. *"Hey! Let us out. Hey!"* His kick didn't budge the lid, didn't make a dent. But now Barbara's eyes were growing accustomed to the dark.

"Levon, look! See that? The trunk release."

The two turned painfully by inches, scraping cheeks and elbows against the carpeting, Barb working off her shoes, pulling at the release lever with her toes. The lever moved, but there was no resistance, no release of the lock.

"Oh, God, please," Barbara wailed, her asthma kicking in, her voice trailing into a wheeze, then a burst of coughs.

"The cables are cut," said Levon. "The *backseat*. We can kick through the backseat."

"And then what? We're tied up!" Barb gasped.

Still they tried, the two of them kicking without full use of their legs, getting nowhere.

"It's latched, goddammit," said Levon.

Barb was fighting to take one breath and then another, trying to stop herself from going into a full-blown gag attack. Why had Hogan taken them? Why? What was he going to do with them? What was to be gained from kidnapping them?

Levon said, "I read somewhere, you kick out the taillights and you can stick a hand out, wave until someone notices. Even if we just bust the lights, maybe a cop will pull the car over. Do it, Barb. *Try.*"

Barb kicked, and plastic shattered. "Now you!" she shouted.

As Levon broke through the taillight on his side of the trunk, Barbara turned so that her face was near the shards and wires.

She actually could see blacktop streaming below the tires. If the car stopped, she'd scream. They weren't helpless, not anymore. They were still alive and dammit, they would fight!

"What's that sound? A cell phone?" Levon asked. "In the trunk with us?"

Barb saw the glowing faceplate of a phone by her feet. "We're getting out of here, honey. Hogan made a big mistake."

She struggled to position her hands as the first ring became the second, thumbing the buttons blindly behind her back, hitting the Send key, turning on the phone.

Levon yelled, "Hello! Hello! Who's there?"

"Mr. McDaniels, it's me. *Marco*. From the Wailea Princess."

"Marco! Thank God. You've got to find us. We've been kidnapped."

"I'm sorry. I know you're uncomfortable back there. I'll explain everything momentarily."

The phone went dead.

The car slowed to a stop.

Chapter 50

HENRI FELT BLOOD charging through his veins. He was tense in the best possible way, adrenalized, mentally rehearsed, ready for the next scene to play itself out.

He checked the area again, glancing up to the road, then taking in the 180 degrees of shoreline. Satisfied that the area was deserted, he hauled his duffel bag out of the backseat, tossed it under a tangle of brush before returning to the car.

Walking around the all-wheel-drive sedan, he stooped beside each tire, reducing the air pressure from eighty to twenty pounds, slapping the trunk when he passed it, then opening the front door on the passenger side. He reached into the glove box, tossed the rental agreement to the floor, and removed his ten-inch buck knife. It felt like it was part of his hand.

He grabbed the keys and opened the trunk. Pale

moonlight shone on Barbara and Levon. Henri, as Andrew, said, "Is everyone all right back here in coach?"

Barbara launched a full-throated, wordless scream until Henri leaned in and held the knife up to her throat. "Barb, *Barb*. Stop yelling. No one can hear you but me and Levon, so call off the histrionics, okay? I don't like it."

Barb's scream became a wheeze and a cry.

"What the hell are you doing, Hogan?" Levon demanded, wrenching his body so he could see his captor's face. "I'm a reasonable man. Explain yourself."

Henri put two fingers under his nose to resemble a mustache. He lowered his voice and thickened it, said, "Sure, I will, Mr. McDaniels. You're my number one priority."

"My dear Christ. You're *Marco*? You're him! I don't believe it. How could you scare us like this? What do you want?"

"I want you to behave, Levon. You, too, Barb. Act up, and I'll have to take strong measures. Be good and I'll move you up to first class. Deal?"

Henri sawed through the nylon ropes around Barbara's legs and helped her out of the car and into the backseat. Then he went back for Levon, cutting the restraints, walking the man to the back of the car, strapping them both in with the seat belts.

Then Henri got into the driver's seat. He locked the doors, turned on the dome light, reached up to the camera behind the rearview mirror, and switched it on.

"If you like, you can call me Henri," he said to the McDanielses, who were staring at him with unblinking eyes. He reached into the pocket of his windbreaker, pulled out a dainty, bracelet-style wristwatch, and held it up in front of them.

"See? As I promised. Kim's watch. The Rolex. Recognize it?"

He stuffed it into Levon's jacket pocket.

"Now," Henri said, "I'd like to tell you what's going on and why I have to kill you. Unless you have questions so far."

Chapter 51

WHEN I WOKE UP that morning and snapped on the local news, Julia Winkler was all over it. There, filling the TV screen, was her achingly beautiful face and a headline in bold italics running under her picture: *Supermodel Found Murdered.*

How could Julia Winkler be dead?

I bolted upright in bed, goosed up the sound, stared at the next shot, this one of Kim and Julia posing together for the *Sporting Life* photo-story, their lovely faces pressed together, laughing, both absolutely radiant with life.

The TV anchors were going back over the breaking news "for those who've just tuned in."

I stared at the tube, gathering in the stunning details: Julia Winkler's body had been found in a room at the Island Breezes Hotel, a five-star resort on Lanai. A housekeeper had run through the hotel shouting that a woman had been strangled, that there were bruises around her neck, blood all over the linens.

Next up, a waitress was interviewed. Emma Laurent. She'd waited on tables in the Club Room last night and recognized Julia Winkler. She'd been having dinner with a good-looking man in his thirties, Laurent said. He was white, brown-haired with a good build. "He definitely works out."

Winkler's date signed the check with a room number, 412, registered to Charles Rollins. Rollins left a good tip, and Julia had given the waitress her autograph. Personalized it. *To Emma from Julia.* Emma held up the signed napkin for the camera.

I got a POG out of the fridge, guzzled it, watched the camera cut now to live shots outside the Island Breezes Hotel. Cruisers were everywhere, the loud garble of police radios squawked in the background. The camera held on a reporter with the local NBC affiliate.

The reporter, Kevin de Martine, was well respected, had been embedded with a military unit in Iraq in '04. He was now standing with his back to a sawhorse barrier, rain falling softly on his bearded face, palm fronds waving dramatically behind him.

De Martine said, "This is what we know. Nineteen-year-old supermodel Julia Winkler, *former roommate* of the still-missing top model Kimberly McDaniels, was found dead this morning in a room registered to a Charles Rollins of Loxahatchee, Florida."

De Martine went on to say that Charles Rollins was not

in his room, that he was sought for questioning, that any information about Rollins should be phoned in to the number at the bottom of the screen.

I tried to absorb this horrendous story. Julia Winkler was dead. There was a suspect—but he was missing. Or how the police like to describe it—*he was in the wind.*

Chapter 52

THE PHONE RANG next to my ear, jarring the hell out of me. I grabbed the receiver. "Levon?"

"It's Dan Aronstein. Your paycheck. Hawkins, are you on this Winkler story?"

"Yep. I'm on the case, chief. If you hang up and let me work, okay?"

I glanced back at the TV. The local anchors, Tracy Baker and Candy Ko'alani, were on screen, and a new face had been patched in from Washington. Baker asked the former FBI profiler John Manzi, "Could the killings of Rosa Castro and Julia Winkler be connected? Is this the work of a serial killer?"

Those two potent and terrifying words. "Serial killer." Kim's story was now going global. The whole wide world was going to be focused on Hawaii and the mystery of two beautiful girls' deaths.

Former agent Manzi tugged at his earlobe, said serial killers generally had a signature, a preferred method for killing.

"Rosa Castro was strangled, but with ropes," he said. "Her actual manner of death was *drowning*. Without speaking to the medical examiner, I can only go by the witness reports that Julia Winkler was manually strangled. That is, she was killed by someone choking her with his hands.

"It's too soon to say if these killings were done by the same person," Manzi continued, "but what I can say about manual strangulation is that it's personal. The killer gets more of a thrill because unlike a shooting, it takes a long time for the victim to die."

Kim. Rosa. Julia. Was this coincidence or a wildfire? I wanted desperately to talk to Levon and Barbara, to get to them before they saw Julia's story on the news, prepare them somehow—but I didn't know where they were.

Barbara had called me yesterday morning to say that she and Levon were going to Oahu to check out what was probably a bum lead, and I hadn't heard from them since.

I turned down the TV volume, called Barb's cell phone number, and, when she didn't answer, I hung up and called Levon. He didn't answer, either. After leaving a message, I called their driver, and when I got forwarded to Marco's voice mail, I left my number and told him that my call was urgent.

I showered and dressed quickly, collecting my thoughts, feeling an elusive and important *something* I should pay attention to, but I couldn't nail it down.

It was like a horsefly you can't swat. Or the faint smell of gas, and you don't know where it's coming from. What was it?

I tried Levon again, and when I got his voice mail I called Eddie Keola. He had to know how to reach Barbara and Levon.

That was his job.

Chapter 53

KEOLA BARKED his name into the phone.

"Eddie, it's Ben Hawkins. Have you seen the news?"

"Worse than that. I've seen the real thing."

Keola told me he'd been to the Island Breezes since the news of Julia Winkler's death had gone over the police band. He'd been there when the body was taken out and he had spoken with the cops on the scene.

He said, "Kim's roommate was murdered. Do you believe it?"

I told him I'd had no luck reaching the McDanielses or their driver and asked if he knew where Barb and Levon were staying.

"Some dive on the eastern shore of Oahu. Barb told me she didn't know the name."

"Maybe I'm paranoid," I told Keola, "but I'm worried. It isn't like them to be incommunicado."

"I'll meet you at their hotel in an hour," Keola said.

I arrived at the Wailea Princess just before eight a.m. I was heading to the front desk when I heard Eddie Keola calling my name. He came across the marble floor at a trot. His bleached hair was damp and wind-combed, and fatigue dragged at his face.

The hotel's day manager was a young guy wearing a smart hundred-dollar tie and a blue gabardine jacket with a name-tag reading "Joseph Casey."

When he got off the phone, Keola and I told Casey our problem—that we couldn't locate two of the hotel guests and we couldn't locate their hotel-comped driver, either. I said that we were concerned for the McDanielses' safety.

The manager shook his head, and said, "We don't have any drivers on staff and we never hired anyone to drive Mr. and Mrs. McDaniels. Not somebody named Marco Benevenuto. Not anyone. We don't do that and never have."

I was stunned into an openmouthed silence. Keola asked, "Why would this driver tell the McDanielses he'd been hired and paid for by your hotel?"

"I don't know the man," said the manager. "I have no idea. You'll have to ask him."

Keola flashed his ID, saying he was employed by the McDanielses, and asked to be let into their room.

After clearing Keola with the head of security, Casey agreed. I took a phone book to a plush chair in the lobby.

There were five limousine services on Maui, and I'd worked my way through all of them by the time Eddie Keola sat down heavily in the chair beside me.

"No one's ever heard of Marco Benevenuto," I told him. "I can't find a listing for him in all of Hawaii."

"The McDanielses' room is empty, too," Keola said. "Like they were never there."

"What the hell is this?" I asked him. "Barbara and Levon left town, and you didn't know where they were going?"

It sounded like an accusation. I didn't mean it that way, but my panic had risen to the high-water mark and it was still climbing. Hawaii had a low crime rate. And now, in the space of a week, two girls were dead. Kim was still missing, and her parents and driver were missing, too.

"I *told* Barbara it should be me following that lead on Oahu," Keola said. "Those backpacker joints are remote and kind of rough. But Levon talked me out of it. He said that he wanted me to spend my time *here* looking for Kim."

Keola was snapping his wristband, chewing his lip. The two of us, ex-cops without portfolio, were trying desperately to make sense out of thin air.

Chapter 54

IT WAS BECOMING a three-ring circus in the lobby of the Wailea Princess. A queue of German tourists had lined up at the desk, a flock of little kids were begging the gardener to let them feed the koi, even a presentation on tourist attractions was going on thirty feet away, slides and film and native music.

Eddie Keola and I might as well have been invisible. No one even looked at us.

I started ticking off the facts, linking Rosa to Kim, Kim to Julia, and to the driver, Marco Benevenuto, who had lied to me and the McDanielses—who were missing.

"What do you think, Eddie? Do you see the connection? Or am I fanning the flames of my overheated imagination?"

Keola sighed loudly, and said, "Tell you the truth, Ben, I'm in over my head. Don't look at me like that. I do cheating husbands. Insurance claims. What do you think? Maui is Los Angeles?"

I said, "Work on your friend, Lieutenant Jackson, why don't you?"

"I will. I'll get him to reach out to the PD in Oahu, get a serious search going for Barb and Levon. If he won't do it, I'll go over his head. My dad's a judge."

"That must come in handy."

"Damned right it does."

Keola said he'd call me, then left me sitting with my phone in my lap. I stared across the open lobby to the dark aqua sea. I could see the outline of Lanai through the morning mist, the small island where Julia Winkler's life had been snuffed out.

It was five a.m. in L.A., but I had to talk to Amanda.

"Wassup, buttercup?" she slurred into the phone.

"Bad stuff, honeybee."

I told her about this latest shocker, how it felt like spiders were using my spine as a speedway, and no, I hadn't had anything stronger to drink than guava juice in three days.

"Kim would have shown up by now if she could do it," I told Amanda. "I don't know the who, where, why, when, or how, but honest to God, honey, I think I know the what."

" 'Serial Killer in Paradise.' The story you've been waiting for. Maybe a book."

I hardly heard her. The elusive fact that had been bothering me since I turned on the TV two hours before lit up in my mind like it was made of bright red neon. *Charles Rollins*. The name of the man last seen with Julia Winkler.

I knew that name.

I told Amanda to hold on a sec, got my wallet out of my back pocket, and, with a shaking hand, I sorted through the business cards I'd stashed behind the small plastic window.

"Mandy."

"I'm here. Are you?"

"A photographer named Charles Rollins came up to me at the Rosa Castro crime scene. He was from a *Talk Weekly* magazine, Loxahatchee, Florida. The cops think he may have been the last person to have seen Julia Winkler alive. He's nowhere to be found."

"You talked to him? You could identify him?"

"Maybe. I need a favor."

"Boot up my laptop?"

"Please."

I waited, my cell phone pressed so hard against my ear that I could hear the toilet flush in L.A. Finally, my beloved's voice came back on the line.

She cleared her throat, said, "Benjy, there are forty pages of Charles Rollinses on Google, gotta be two thousand guys by that name, a hundred in Florida. But there's no listing for a magazine called *Talk Weekly*. Not in Loxahatchee. Not anywhere."

"For the hell of it, let's send him an e-mail."

I read her Rollins's e-mail address, dictated a message.

Seconds later Amanda said, "It bounced back, Benjy. 'Mailer-Daemon. Unknown e-mail address.' What now?"

"I'll call you later. I've got to go to the police."

Chapter 55

HENRI SAT two rows back from the cockpit in a spanking new charter jet that was almost empty. He watched through the window as the sleek little aircraft lifted smoothly off the runway and took to the wide blue and white sky above Honolulu.

He sipped champagne, said yes to caviar and toast points from the hostess, and when the pilot made his all-clear announcement Henri opened his laptop on the tabletop in front of him.

The miniature video camera he'd affixed to the rearview mirror of the car had been sacrificed, but before it was destroyed by the flooding seawater, it had sent the video wirelessly to his computer.

Henri was dying to see the dailies.

He put in his earbuds and opened the MPV file.

He almost said "wow" out loud. The pictures unfurling on his computer screen were *that* beautiful. The interior of the car glowed from the dome light. Barbara and Levon were softly lit, and the sound quality was excellent.

Because Henri had been in the front seat, he was not in the shot—and he liked that. No mask. No distortion. Just his disembodied voice, sometimes as Marco, sometimes as Andrew, at all times reasoning with the victims.

"I told Kim how beautiful she was, Barbara, as I made love to her. I gave her something to drink so she wouldn't feel pain. Your daughter was a lovely person, very sweet. You don't have to think she did anything to deserve being killed."

"I don't believe you killed her," Levon said. "You're a freak. A pathological liar!"

"I gave you her watch, Levon.... Okay, then, *look at this.*"

Henri had opened his cell phone, and showed them the photo of his hand holding Kim's head by the roots of her wild blond hair.

"Try to understand," he said, talking over Barb and Levon's insufferable wailing and snuffling. "This is business. The people I work for pay a lot of money to see people die."

Barbara was gagging and sobbing, telling him to stop, but Levon was in a different kind of hell, clearly trying to balance his grief and horror with a desire to keep the two of them alive.

He'd said, "Let us go, Henri. We don't know who you really are. We can't hurt you."

Henri had said, "It's not that I *want* to kill you, Levon. It's about the money. Yes. I make money by killing *you.*"

"I can get you money," Levon said. "I'll beat their offer. I will!"

And now there on his laptop, Barbara was pleading for her boys. Henri stopped her, saying it was time for him to go.

He'd stepped on the gas, the soft tires rolling easily over the sand, the car plowing into the surf. When it had good momentum, Henri had gotten out of the car, walked alongside it, until the water rose up to the windshield.

Inside, the camera on the rearview had recorded the McDanielses begging, the water sloshing over the window frames, rising up the seats where the McDanielses' arms were locked behind them, their bodies lashed in place with the seat belts.

Still he'd given them hope.

"I'm leaving the light on so you can record your goodbyes," he heard himself saying on the small screen. "And someone on the road *could* see you. You could be rescued. Don't count it out. But if I were you, I'd pray for that."

He had wished them luck, then waded back up to the beach. He'd stood under the trees and watched the car sink completely in only about three minutes. Faster than he would have guessed. Merciful. So maybe there was a God after all.

When the dome light winked out, he'd changed his clothes, then walked up the highway until he caught a ride.

Now he closed his laptop, finished the champagne as the hostess handed him the lunch menu. He decided on the duck *à l'orange,* put on his Bose speakers, and listened to some Brahms. Soothing. Beautiful. Perfect.

The last few days had been exceptional, a fantastic drama every minute, a highlight of his life.

He was quite sure everybody would be happy.

Chapter 56

HOURS LATER, Henri Benoit was in the washroom of the first-class flight lounge at Honolulu International. The first leg of his flight had been a pleasure, and he was looking forward to the same for his flight to Bangkok.

He washed his hands, checked out his new persona in the mirror. He was a Swiss businessman based in Geneva. His white-blond hair was short, his eyeglass frames were large and horn-rimmed, giving him an erudite look, and he wore a five-thousand-dollar suit with some fine handmade English shoes.

He had just sent a few frames of the McDanielses' last moments to the Peepers, knowing that by this time tomorrow, there would be a good many more euros in his bank account in Zurich.

Henri left the washroom, went to the main waiting area

in the lounge, set his briefcase beside him, and relaxed in a soft gray chair. Breaking news was coming over the television, a cable news special. The anchorwoman Gloria Roja was reporting on a crime that she said "evoked horror and outrage."

She went on, "A young woman's decapitated body has been founded in a rental cabin on a beach in Maui. Sources close to the police department say the victim has been dead for several days."

Roja turned to the large screen behind her and introduced a local reporter, Kai McBride, on the ground in Maui.

McBride said into the camera, "This morning, Ms. Maura Aluna, the owner of this beach camp, found the decapitated head and body of a young woman inside. Ms. Aluna told police that she had rented her house to a man over the telephone and that his credit card cleared. Any minute now, we expect Lieutenant Jackson of the Kihei PD to make a statement."

McBride turned away briefly from the camera, then said, "Gloria, Lieutenant James Jackson is coming out of the house *now*."

McBride ran, and her cameraman ran right alongside her, the picture jiggling. McBride shouted, "Lieutenant, Lieutenant Jackson, can you give us a minute?"

The camera closed in on the lieutenant.

"I have nothing to say to the press at this time."

"I have just *one* question, sir."

Henri leaned forward in his seat in the flight lounge, transfixed by the dramatic scene that was unfolding on the large screen.

He was witnessing the endgame in real time. This was just too good to be true. What he'd do later is lift the broadcast from the network's Web site, cut it into his video. He'd have the whole Hawaiian saga, the beginning, middle, phenomenal ending, and now — this epilogue.

Henri quashed a giddy desire to say to the guy sitting two seats away, "Look at that cop, would you? That Lieutenant Jackson. His skin is *green*. I think he's going to throw up."

On screen, the reporter persisted.

"Lieutenant Jackson, is it Kim? Is the body you found that of the supermodel Kim McDaniels?"

Jackson spoke, tripping over his words. "No comment at this, *on* this. We're right in the middle of something," he said. "We've got a lot of moves we have to make. Will you turn that thing off? We never comment on an ongoing investigation, McBride. You *know* that."

Kai McBride turned back to the camera.

"I'm going to take a wild flying leap and say that Lieutenant Jackson's no-comment dodgeball was a confirmation, Gloria. We're all waiting now for a positive ID that the victim *was* Kim McDaniels. This is Kai McBride, reporting from Maui."

Chapter 57

THAT MORNING at low tide the roof of a car had looked at first to the passing jogger like the shell of a giant sea turtle. When he realized what it was, he'd called the police and they'd responded in force.

Now the crane had lowered the waterlogged car to the beach. The fire department crew, search and rescue, and cops from two islands were standing in groups on the sand, watching the Pacific flow out of the chassis.

A cop opened one of the back doors and called out, "Two DBs wearing their seat belts. I recognize them. Jesus God. It's the McDanielses. The parents."

My stomach dropped, and I spewed a string of curse words that didn't make any literal sense, just me venting all the bile I could without getting physically violent or sick.

Eddie Keola was standing beside me outside the yellow

tape that ran from a branch of driftwood to a chunk of lava rock thirty yards away. Keola was not only my ticket to police intel and crime scenes, but I was starting to think of him as the younger brother I never had.

Actually, we looked nothing alike, except that we both looked like shit right now.

More vehicles pulled up, some with sirens, some without, all braking on the potholed asphalt running above and parallel to the beach, a road that had been closed for repairs.

These new additions to the law enforcement fleet were black SUVs, and the men who got out of them wore jackets stenciled "FBI."

A cop friend of Eddie's came over to us, said, "Only thing I can tell you is that the McDanielses were seen having dinner at the Kamehameha Hostel. They were with a white man, six foot or so, grayish hair and glasses. They left with him, and that's all we've got. Based on that description, the guy they had dinner with could've been anyone."

"Thanks," said Eddie.

"It's okay, but now you guys really have to leave."

Eddie and I walked up a sandy ramp to Eddie's Jeep.

I was glad to go.

I didn't want to see the corpses of those two good people I'd come to care about so very much. Eddie drove me back to the Marriott, and we sat in the lot for a while just chewing it over.

The deaths of everyone attached to this crime spree had been premeditated, calculated, almost artistic, the work of a very smart and practiced killer who'd left no clues behind. I felt sorry for the people who had to solve this crime. And now Aronstein was terminating my all-expenses-paid Hawaiian holiday.

"When's your flight?" Keola asked.

"Around two."

"Want me to drive you? I'd be happy to do it."

"Thanks, anyway. I've got to return my car."

"I'm sorry how this turned out," said Keola.

"This is going to be one of those cases, if it gets solved at all, it'll be like . . . seventeen years from now. A deathbed confession," I said. "Or a deal with a jailhouse snitch."

A little while later, I said good-bye to Eddie, threw my things together, and checked out of the hotel. I was going back to L.A. unresolved and disconsolate, feeling like I'd left a big piece of myself behind. I would've bet anything I owned that for me, at least, the story was over.

I was wrong again.

Part Three

BODY COUNT

Chapter 58

THE VERY GOOD-LOOKING gentleman with the white-blond hair walked down a red, silk-lined corridor ending in a breeze-swept lobby. A stone desk rose out of the floor at the far end of the room, and a young clerk received the guest with a smile and lowered eyes.

"Your suite is ready for you, Mr. Meile. Welcome back to the Pradha Han."

"Delighted to be here," Henri said. He pushed his horn-rimmed glasses to the top of his head as he signed the credit card slip. "Did you keep the gulf warm for me, Rahpee?"

"Oh, yes sir. We would not disappoint our precious guest."

Henri opened the door to the luxury suite, undressed in the lavish bedroom, tossing his clothes onto the king-size bed under the mosquito netting. He wrapped himself in a silk robe and sampled chocolates and dried mango as he watched *BBC World News,* thrilling to the update on "the killing spree in Hawaii that continues to confound police."

He was thinking, *That* should make the Peepers happy, when the door chimes announced the arrival of his special friends.

Aroon and Sakda, slight boys in their early teens with short hair and golden skin, bowed to greet the man they knew as Mr. Paul Meile. Then they laughed and threw their arms around him as he called them by name.

The massage table was set up on the private balcony facing the beach, and as the boys smoothed the sheets and got oils and lotions out of their bags, Henri set up his video camera and framed the scene.

Aroon helped Henri out of his robe, and Sakda folded the sheets over his lower body, and then the boys began the specialty of the Pradha Han spa, *the four-hand massage.*

Henri sighed as the boys worked in tandem, stroking across the grain of his muscles, working in the Hmong cream, rubbing away his tensions of the past week. Hornbills screeched in the jungle, and the air was scented with jasmine. This was one of the most delicious of sensory experiences, and it was why he came to Hua Hin at least once a year.

The boys turned Henri over and pulled at his arms down to the pads of his fingers in unison, did the same with his legs and feet, stroked his brow, until Henri opened his eyes, and said in Thai, "Aroon, will you bring me my wallet from the dresser?"

When Aroon returned, Henri took a stack of bills out of the wallet, quite a lot more than the few hundred baht he owed for the massage. He waggled the money in front of the boys' faces, asked, "Would you like to stay and play some games?"

The boys giggled and helped the rich gentleman sit up on the massage table.

"What games would you like to play, Daddy?" Sakda asked.

Henri explained what he was thinking, and they nodded and clapped their hands, seeming very excited to be part of his enjoyment. He kissed their palms, each in turn.

He just loved these sweet boys.

It was a true joy to be with them.

Chapter 59

HENRI WOKE UP alone, hearing the chimes, then calling out, "Come in."

A girl with a red flower in her hair entered, bowed, and served his morning meal on a bed tray: *nam prik* — rice noodles in a chili and peanut sauce — plus fresh fruit and a pot of strong black tea.

Henri's mind was churning as he ate, thinking over the night before, getting ready to edit his video for the Alliance.

Taking his tea to the desk, he called up the raw footage on his laptop, scrolled through the scene of the massage. He cut away to the shots of water flowing into the soaking tub under the round eye of the skylight, putting a title over the running water, "Ochiba Shigure."

His next scene was a loving and long tracking shot starting at the boys' innocent faces, panning down their nude

194

young bodies, lingering on the ropes that bound their limbs behind them.

When his own face showed on the screen, Henri used the blur tool to obscure his features as he lifted and lowered the boys into the bath. This shot was a beauty.

He cut and pasted the next sequence, making sure to edit the action so that it appeared seamless: a tight shot on his hands holding down the boys' heads as they fought and floundered, the bubbles coming from their mouths, then angles on their bodies floating, *ochiba shigure*, Japanese for "like leaves floating on a pond."

Next a jump cut to Sakda's slack face, droplets of water clinging to his hair and skin. Then the camera pulled back to reveal both boys lying limp on chaises beside the tub, their arms and legs splayed out as if in a dance.

A fly made a four-point landing on Sakda's dewy cheek.

The camera zoomed in, then the screen faded to black. Off camera, Henri whispered his signature line, *"Is everybody happy?"*

Henri ran the film again, tweaked it, and cut it to ten minutes of savagely beautiful videography for Horst and his company of pervs, a teaser to get them hot for another film.

He composed an e-mail, attached a still shot from the video: the two boys open-eyed, underwater, their faces contorted in terror.

"Offered for your viewing pleasure," he wrote, "two young princes for the price of one." He sent the e-mail as the door chimes rang again.

Henri tightened the sash of his robe and opened the door.

The boys burst out laughing, Aroon saying, "So, are we dead, Daddy? We don't feel dead."

"No, you look *very* much alive. My two good, lively boys. Let's go to the beach," Henri said, putting a hand on each of their slender shoulders, leading the boys out the back door of his villa.

"No games, Daddy?"

He tousled the boy's hair, and Sakda grinned up at him. "No, just swimming and splashing," Henri said. "And then back here for my lovely massage."

Chapter 60

HENRI'S WELL-EARNED HOLIDAY continued in Bangkok, one of his favorite cities in all the world.

He met the Swedish girl in the night market, where she was struggling to translate baht into euros so that she could decide whether to buy a small wooden elephant. His Swedish was good enough that she spoke to him in her own language until, laughing, he said, "I've used up all of my Swedish."

"Let's try this," she said in perfect, British-inflected English. She introduced herself as Mai-Britt Olsen, telling Henri that she was on holiday with classmates from Stockholm University.

The girl was striking, nineteen or twenty and nearly six feet tall. She wore her flaxen hair cut straight at the shoulders, drawing his attention to her lovely throat.

"You have remarkable blue eyes," he said.

She said, "Oooh," and batted her lashes comically, and Henri laughed. She waggled her little elephant, and said, "I'm looking for a monkey, also."

She took Henri's arm and they strolled down the aisles of colorfully lit stalls of fruit and costume jewelry and sweets.

"My girlfriends and I went to the elephant polo today," Mai-Britt told him, "and tomorrow we're invited to the palace. We are volleyball players," she explained. "The 2008 Olympics."

"Truly? That's fantastic. Hey, I hear the palace is really stupendous. As for me, tomorrow morning I'm going to be strapped into a projectile heading to California."

Mai-Britt laughed. "Let me guess. You're flying to L.A. on business."

Henri grinned. "That's a very good guess. But that's tomorrow, Mai-Britt. Have you had dinner?"

"Just little bites in the market."

"There's a place close by that few people know. Very exclusive and a little risqué. Are you up for an adventure?"

"You are taking me to dinner?" Mai-Britt asked.

"Are you saying yes?"

The street was lined with open-air restaurants. They passed the boisterous bars and nightspots on Selekam Road and headed to an almost hidden doorway that opened into a Japanese restaurant, the Edomae.

The maitre d' walked Henri and Mai-Britt into the glowing, green-glass-lined interior, partitioned with aquariums of jewel-colored fish from floor to ceiling.

Mai-Britt suddenly grabbed Henri's arm, making him stop so she could really see.

"What are they *doing?*"

She jutted her chin toward the naked girl lying gracefully on the sushi bar and a customer drinking from the cup made by the cleft of her closed thighs.

"It's called *wakesame,*" Henri explained. "It means 'floating seaweed.'"

"Hah! That is quite new to me," she said. "Have you done that, Paul?"

Henri winked at her, then pulled out a chair for his dinner companion who was not just beautiful, but had a daring streak, was willing to try the horsemeat sashimi and the edomae, the raw, marinated fish that the restaurant was named for.

Henri had already fallen half in love with her—when he noticed the eyes of a man at another table fixed on him.

It was a shock, as though someone had dumped ice down the back of his shirt. *Carl Obst.* A man Henri had known many years ago, now sitting with a lady-boy, a high-priced, very polished, transvestite prostitute.

Henri was sure that his own looks had changed so much that Obst wouldn't recognize him. But it would be very bad if he did.

Obst's attention swung back to his lady-boy, and Henri

let his eyes slip away from Obst. Henri thought he was safe, but his good mood was gone.

The enchanting young woman and the rare and beautiful setting faded as his thoughts were hurled back to a time when he was dead—and yet somehow he still breathed.

Chapter 61

HENRI HAD TOLD Marty Switzer that being in an isolation cell was like being inside his own bowel. It was that dark and stinking, and that's where the analogy ended. Because nothing Henri had ever seen or heard about or imagined could be compared to that filthy hole.

It had started for Henri before the Twin Towers came down, when he was hired by Brewster-North, a private military contractor that was stealthier and deadlier than Blackwater.

He'd been on a reconnaissance mission with four other intelligence analysts. As the linguist, Henri was the critical asset.

His unit had been resting in a safe house when their lookout was gutted outside the door where he stood guard. The rest of the team was taken captive, beaten just short of death, and locked away in a prison with no name.

By the end of his first week in hell, Henri knew his captors by name, their tics and preferences. There was the Rapist, the one who sang while hanging his prisoners like spiders, their arms chained above their heads for hours. Fire liked to use burning cigarettes; Ice drowned prisoners in freezing cold water. Henri had long conversations with one soldier, Cocktease, who made tantalizing offers of phone calls, and letters home, and possible freedom.

There were the brutes and the ones who were more refined, but all the guards were sadistic. Had to give credit where it was due. They all really enjoyed their work.

One day Henri's schedule was changed.

He was taken from his cell and kicked into the corner of a windowless room—along with the three remaining men from his unit, all bloodied, with broken bones and oozing sores.

Bright lights flashed on, and when Henri could finally see he took in the cameras and the half-dozen hooded men lined up against a wall.

One of those men grabbed his cellmate and friend Marty Switzer, pulled him to the center of the room, and hauled him to his feet.

Switzer answered their questions, saying that he was Canadian, twenty-eight, that his parents and girlfriend lived in Ottawa, that he was a military operative. Yes, he was a spy.

He lied as expected, saying that he was being treated well, and then one of the hooded men threw Switzer to the ground, lifted his head by his hair, and drew a serrated knife across the back of his neck. Blood spouted, and there was a chorus of the *takbir: Allahu Akbar.* Allah is great.

Henri was transfixed by how easily Switzer's head had been severed with a few saws of the blade, an act both infinite and quick.

When the executioner held up Switzer's head for the camera, his friend's expression of despair was fixed on his face. Henri had thought to call out to him — as though Marty could still speak.

There was one other thing that Henri could never forget. How as he waited to die, he felt a flush of excitement. He couldn't understand the emotion, and he couldn't put it down. As he lay on the killing floor, he had wondered if he was elated because soon he'd be free of his misery.

Or maybe he'd just realized who he really was, and what was at his core.

He got a thrill from death — even his own.

Chapter 62

FRESH TEA WAS POURED into his cup at the Edomae, and Henri came back to the present; he thanked the waiter automatically. He sipped the tea but couldn't entirely pull himself back from the memory.

He thought of the hooded tribunal, the headless body of a man who'd been his friend, the stickiness of the killing floor. His senses had been so acute then; he could hear the electricity singing in the light fixtures.

He had kept his eyes on the remaining men in his unit as they were separated from the heap. Raymond Drake, the former marine from Alabama who screamed for God to help him. The other boy, Lonnie Bell, an ex-SEAL from Louisiana, who was in shock and never said a word, never even screamed.

Both men were beheaded to exultant cries, and then

Henri was dragged by his hair to the bloody center of the room. A voice came out of the darkness beyond the lights.

"Say your name for the camera. Say where you are from."

He answered in Arabic, "I will be armed and waiting for you in hell. Send my bottomless contempt to Saddam."

They laughed. They mocked his accent. And then, with the smell of shit in his nostrils, Henri was blindfolded. He waited to be shoved to the ground, but instead a coarse blanket was thrown over his head.

He must have passed out because when he awoke, he was tied with ropes and folded into the rear of a vehicle in which he rode for hours. Then he was dumped at the Syrian border.

He was afraid to believe it, but it was true.

He was alive. He was *alive*.

"Tell the Americans what we have done, infidel. What we *will* do. At least you try to speak our language."

A boot struck him hard in the lower back, and the vehicle sped away.

He returned to the United States through an underground chain of friendly back doors from Syria to Beirut, where he got new documentation, and by cargo plane from Beirut to Vancouver. He hitched a ride to Seattle, stole a car, and made his way to a small mining town in Wisconsin. But Henri didn't contact his controller at Brewster-North.

He never wanted to see Carl Obst again.

Still, Brewster-North had done great things for Henri. They'd eradicated his past when they hired him, had thoroughly expunged his real name, his fingerprints, his entire history from the records. And now he was presumed dead.

He counted on that.

Across from him now, inside an exclusive Japanese club in Thailand, the lovely Mai-Britt had noticed that Henri's mind had drifted far away from her.

"Are you okay, Paul?" she asked. "Are you angry that that man was staring at me?"

Together they watched Carl Obst leave the restaurant with his date. He didn't look back.

Henri smiled, said, "No, I'm not angry. Everything is fine."

"Good, because I was wondering if we should continue the evening more privately?"

"Hey, I'm sorry. I wish I could," Henri told the girl with the most elegant neck since Henry VIII's second wife. "I really wish I had the time," he said, taking her hand. "I have that early flight tomorrow morning."

"Screw business," Mai-Britt joked. "You're on holiday tonight."

Henri leaned across the table and kissed her cheek.

He imagined her nakedness under his hands—and he let the fantasy go. He was already thinking ahead to his business in L.A., laughing inside at how surprised Ben Hawkins would be to see him.

Chapter 63

HENRI SPENT a three-day weekend at the airport Sheraton in L.A., moving anonymously among the other business travelers. He used the time to reread Ben Hawkins's novels and every newspaper story Ben had written. He'd purchased supplies and made dry runs to Venice Beach and the street where Ben lived, right around the corner from Little Tokyo.

At just after five that Monday afternoon, Henri took his rental car onto the 105 Freeway. The yellowing cement walls lining the eight-laner were illuminated by a golden light, randomly splashed with spiky vines of red and purple bougainvillea and gothic Latino gang graffiti, giving the drab Los Angeles highway a Caribbean flavor, at least in his mind.

Henri took the 105 to the 110 exit at Los Angeles Street,

and from there he made his way through stop-and-go traffic to Alameda, a major artery running to the heart of downtown.

It was rush hour, but Henri was in no rush. He was keyed up, focused on an idea that over the last three weeks had taken on potential for life-changing drama and a hell of a finale.

The plan centered on Ben Hawkins, the journalist, the novelist, the former detective.

Henri had been thinking about him since that evening in Maui, outside the Wailea Princess, when Ben had stretched out his hand to touch Barbara McDaniels.

Henri waited out the red light, and when it changed he took a right turn onto Traction, a small street near the Union Pacific tracks that ran parallel to the Los Angeles River.

Following the poky SUV in front of him, Henri trawled down the middle of Ben's homey neighborhood, with its L.A. hipster restaurants and vintage clothing shops, finding a parking spot across from the eight-story, white-brick building where Ben lived.

Henri got out of the car, opened the trunk, and took a sports jacket from his bag. He stuck a gun into the waistband of his slacks, buttoned his jacket, and raked back his brown and silver-streaked hair.

Then he got back into the car and found a good music station, spent about twenty minutes watching pedestrians meander along the pleasant street, listening to Beethoven and Mozart, until he saw the man he was waiting for.

Ben was in Dockers and a polo shirt and was carrying a beat-up leather briefcase in his right hand. He entered a restaurant called Ay Caramba, and Henri waited patiently until Ben emerged with his take-out Mexican dinner in a plastic bag.

Henri got out of his car, locked it, followed Ben across Traction right up the short flight of stairs to where Ben was fitting his key into the lock.

Henri called out, "Excuse me. Sorry. Mr. Hawkins?"

Ben turned, a look of mild alertness on his face.

Henri smiled and, pulling aside the front of his jacket, showed Ben his gun. He said, "I don't want to hurt you."

Ben spoke in a voice that still reeked of cop. "I've got thirty-eight dollars on me. Take it. My wallet's in my back pocket."

"You don't recognize me, do you?"

"Should I?"

"Think of me as your godfather, Ben," Henri said, thickening his speech. "I'm gonna make you an offer—"

"I can't refuse? I know who you are. You're Marco."

"Correct. You should invite me inside, my friend. We need to talk."

Chapter 64

"SO, what the fuck is this, Marco?" I shouted. "Suddenly you have information about the McDanielses?"

Marco didn't answer my question. He didn't even flinch.

He said, "I mean it, Ben," and standing with his back to the street, he drew the gun from his waistband and leveled it at my gut. "Open the door."

I couldn't move my feet, I was that stuck. I'd known Marco Benevenuto a bit, had spent time sitting next to him in a car, and now he'd taken off the chauffeur's cap, the mustache, put on a six-hundred-dollar jacket, and completely skunked me.

I was ashamed of myself and I was confused.

If I refused to let him into my building, would he shoot me? I couldn't know. And I was having the irrational thought that I *should* let him in.

My curiosity was overriding caution big-time, but I wanted to satisfy my curiosity with a gun in *my* hand. My well-oiled Beretta was in my nightstand, and I was confident that once I was inside with this character I could get my hands on it.

"You can put that thing away," I said, shrugging when he gave me a bland, you-gotta-be-kidding smile. I opened the front door, and with the McDanielses' former driver right behind me, we climbed up three flights to the fourth floor.

This building was one of several former warehouses that had gone residential in the past ten years. I loved it here. One unit per floor, high ceilings, and thick walls. No nosy neighbors. No unwanted sounds.

I unlocked the heavy-duty dead bolts on my front door and let the man in. He locked the door behind us.

I put my briefcase down on the cement floor, said "Have a seat," then headed into the kitchen area. Perfect host, I called out, "What can I get you to drink, Marco?"

He said from behind my shoulder, "Thanks anyway. I'll pass."

I quashed my jump reflex, took an Orangina out of the fridge, and led the way back to the living room, sitting at one end of the leather sectional. My "guest" took the chair.

"Who are you really?" I asked this man who was now looking my place over, checking out the framed photos, the old newspapers in the corner, every title of every book. I had the sense that I was in the presence of a highly observant operator.

He finally set his Smith and Wesson down on my coffee

table, ten feet from where I was sitting, out of my reach. He fished in his breast pocket, took out a business card held between his fingers, slid it across the glass table toward me.

I read the printed name, and my heart almost stopped.

I knew the card. I'd read it before: Charles Rollins. Photographer. *Talk Weekly*.

My mind was doing backflips. I imagined Marco without the mustache, and then envisioned Charles Rollins's half-seen face the night when Rosa Castro's twisted body had been brought up from the deep.

That night, when Rollins had given me his card, he'd been wearing a baseball cap and, maybe, shades. It had been another disguise.

The prickling at the back of my neck was telling me that the slick, good-looking guy sitting on my sofa had been *this* close to me the whole time I was in Hawaii. Almost from the moment I arrived.

I'd been completely unaware of him, but he'd been watching me.

Why?

Chapter 65

THE MAN SITTING in my favorite leather chair watched my face as I desperately tried to fit the pieces together.

I was remembering that day in Maui when the McDanielses had gone missing and Eddie Keola and I had tried to find Marco, the driver who didn't exist.

I remembered how after Julia Winkler's body was found in a hotel bed in Lanai, Amanda had tried to help me locate a tabloid paparazzo named Charles Rollins because he'd been the last person seen with Winkler.

The name Nils Bjorn jumped into my mind, another phantom who'd been staying at the Wailea Princess at the same time as Kim McDaniels. Bjorn had never been questioned—because he had conveniently disappeared.

The police hadn't thought Bjorn had anything to do with

Kim's abduction, and when I'd researched Bjorn, I was sure he was using a dead man's name.

Those facts alone told me that at the very least, Mr. Smooth on my chair was a con artist, a master of disguise. If that were true, if Marco, Rollins, and maybe Bjorn were all the same man, what did it mean?

I fought off the tsunami of black thoughts that were swamping my mind. I unscrewed the top of the soda bottle with a shaking hand, wondering if I'd kissed Amanda for the last time.

I thought about the messiness of my life, the overdue story Aronstein was waiting for, the will I'd never drawn up, my life insurance policy—had I paid the latest premium?

I was not only scared, I was furious, thinking, *Shit, this can't be the last day of my life. I need time to put my damned affairs in order.*

Could I make a break for my gun?

No, I didn't think so.

Marco-Rollins-Bjorn was two feet from his Smith and Wesson. And he was maddeningly relaxed about everything. His legs were crossed, ankle over knee, watching me like I was on TV.

I used that fearful moment to memorize the prick's bland, symmetrical face. In case somehow I got out of here. In case I had a chance to describe him to the cops.

"You can call me Henri," he said now.

"Henri what?"

"Don't worry about it. It's not my real name."

"So what now, Henri?"

He smiled, said, "How many times has someone said to you, 'You should write a book about my life'?"

"Probably at least once a week," I said. "Everyone thinks they have a blockbuster life story."

"Uh-huh. And how many of those people are contract killers?"

Chapter 66

THE TELEPHONE RANG in my bedroom. It was probably Amanda. Henri shook his head, so I let my sweetheart's voice send her love to the answering machine.

"I've got a lot of things to tell you, Ben. Get comfortable. Tune in to the present only. We could be here for a while."

"Mind if I get my tape recorder? It's in my bedroom."

"Not now. Not until we work out our deal."

I said, "Okay. Talk to me," but I was thinking, *Was he serious? A contract killer wanted a contract with me?*

Henri's gun was a half second away from Henri's hand. All I could do was play along with him until I could make a move.

The worst of amateur autobiographies start with "I was born...," so I leaned back in my seat, prepared myself for a saga.

And Henri didn't disappoint. He started his story from *before* he was born.

He gave me a little history: In 1937 there was a Frenchman, a Jewish man who owned a print shop in Paris. He was a specialist in old documents and inks.

Henri said that very early on, this man understood the real danger of the Third Reich and that he and others got out before the Nazis stormed Paris. This man, this printer, had fled to Beirut.

"So this young Jew married a Lebanese woman," Henri told me. "Beirut is a large city, the Paris of the Middle East, and he blended in fairly well. He opened another print shop, had four children, lived a good life.

"No one questioned him. But other refugees, friends of friends of friends, would find him. They needed papers, false identification, and this man helped them so that they could start new lives. His work is excellent."

"*Is* excellent?"

"He's still living, but no longer in Beirut. He was working for the Mossad, and they've moved him for safekeeping. Ben, there's no way for you to find him. Stay in the present, stay with me, my friend.

"I'm telling you about this forger because he works for me. I keep food on his table. I keep his secrets. And he has given me Marco and Charlie and Henri and many others. I can become someone else when I walk out of this room."

Hours whipped by.

I turned on more lights and came back to my seat, so absorbed by Henri's story that I'd forgotten to be afraid.

Henri told me about surviving a brutal imprisonment in Iraq and how he'd determined that he would no longer be constrained by laws or by morality.

"And so, what is my life like now, Ben? I indulge myself in every pleasure, many you can't imagine. And to do that, I need lots of money. That's where the Peepers come in. It's where you come in, too."

Chapter 67

HENRI'S SEMIAUTOMATIC WAS KEEPING me in my seat, but I was so gripped by his story that I almost forgot about the gun. "Who are the Peepers?" I asked him.

"Not now," he said. "I'll tell you next time. After you come back from New York."

"What are you going to do, muscle me onto a plane? Good luck getting a gun on board."

Henri pulled an envelope from his jacket pocket, slid it across the table. I picked it up, opened the flap, and took out the packet of pictures.

My mouth went dry. They were high-quality snapshots of *Amanda*, recent ones. She was Rollerblading only a block from her apartment, wearing the white tank top and pink shorts she'd had on when I met her for breakfast yesterday morning.

I was in one of the shots, too.

"Keep those, Ben. I think they're pretty nice. Point is, I can get to Amanda anytime, so don't even think about going to the police. That's just a way of committing suicide and getting Amanda killed, too. Understand?"

I felt a chill shoot from the back of my neck all the way down my spine. A death threat with a smile. The guy had just threatened to kill Amanda and made it sound like an invitation to have lunch.

"*Wait a minute,*" I said. I put the pictures down, shoved my hands out, as if pushing Henri and his gun and his damned life story far, far away. "I'm wrong for this. You need a biographer, someone who's done this kind of book before and would see it as a dream job."

"Ben. It *is* a dream job, and *you're* my writer. So turn me down if you want, but I'll have to exercise the termination clause for my own protection. See what I mean?

"Or, you could look at the upside," Henri said, affable now, selling me on the silver lining while pointing a 9-millimeter at my chest.

"We're going to be *partners*. This book is going to be *big*. What did you say a little while ago about blockbusters? Yeah, well that's what we're looking at with my story."

"Even if I wanted to, I can't. Look, Henri, I'm just a writer. I don't have the power you think. Shit, man, you have no idea what you're asking."

Henri smiled as he said, "I brought you something you can use as a sales tool. About ninety seconds of inspiration."

He reached inside his jacket and pulled out a gizmo hanging from a cord around his neck. It was a flash drive, a small media card used to save and transfer data.

"If a picture's worth a thousand words, I'm guessing this is worth, I don't know, *eighty* thousand words and several million dollars. Think about it, Ben. You could become rich and famous...or...you could die. I like clear choices, don't you?"

Henri slapped his knees, stood, asked me to walk him to the door and then to put my face against the wall.

I did it—and when I woke up sometime later, I was lying on the cold cement floor. I had a painful lump at the back of my head and a blinding headache.

Son of a bitch pistol-whipped me before he took off.

Chapter 68

I PULLED MYSELF to my feet, bumped against walls all the way to the bedroom, yanked open the drawer to my nightstand. My heart was clanging in my chest like a fire alarm until my fingers curled around the butt of my gun. I stuck the Beretta into my waistband and went for the phone.

Mandy answered on the third ring.

"Don't open your door for anyone," I said, still panting, perspiring heavily. Had this really happened? Had Henri just threatened to kill me and Mandy if I didn't write his book?

"Ben?"

"Don't answer the door for a neighbor or a Girl Scout or the cable guy, or anyone, okay, Mandy? Don't open it for the *police*."

"Ben, you're scaring me to death! Seriously, honey. What's going on?"

"I'll tell you when I see you. I'm leaving now."

I staggered back to the living room, pocketed the items Henri had left behind, and headed out the door, still seeing Henri's face and hearing his threat.

That's just a way of…getting Amanda killed…I'll have to exercise the termination clause…Understand?

I think I did.

Traction Avenue was dark now, but alive with honking horns, tourists buying goods from racks, gathering around a one-man band on the sidewalk.

I got into my ancient Beemer, headed for the 10 Freeway, worried about Amanda as I drove. Where was Henri now?

Henri was good-looking enough to pass as a solid citizen, his features bland enough to take on any kind of disguise. I imagined him as Charlie Rollins, saw a camera in his hand, taking pictures of me and Amanda.

His camera could just as easily have been a gun.

I thought about the people who'd been murdered in Hawaii. Kim, Rosa, Julia, my friends Levon and Barbara, all tortured and so skillfully dispatched. Not a fingerprint or a trace had been left behind for the cops.

This wasn't the work of a beginner.

How many other people had Henri killed?

The freeway tailed off onto 4th and Main. I turned onto Pico, passed the diners and car repair shops, the two-level crappy apartments, the big clown on Main and Rose—and I was in a different world, Venice Beach, both a playground for the young and carefree and a refuge for the homeless.

It took me another few minutes to circle around Speedway

until I found a spot a block from Amanda's place, a former one-family home now split into three apartments.

I walked up the street listening for the approach of a car or the sound of Italian loafers slapping the pavement.

Maybe Henri was watching me now, disguised as a vagrant, or maybe he was that bearded guy parking his car. I walked past Amanda's house, looked up to the third floor, saw the light on in her kitchen.

I walked another block before doubling back. I rang the doorbell, muttered, *"Please, Mandy, please,"* until I heard her voice behind the door.

"What's the password?"

" 'Cheese sandwich.' Let me in."

Chapter 69

AMANDA OPENED the door, and I grabbed her, kicked the door closed behind me, and held her tight.

"What is it, Ben? What *happened?* Please tell me what's going on."

She freed herself from my arms, grabbed my shoulders, and inventoried my face.

"Your *collar* is bloody. You're *bleeding.* Ben, were you *mugged?*"

I threw the bolts on Amanda's front door, put my hand at her back, and walked her to the small living room. I sat her down in the easy chair, took the rocker a few feet away.

"Start talking, okay?"

I didn't know how to soften it, so I just told it plain and simple. "A guy came to my door with a gun. Said he's a contract killer."

"*What?*"

"He led me to believe that he killed all those people in Hawaii. Remember when I asked you to help me find Charlie Rollins from *Talk Weekly* magazine?"

"The Charlie Rollins who was the last one to see Julia Winkler? That's who came to see you?"

I told Amanda about Henri's other names and disguises, how I had met him not only as Rollins, but that he'd also masqueraded as the McDanielses' driver, calling himself Marco Benevenuto.

I told her that he'd been sitting on my couch and pointing a gun, telling me that he was a professional assassin for hire and had killed many, many times.

"He wants me to write his autobiography. Wants Raven-Wofford to publish it."

"This is unbelievable," Amanda said.

"I know."

"No, I mean, it's *really* unbelievable. Who would confess to murders like that? You've got to call the police, Ben," she said. "You know that, don't you?"

"He warned me not to."

I handed Mandy the packet of pictures and watched the disbelief on her face change to shock and then anger.

"Okay, the bastard has a zoom lens," she said, her mouth clamped into a straight line. "He took some pictures. Proves nothing."

I took the flash drive out of my pocket, dangled it by the cord. "He gave me this. Said it's a sales tool and that it will inspire me."

Chapter 70

AMANDA LEFT THE LIVING ROOM, then came back with her laptop under her arm and holding two glasses and a bottle of Pinot. She booted up while I poured, and when her laptop was humming, I inserted Henri's flash drive into the port.

A video started to roll.

For the next minute and a half, Amanda and I were in the grip of the most horrific and obscene images either of us had ever seen. Amanda clutched my arm so hard that she left bruises, and when it was finally over she threw herself back into the chair, tears flowing, sobbing.

"Oh, my God, Amanda, what an *ass* I am. I'm so sorry. I should have looked at it first."

"You couldn't have known. I wouldn't have believed it if I hadn't seen it."

"That goes for me, too."

I put the media card into my back pocket and went down the hall to the bathroom, sluiced cold water over my face and the back of my scalp. When I looked up, Amanda was standing in the doorway. She said, "Take it all off."

She helped me with my bloody shirt, undressed herself, and turned on the shower. I got into the tub and she got in behind me, put her arms around me as the hot water beat down on us both.

"Go to New York and talk to Zagami," she said. "Do what Henri says. Zagami can't turn this down."

"You're sure about that?"

"Yeah, I'm sure. The thing to do is keep Henri happy while we figure out what to do."

I turned to face her. "I'm not leaving you here alone."

"I can take care of myself. I know, I know, famous last words. But really, I can."

Mandy got out of the shower and disappeared for long enough that I turned off the water, wrapped myself in a bath towel, and went looking for her.

I found her in the bedroom, on her tiptoes, reaching up to the top shelf of her closet. She pulled down a shotgun and showed it to me.

I looked at her stupidly.

"Yeah," she said. "I know how to use it."

"And you're going to carry it around with you in your purse?"

I took her shotgun and put it under the bed.

Then I used her phone.

I didn't call the cops, because I knew that they couldn't

protect us. I had no fingerprint evidence, and my description of Henri would be useless. Six foot, brown hair, gray eyes, could be anyone.

After the cops watched my place and Mandy's for a week or so, we'd be on our own again, vulnerable to a sniper's bullet—or whatever Henri would or could use to silence us.

I saw him in my mind, crouched behind a car, or standing behind me at Starbucks, or watching Amanda's apartment through a gun sight.

Mandy was right. We needed time to make a plan. If I worked with Henri, if he got comfortable with me, maybe he'd slip, give me convictable evidence, something the cops or the Feds could use to lock him up.

I left a voice-mail message for Leonard Zagami, saying it was urgent that we meet. Then I booked tickets for me and Mandy, round trip, Los Angeles to New York.

Chapter 71

WHEN LEONARD ZAGAMI TOOK ME on as one of his authors, I was twenty-five, he was forty, and Raven House was a high-class specialty press that put out a couple dozen books a year. Since then, Raven had merged with the gigantic Wofford Publishing, and the new Raven-Wofford had taken over the top six floors of a skyscraper overlooking Bloomingdale's.

Leonard Zagami had moved up as well. He was now the CEO and president, the crème de la cheese, and the new house brought out two hundred books a year.

Like their competition, the bulk of RW's list either lost money or broke even, but three authors—and I wasn't one of them—brought in more revenue than the other 197 combined.

Leonard Zagami didn't see me as a moneymaker anymore, but he liked me and it cost him nothing to keep me on board. I hoped that after our meeting he'd see me another way, that he'd hear cash registers ringing from Bangor to Yakima.

And that Henri would remove his death threat.

I had my pitch ready when I arrived in RW's spiffy modern waiting room at nine. At noon, Leonard's assistant came across the jaguar-print carpet to say that Mr. Zagami had fifteen minutes for me, to please follow her.

When I crossed his threshold, Leonard got to his feet, shook my hand, patted my back, and told me it was good to see me but that I looked like crap.

I thanked him, told him I'd aged a couple of years while waiting for our nine o'clock meeting.

Len laughed, apologized, said he'd done his best to squeeze me in, and offered me a chair across from his desk. At five feet six, almost child-sized behind the huge desk, Leonard Zagami still radiated power and a no-bullshit canniness.

I took my seat.

"What's this book about, Ben? When last we spoke, you had nothing cooking."

"Have you been following the Kim McDaniels case?"

"The *Sporting Life* model? Sure. She and some other people were killed in Hawaii a few...Hey. You were covering that story? Oh. I see."

"I was very close to some of the victims—"

"Look, Ben," Zagami interrupted me. "Until the killer is caught, this is still tabloid fodder. It's not a book, not yet."

231

"It's not what you're thinking, Len. This is a first-person tell-all."

"Who's the first person? You?"

I made my pitch like my life depended on it.

"The killer approached me incognito," I said. "He's a very cool and clever maniac who wants to do a book about the murders, and he wants me to write it. He won't reveal his identity, but he'll tell how he did the killings and why."

I expected Zagami to say *something,* but his expression was flat. I crossed my arms over his leather-topped desk, made sure my old friend was looking me in the eyes.

"Len, did you hear me? This guy could be the most-wanted man in America. He's smart. He's at liberty. And he kills with his *hands*. He says he wants me to write about what he's done because he wants the money and the notori-ety. Yeah. He wants some kind of credit for a job well done. And if I won't write the book, he'll kill *me*. Might kill Amanda, too.

"So I need a simple yes or no, Len. Are you interested or not?"

Chapter 72

LEONARD ZAGAMI LEANED back in his chair, rocked a couple of times, smoothed back what remained of his white hair, then turned to face me. When he spoke, it was with heartbreaking sincerity, and that's what really hurt.

"You know how much I like you, Ben. We've been together for what, twelve years?"

"Almost fifteen."

"Fifteen good years. So, as your friend, I'm not going to bullshit you. You deserve the truth."

"Agreed," I said, but my pulse was booming so loudly that I could hardly hear what Len said.

"I'm verbalizing what any good businessman would be *thinking*, so don't take this wrong, Ben. You've had a promising but quiet career. So now you think you've got a breakout book that'll raise your profile here at RW and in the industry. Am I right?"

"You think this is a stunt? You think I'm that desperate? Are you kidding?"

"Let me finish. You know what happened when Fritz Keller brought out Randolph Graham's so-called true story."

"It blew up, yeah."

"First the 'startling reviews,' then Matt Lauer and Larry King. Oprah puts Graham in her book club—and then the truth starts leaking out. Graham wasn't a killer. He was a petty thug and a pretty good writer who embellished the hell out of his life story. And when it exploded, it exploded all over Fritz Keller."

Zagami went on to say that Keller got late-night threats at home, TV producers calling his cell phone. His company's stock went down the toilet, and Keller had a heart attack.

My own heart was starting to fibrillate. Leonard thought that either Henri was lying or I was stretching a newspaper article beyond reality.

Either way, he was turning me down.

Hadn't Leonard heard what I said? *Henri had threatened to kill me and Amanda.* Len took a breath, so I seized the moment.

"Len, I'm going to say something very important."

"Go ahead, because unfortunately, I only have five more minutes."

"I questioned it, too. Wondered if Henri was really a killer, or if he's a talented con man, seeing in me the grift of a lifetime."

"Exactly," Len said.

"Well, Henri is for real. And I can prove it to you."

I put the media card on the desk.

"What's that?"

"Everything you need to know and more. I want you to meet Henri for yourself."

Len inserted the flash drive, and his computer screen went from black to a shot of a dusky yellow room, candles burning, a bed centered on a wall. The camera zoomed in on a slender young woman lying belly-down on the bed. She had long, pale blond hair, wore a red bikini and black shoes with red soles. She was hog-tied with intricately knotted ropes. She seemed drugged or sleeping, but when the man entered the frame she began crying.

The man was naked except for a plastic mask and blue latex gloves.

I didn't want to see the video again. I walked to the glass wall that looked straight down the well of the atrium, from the forty-third floor to the tiny people who crossed the plaza on the ground floor below.

I heard the voices coming from the computer, heard Leonard gag. I turned to see him make a run for the door. When he returned a few minutes later, Leonard was as pale as a sheet of paper, and he was changed.

Chapter 73

LEONARD DROPPED BACK into the seat behind his desk, yanked out the flash drive, stared at it like it was the snake in the Garden of Eden.

"Take this back," he said. "Let's agree that I never saw it. I don't want to be any kind of accessory after the fact or God knows what. Have you told the police? The FBI?"

"Henri said that if I did, he'd kill me, kill Amanda, too. I can't take that chance."

"I understand now. You're sure that the girl in that video is Kim McDaniels?"

"Yeah. That's Kim."

Len picked up the phone, canceled his twelve-thirty meeting, and cleared the rest of his afternoon. He ordered sandwiches from the kitchen, and we moved to the seating area at the far side of his office.

Len said, "Okay, start at the beginning. Don't leave out a bloody period or comma."

So I did. I told Len about the last-minute Hawaiian boondoggle that had turned out to be a murder mystery times five. I told him about becoming friends with Barbara and Levon McDaniels and about being deceived by Henri's alter egos, Marco Benevenuto and Charlie Rollins.

Emotion jammed up my voice box when I talked about the dead bodies, and also when I told Len how Henri had forced me into my apartment at gunpoint, then showed me the pictures he'd taken of Amanda.

"How much does Henri want for his story? Did he give you a number?"

I told Len that Henri was talking about multimillions, and my editor didn't flinch. In the past half hour, he had gone from skeptic to inside bidder. From the light in his eyes, I thought he'd sized up the market for this book and saw his budget gap being overwhelmed by a mountain of cash.

"What's the next step?" he asked me.

"Henri said he'd be in touch. I'm certain he will be. That's all I know so far."

Len called Eric Zohn, Raven-Wofford's chief legal counsel, and soon a tall, thin, nervous man in his forties joined our meeting.

Len and I briefed Eric on "the assassin's legacy," and Zohn threw up objections.

Zohn cited the "Son of Sam" law that held that a killer can't profit from his crimes. He and Len discussed Jeffrey

MacDonald, who had sued his ghostwriter, and then the O.J. book, since the Goldman family had claimed the book's earnings to satisfy their civil suit against the author.

Zohn said, "I worry that we'll be financially responsible to each and every one of the victims' families."

I was the forgotten person in the room, as loopholes and angles were discussed, but I saw that Len was fighting for the book.

He said to Zohn, "Eric, I don't say this lightly. This is a guaranteed monster bestseller in the making. Everyone wants to know what's actually in the mind of a killer, and this killer will talk about crimes that are current and *unsolved*. What Ben's got isn't *If I Did It*. It's *I Damn Well Did It*."

Zohn wanted more time to explore the ramifications, but Leonard used his executive prerogative.

"Ben, for now, you're Henri's anonymous ghostwriter. If anyone says they saw you in my office, say you came to pitch a new novel. That I turned it down.

"When Henri contacts you, tell him that we're fine-tuning an offer I think he'll like."

"That's a yes?"

"That's a yes. You have a deal. This is the scariest book I've ever taken on, and I can't wait to publish it."

Chapter 74

THE NEXT EVENING, in L.A., the unreality was still settling in. Amanda was cooking a four-star dinner in her
minuscule kitchen while I sat at her desk working the Internet. I had indelible pictures in my mind of the execution of
Kim McDaniels, and that led me to multiple Web sites that
discussed personality disorders. I quickly homed in on the
description of serial killers.

A half-dozen experts agreed that serial killers almost
always learn from their mistakes. They evolve. They com-
partmentalize and don't feel their victims' pain. They keep
upping the danger and increasing the thrill.

I could see why Henri was so happy and self-satisfied. He
was being paid for doing what he loved to do, and now a
book about his passion would be a kind of victory lap.

I called out to Mandy, who came into the living room with a wooden spoon in her hand.

"The sauce is going to burn."

"I want to read you something. This is from a psychiatrist, a former Viet Nam vet who's written extensively on serial killers. Here. Listen, please.

"'All of us have some of the killer in us, but when you get to the proverbial edge of the abyss, you have to be able to take a step back. These guys who kill and kill again have jumped right into the abyss and have lived in it for years.'"

Mandy said, "But Ben, what's it going to be like to work with this...*creature*?"

"If I could walk away from it, Mandy, I'd run. I'd run."

Mandy kissed the top of my head and went back to her sauce. A moment later, the phone rang. I heard Mandy say, "Hang on. I'll get him."

She held out the phone to me with a look on her face that I can describe only as one of pure horror.

"It's for *you*."

I took the phone, said, "Hello."

"So how did our big meeting in New York go?" Henri asked me. "Do we have a book deal?"

My heart almost jumped out of my chest. I did my best to keep calm as I told him, "It's in the works. A lot of people have to be consulted for the kind of money you're asking."

Henri said, "I'm sorry to hear that."

I had a green light from Zagami, and I could have told Henri that, but I was looking at the twilight coming through

240

the windows, wondering where Henri was, how he'd known that Amanda and I were here.

"We're going to do the book, Ben," Henri was saying. "If Zagami isn't interested, we'll have to take it somewhere else. But either way, remember your choices. Do or die."

"Henri, I didn't make myself clear. We have a deal. The contract is in the works. Paperwork. Lawyers. A number has to be worked up and an offer made. This is a big corporation, Henri."

"Okay, then. Break out the champagne. When will we have a solid offer?"

I told him I expected to hear from Zagami in a couple of days and that a contract would follow. It was the truth, but still my mind was reeling.

I was going into partnership with a great white shark, a killing machine that never slept.

Henri was watching us right now, wasn't he?

He was watching us all the time.

Chapter 75

HENRI HADN'T GIVEN me my final destination when he mapped out my drive, just said, "Get on the Ten and go east. I'll tell you what to do after that."

I had the papers in my briefcase, the contract from Raven-Wofford, the releases, signature lines with flags marked "sign here." I also had a tape recorder, notepads, and laptop, and in the zipped pocket at the back of the briefcase, right next to my computer's power pack, was my gun. I hoped to God I would get the chance to use it.

I got into my car and headed out to the freeway. It wasn't funny, but the situation was so weird that I wanted to laugh.

I had a contract for a "guaranteed monster bestseller," what I'd been looking for and dreaming about for years, only this contract had a very literal termination clause.

Write it or die.

Had any author in modern history had a book deal attached to a death penalty? I was pretty sure this was unique, and it was all mine.

It was sunny, a Saturday in mid-July. I set off on the freeway, checking my rearview mirror every minute or so, looking for a tail, but I never saw one. I stopped for gas, bought coffee, a doughnut, got back on the road.

Fifty miles and an hour later, my cell phone rang.

"Take the One-eleven to Palm Springs," he said.

I'd put another twenty miles on the odometer when I saw the turnoff for the 111. I took the exit ramp and continued on the highway until it became Palm Canyon Drive.

My phone rang again, and again I got directions from my "partner."

"When you get to the center of town, turn right on Tahquitz Canyon, then a left on Belardo. Don't hang up the phone."

I made the turns, sensing that we were near our meeting spot, when Henri said, "You should be seeing it now. The Bristol Hotel."

We were going to be meeting in a public place.

This was good. It was a relief. I felt a burst of elation.

I pulled up to the hotel, handed my keys to the valet at the entrance of this famous old luxury resort and spa, known for its high-end amenities.

Henri spoke into my ear. "Go to the restaurant out by the pool. The reservation is in my name. Henri Benoit. I hope you're hungry, Ben."

This was news.

He'd given me a last name. Real or fictitious, I didn't know, but it struck me as an offering of trust.

I headed through the lobby to the restaurant, thinking, Yes. This was going to be very civilized.

Break out the champagne.

Chapter 76

THE DESERT ROSE RESTAURANT was situated under a long blue canopy near the swimming pool. Light bounced off the white stone patio, and I had to shield my eyes from the glare. I told the maitre d' that I was having lunch with Henri Benoit, and he said, "You're the first to arrive."

I was shown to a table with a perfect view of the pool, the restaurant, and a path that wound around the hotel and led to the parking lot. I had my back to the wall, my briefcase open by my right side.

A waiter came to the table, told me about the various drinks, including the specialty of the house, a cocktail with grenadine and fruit juice. I asked for a bottle of San Pellegrino, and when it came I slugged down a whole glass, refilled it, and waited for Henri to appear.

I looked at my watch, saw that I'd been waiting for only ten minutes. It seemed at least twice that long. With an eye on my surroundings, I called Amanda, told her where I was. Then I used my phone to do an Internet search, looking for any mention of Henri Benoit.

I came up with nothing.

I called Zagami in New York, told him I was waiting for Henri, got a crackly connection. I killed another minute as I filled Len in on the drive into the desert, the beautiful hotel, the state of my mood.

"I'm starting to get excited about this," I said. "I'm just hoping he signs the contract."

"Be careful," said Zagami. "Listen to your instincts. I'm surprised he's late."

"I'm not. I don't like it, but I'm not surprised."

I took a bathroom break and then went back to the table with trepidation. I was expecting that while I was gone, Henri would have arrived and would be sitting across from my empty chair.

I wondered whether Henri was donning a new disguise, whether he was undergoing another metamorphosis—but the seat was still empty.

The waiter came toward me again, said that Mr. Benoit had phoned to say he was delayed and that I was to start without him.

So I ordered lunch. The Tuscan bean soup with black kale was fine. I took a few bites of the penne, ate without tasting what I imagined was excellent cuisine. I'd just asked for an espresso when my cell phone rang.

I stared at it for a moment, then, as if my nerves weren't frayed down to the stumps, said, "Hawkins" into the mouthpiece.

"Are you ready, Ben? You've got a little more driving to do."

Chapter 77

COACHELLA, California, is twenty-eight miles east of Palm Springs and has a population of close to forty thousand. For a couple of days every year in April, that number swells during the annual music festival, a mini-Woodstock, without the mud.

When the concert is over, Coachella reverts to an agricultural flatland in the desert, home to young Latino families and migrant workers, a drive-through for truckers, who use the town as a pit stop.

Henri had told me to look for the Luxury Inn, and it was easy to find. Off by itself on a long stretch of highway, the Lux was a classic U-shaped motel with a pool.

I pulled the car around to the back as directed, looked for the room number I'd been given, 229.

There were two vehicles in the parking lot. One was a

late-model Mercedes, black, a rental. I guessed that Henri must've driven it here. The other was a blue Ford pickup hitched to an old house trailer about twenty-six feet long. Silver with blue stripes, air conditioner on top, Nevada plates.

I turned off my engine and reached for my briefcase, opened the car door.

A man appeared on the balcony above me. It was Henri, looking the same as the last time I saw him. His brown hair was combed back, and he was clean-shaven, wore no glasses. In short, he was a good-looking Mr. Potato Head of a guy who could morph into another identity with a mustache or an eye patch or a baseball cap.

He said, "Ben, just leave your briefcase in the car."

"But the contract—"

"I'll get your briefcase. But right now, get out of your car and please leave your cell phone on the driver's seat. Thanks."

One part of me was screaming, *Get out of here. Jam on the gas and go.* But an opposing inner voice was insisting that if I quit now, nothing would have been gained. *Henri would still be out there. He could still kill me and Amanda at any time, for no reason other than that I'd disobeyed him.*

I took my hand off my briefcase, left it in my car along with my cell phone. Henri jogged down the stairs, told me to put my hands on the hood. Then he expertly frisked me.

"Put your hands behind your back, Ben," he said. Very casual and friendly.

Except that a gun muzzle was pressed against my spine.

The last time I turned my back to Henri, he'd coldcocked me with a gun butt to the back of my head. I didn't even think it through, just used instinct and training. I side-stepped, was about to whip around and disarm him, but what happened next was a blur of pain.

Henri's arms went around me like a vise, and I went airborne, crashing hard on my shoulders and the back of my head.

It was a hard fall, painfully hard, but I didn't have time to check myself out.

Henri was on top of me, his chest to my back, his legs interwoven with mine. His feet were hooked into me so that our bodies were fused, and his full weight crushed me against the pavement.

I felt the gun muzzle screw into my ear.

Henri said, "Got any more ideas? Come on, Ben. Give me your best shot."

Chapter 78

I WAS SO IMMOBILIZED by the takedown, it was as if my spinal cord had just been cut. No weekend black belt could have thrown me like that.

Henri said, "I could easily snap your neck. Understand?"

I wheezed "yes," and he stood, grasped my forearm, and hauled me to my feet.

"Try to get it right this time. Turn around and put your hands behind your back."

Henri cuffed me, then yanked upward on the cuffs, nearly popping my shoulders out of their joints.

Then he shoved me against the car and set my briefcase on the roof. He unlatched the case, found my gun, tossed it into the footwell. Then he locked the car, grabbed my case, and marched me toward the trailer.

"What the hell *is* this?" I asked. "Where are we going?"

"You'll know when you know," said the monster.

He opened the trailer door, and I stumbled inside.

The trailer was old and well used. To my left was the galley: a table attached to the wall, two chairs bolted to the floor. To my right was a sofa that looked like it doubled as a foldaway bed. There was a closet that housed a toilet and a cot.

Henri maneuvered me so one of the chairs clipped me at the back of my knees and I sat down. A black cloth bag was dropped over my head and a band was cinched around my legs. I heard a chain rattle and the snap of a lock.

I was shackled to a hook in the floor.

Henri patted my shoulder, said, "Relax, okay? I don't want to hurt you. I want you to write this book more than I want to kill you. We're partners now, Ben. Try to trust me."

I was chained down and essentially blind. I didn't know where Henri was taking me. *And I definitely didn't trust him.*

I heard the door close and lock. Then Henri started up the truck. The air conditioner pumped cold air into the trailer through a vent overhead.

We rolled along smoothly for about a half hour, then took a right turn onto a bumpy road. Other turns followed. I tried to hang onto the slick plastic seat with my thighs, but got slammed repeatedly against the wall and into the table.

After a while, I lost track of the turns and the time. I was mortified by how thoroughly Henri had disabled me. There was no way around the bald and simple truth.

Henri was in charge. This was his game. I was only along for the ride.

Chapter 79

MAYBE AN HOUR, hour and a half, had gone by when the trailer stopped and the door slid open. Henri ripped off my hood, and said, "Last stop, buddy. We're home."

I saw flat, uninviting desert through the open door: sand dunes out to the horizon, mop-headed Joshua trees, and buzzards circling on the updraft.

My mind also circled around one thought: *If Henri kills me here, my body will never even be found.* Despite the refrigerated air, sweat rolled down my neck as Henri leaned back against the narrow Formica counter a few feet away.

"I've done some research on collaborations," Henri said. "People say it takes about forty hours of interviews to get enough material for a book. Sound right?"

"Take off the cuffs, Henri. I'm not a flight risk."

He opened the small fridge beside him, and I saw that it

was stocked with water, Gatorade, some packaged food. He took out two bottles of water, put one on the table in front of me.

"Say we work about eight hours a day, we'll be here for about five days—"

"Where's here?"

"Joshua Tree. This campsite is closed for road repairs, but the electric hookup works," Henri told me.

Joshua Tree National Park is eight hundred thousand acres of desert wilderness, miles of nothing but yucca and brush and rock formations in all directions. The high views are said to be spectacular, but normal folk don't camp here in the white heat of high summer. I didn't understand people who came here at all.

"In case you think you can get out of here," Henri said, "let me save you the trouble. This is Alcatraz, desert-style. This trailer is sitting on a sea of sand. Daytime temperatures can climb to a hundred and twenty. Even if you got out at night, the sun would fry you before you reached a road. So, please, and I mean this sincerely, stay put."

"Five days, huh?"

"You'll be back in L.A. for the weekend. Scout's honor."

"Okay. So how about it?"

I held out my hands, and Henri took off the cuffs. Then he removed the cinch around my legs and unshackled me.

Chapter 80

I RUBBED my wrists, stood up, drank down a bottle of cold water in one continuous swallow, those small pleasures giving me a boost of unexpected optimism. I thought about Leonard Zagami's enthusiasm. I imagined dusty old writing dreams coming true for me.

"Okay, let's do this," I said.

Henri and I set up the awning against the side of the trailer, put out a couple of folding chairs and a card table in the thin strip of shade. With the trailer door open, cool air tickling our necks, we got down to business.

I showed Henri the contract, explained that Raven-Wofford would only make payments to the writer. I would pay Henri.

"Payments are made in installments," I told him. "The

first third is due on signing. The second payment comes on acceptance of the manuscript, and the final payment is due on publication."

"Not a bad life insurance policy for you," Henri said. He smiled brightly.

"Standard terms," I said to Henri, "to protect the publisher from writers crashing in the middle of the project."

We discussed our split, a laughably one-sided negotiation.

"It's my book, right?" Henri said, "and your name's going on it. That's worth more than money, Ben."

"So why don't I just work for free?" I said.

Henri smiled, said, "Got a pen?"

I handed one over, and Henri signed his nom de jour on the dotted lines, gave me the number of his bank account in Zurich.

I put the contract away, and Henri ran an electric cord out from the trailer. I booted up my laptop, turned on my tape recorder, gave it a sound test.

I said, "Ready to start?"

Henri said, "I'm going to tell you everything you need to know to write this book, but I'm not going to leave a trail of breadcrumbs, understand?"

"It's your story, Henri. Tell it however you want."

Henri leaned back in his canvas chair, folded his hands over his tight gut, and began at the beginning.

"I grew up in the sticks, a little farming town on the edge of nothing. My parents had a chicken farm, and I was their only child. They had a crappy marriage. My father drank.

He beat my mother. He beat me. *She* beat me, and she also took some shots at him."

Henri described the creaking four-room farmhouse, his room in the attic over his parents' bedroom.

"There was a crack between two floorboards," he told me. "I couldn't actually see their bed, but I could see shadows, and I could hear what they were doing. Sex and violence. Every night. I slept over that."

Henri described the three long chicken houses—and how at the age of six, his father put him in charge of killing chickens the old-fashioned way, decapitation with an axe on a wooden block.

"I did my chores like a good boy. I went to school. I went to church. I did what I was told and tried to duck the blows. My father not only clocked me regularly, but he also humiliated me.

"My mom. I forgive her. But for years I had a recurring dream about killing them both. In the dream, I pinned their heads to that old stump in the chicken yard, swung the axe, and watched their headless bodies run.

"For a while after I woke up from that dream, I'd think it was true. That I'd really done it."

Henri turned to me.

"Life went on. Can you picture me, Ben? Cute little kid with an axe in my hand, my overalls soaked with blood?"

"I can see you. It's a sad story, Henri. But it sounds like a good place to start the book."

Henri shook his head. "I've got a better place."

"Okay. Shoot."

Henri hunched over his knees and clasped his hands. He said, "I would start the movie of my life at the summer fair. The scene would center on me and a beautiful blond girl named Lorna."

Chapter 81

I CONSTANTLY CHECKED the recorder, saw that the wheels were slowly turning.

A dry breeze blew across the sands, and a lizard ran across my shoe. Henri raked both hands through his hair, and he seemed nervous, agitated. I hadn't seen this kind of fidgety behavior in him before. It made me nervous, too.

"Please set the scene, Henri. This was a county fair?"

"You could call it that. Agriculture and animals were on one side of the main path. Carnival rides and food were on the other. No breadcrumbs, Ben. This could have happened outside Wengen or Chipping Camden or Cowpat, Arkansas.

"Don't worry about where it was. Just see the bright lights on the fairgrounds, the happy people, and the serious animal competitions. Business deals were at stake here, people's farms and their futures.

"I was fourteen," he continued. "My parents were show-ing exotic chickens in the fowl tent. It was getting late, and my father told me to get the truck from the private lot for exhibitor's vehicles, upfield from the fairgrounds.

"On the way, I cut through one of the food pavilions and I saw Lorna selling baked goods," he said.

"Lorna was my age and was in my class at school. She was blond, a little shy. She carried her books in front of her chest, so you couldn't see her breasts. But you could see them anyway. There was nothing about Lorna I didn't want."

I nodded, and Henri went on with his story.

"That day I remember she was wearing a lot of blue. Made her hair look even more blond, and when I said hi to her, she seemed glad to see me. Asked me if I wanted to get some-thing to eat at the fairgrounds.

"I knew my father would kill me when I didn't come back with the truck, but I was willing to take the beating, that's how crazy I was about that beautiful girl."

Henri described buying Lorna a cookie and said that they'd gone on a ride together, that she'd grabbed his hand when the roller coaster made its swooping descent.

"All the while I felt a wild kind of tenderness toward this girl. After the ride," Henri said, "another boy came over, Craig somebody. He was a couple of years older. He looked right past me and told Lorna that he had tickets to the Ferris wheel, that it was unreal how the fairgrounds looked with the stars coming out and everything lit up down below.

"Lorna said, 'Oh, I'd love to do that,' and she turned to

me, and said, 'You don't mind, do you?' and she took off with this guy.

"Well, I did mind, Ben.

"I watched them go, and then I went to get the truck and my beating. It was dark up in that lot, but I found my dad's truck next to a livestock trailer.

"Standing outside the trailer was another girl I knew from school, Molly, and she had a couple of calves with show ribbons on their halters. She was trying to load them into the trailer, but they wouldn't go.

"I offered to help her," Henri told me. "Molly said, 'No, thanks. I've got it,' something like that, and tried to shove those calves up the ramp by herself.

"I didn't like the way she said that, Ben. I felt she had crossed a line.

"I grabbed a shovel that was leaning against the trailer, and as Molly turned her back to me, I swung the shovel against the back of her head. There was the one loud smack, a sound that thrilled me, and she went down."

Henri stopped speaking. A long moment dragged on, but I waited him out.

Then he said, "I dragged her into the trailer, shut the tailgate. By now she'd started to wail. I told her no one would hear her, but she wouldn't stop.

"My hands went around her neck, and I choked her as naturally as if I was reenacting something I'd done before. Maybe I had, in my dreams."

Henri twisted his watchband and looked away into the desert. When he turned back, his eyes were flat.

"As I was choking her, I heard two men walking by, talking. Laughing. I was squeezing her neck so hard that my hands hurt, so I adjusted my grip and choked her again until Molly stopped breathing.

"I let go of her throat, and she took another breath, but she wasn't wailing anymore. I slapped her—and I got hard. I stripped off her clothes, turned her over, and did her, my hands around her throat the whole time, and when I was done, I strangled her for good."

"What went through your mind as you were doing this?"

"I just wanted it to keep going. I didn't want the feeling to *stop*. Imagine what it was like, Ben, to climax with the power of life and death in your hands. I felt I had earned the *right* to do this. Do you want to know how I felt? *I felt like God*."

Chapter 82

I WAS AWOKEN the next morning when the trailer door rolled open, and light, almost white sunlight, poured in. Henri was saying, "I've got coffee and rolls, for you, bud. Eggs, too. Breakfast for my partner."

I sat up on the foldaway bed, and Henri lit the stove, beat the eggs in a bowl, made the frying pan sizzle. After I'd eaten, we began work under the awning. I kept turning it over in my mind: Henri had confessed to a murder. Somewhere, a fourteen-year-old girl had been strangled at a county fair. A record of her death would still exist.

Would Henri really let me live knowing about that girl?

Henri went back to the story of Molly, picked up where he'd left off the night before.

He was animated, using his hands to show me how he'd dragged Molly's body into the woods, buried it under piles of leaves, said that he was imagining the fear that would spread from the fairgrounds to the surrounding towns when Molly was reported missing.

Henri said that he'd joined the search for Molly, put up posters, went to the candlelight vigil, all the while cherishing his secret, that he'd killed Molly and had gotten away with it.

He described the girl's funeral, the white coffin under the blanket of flowers, how he'd watched the people crying, but especially Molly's family, her mother and father, the siblings.

"I wondered what it must be like to have those feelings," he told me.

"You know about the most famous of the serial killers, don't you, Ben? Gacy, BTK, Dahmer, Bundy. They were all run by their sexual compulsions. I was thinking last night that it's important for the book to make a distinction between those killers and me."

"Wait a minute, Henri. You told me how you felt raping and killing Molly. That video of you and Kim McDaniels? Are you telling me now you that you're not like those other guys? How does that follow?"

"You're missing the point. Pay attention, Ben. This is critical. I've killed dozens of people and had sex with most of them. But except for Molly, when I've killed I've done it for money."

It was good that my recorder was taking it all down because my mind was split into three parts: The writer, figuring out how to join Henri's anecdotes into a compelling narrative. The cop, looking for clues to Henri's identity from what he told me, what he left out, and from the psychological blind spots he didn't know that he had. And the part of my brain that was working the hardest, the survivor.

Henri said that he killed for money, but he'd killed Molly out of anger. He'd warned me that he would kill me if I didn't do what he said. He could break his own rules at any time.

I listened. I tried to learn Henri Benoit in all of his dimensions. But mostly, I was figuring out what I had to do to survive.

Chapter 83

HENRI CAME BACK to the trailer with sandwiches and a bottle of wine. After he uncorked the bottle, I asked him, "How does your arrangement with the Peepers work?"

"They call themselves the Alliance," Henri said. He poured out two glasses, handed one to me.

"I called them 'the Peepers' once and was given a lesson: no work, no pay." He put on a mock German accent. "You are a bad boy, Henri. Don't trifle with us."

"So the Alliance is German."

"One of the members is German. Horst Werner. That name is probably an alias. I never checked. Another of the Peepers, Jan Van der Heuvel, is Dutch.

"Listen, that could be an alias, too. It goes without saying, you'll change all the names for the book, right, Ben? But these people are not so stupid as to leave their own bread-crumbs."

"Of course. I understand."

He nodded, then went on. His agitation was gone, but his voice was harder now. I couldn't find a crack in it.

"There are several others in the Alliance. I don't know who they are. They live in cyberspace. Well, one I know very well. Gina Prazzi. She recruited me."

"That sounds interesting. You were recruited? Tell me about Gina."

Henri sipped at his wine, then began to tell me about meeting a beautiful woman after his four years in the Iraqi prison.

"I was having lunch in a sidewalk bistro in Paris when I noticed this tall, slender, extraordinary woman at a nearby table.

"She had very white skin, and her sunglasses were pushed up into her thick brown hair. She had high breasts and long legs and three diamond watches on one wrist. She looked rich and refined and impossibly inaccessible, and I wanted her.

"She put money down for the check and stood up to leave. I wanted to talk to her, and all I could think to say was, 'Do you have the time?'

"She gave me a long, slow look, from my eyes down to my shoes and back up again. My clothes were cheap. I had been out of prison for only a few weeks. The cuts and bruises had healed, but I was still gaunt. The torture, the things I'd seen, the afterimages, were still in my eyes. But she recognized something in me.

"This woman, this angel whose name I did not yet know, said, 'I have Paris time, New York time, Shanghai time . . . and I also have time for *you*.'"

Henri's voice was softened now as he talked about Gina Prazzi. It was as if he'd finally tasted fulfillment after a lifetime of deprivation.

He said that they'd spent a week in Paris. Henri still visited every September. He described walking with her through the Place Vendôme, shopping with her there. He said that Gina paid for everything, bought him expensive gifts and clothing.

"She came from very old money," Henri told me. "She had connections to a world of wealth I knew nothing about."

After their week in Paris, Henri told me, they cruised the Mediterranean on Gina's yacht. He called up images of the Côte d'Azur, one of the most beautiful spots in the world, he said.

He recalled the lovemaking in her cabin, the swell of the waves, the wine, the exquisite meals in restaurants with high views of the Mediterranean.

"I had nineteen fifty-eight Glen Garioch whisky at twenty-six hundred dollars a bottle. And here's a meal I'll never forget: sea urchin ravioli, followed by rabbit with fennel, mascarpone, and lemon. Nice fare for a country boy and ex–Al Qaeda POW."

"I'm a steak and potatoes man myself."

Henri laughed, said, "You just haven't had a real gastronomic tour of the Med. I could teach you. I could take you to a pastry shop in Paris, Au Chocolat. You would never be the same, Ben.

"But I was talking about Gina, a woman with refined appetites. One day a new guy appeared at our table. The Dutchman—Jan Van der Heuvel."

Henri's face tightened as he talked about Van der Heuvel, how he had joined them in their hotel room, called out stage directions from his chair in the corner as Henri made love to Gina.

"I didn't like this guy or this routine, but a couple of months before I'd been sleeping in my own shit, eating bugs. So what wouldn't I do to be with Gina, Jan Van der Heuvel or not?"

Henri's voice was drowned out by the roar of a helicopter flying over the valley. He warned me with his eyes not to move from my chair.

Even after the silence of the desert returned, it was several moments before he continued his story about Gina.

Chapter 84

"I DIDN'T LOVE GINA," Henri said to me, "but I was fascinated by her, obsessed with her. Okay. Maybe I did love her in some way," Henri said, admitting to having a human vulnerability for the first time.

"One day in Rome, Gina picked up a young girl—"

"And the Dutchman? He was out of the picture?"

"Not entirely. He'd gone back to Amsterdam, but he and Gina had some strange connection. They were always on the phone. She'd be whispering and laughing when she spoke with him. You can imagine, right? The guy liked to *watch*. But in the flesh, she was with *me*."

"You were with Gina in Rome." I prompted him to continue with the main narrative.

"Yes, of course. Gina picked up a student who was screwing her way through college, as they say. A first-semester prostitute from Prague, at Università degli Studi di Roma. I don't remember her name, only that she was hot and too trusting.

"We were in bed, the three of us, and Gina told me to close my hands around the girl's neck. It's a sex game called 'breath play.' It enhances the orgasm, and yes, Ben, before you ask, it was exciting to revisit my singular experience with Molly. This girl passed out, and I loosened my grip so that she could breathe.

"Gina reached out, took my cock in her hand, and kissed me. And then she said, 'Finish her, Henri.'

"I started to mount the girl, but Gina said, 'No, Henri, you don't understand. *Finish* her.'

"She reached over to the bedside table, held up the keys to her Ferrari, swung the keys in front of my eyes. It was an offer, the car for the girl's life.

"I killed that girl. And I made love to Gina with the dead girl beside us. Gina was electrified and wild under my hands. When she came, it was like a death and a rebirth as a softer, sweeter woman."

Henri's body language relaxed. He told me about driving the Ferrari, a leisurely three-day ride to Florence with many stops along the way, and about a life he believed was becoming his.

"Not long after that trip to Florence, Gina told me about the Alliance, including the fact that Jan was an important member."

The travelogue of Western Europe had ended. Henri's

posture straightened, and the tempo of his voice changed from languid to clipped.

"Gina told me that the Alliance was a secret organization composed of the very best people, by which she meant wealthy, filthy rich. She said that they could use me, 'make use of my talents' is the way she put it. And she said that I would be rewarded handsomely.

"So Gina didn't love me. She had a purpose for me. Of course, I was a little hurt by that. At first, I thought I might kill her. But there was no need for that, was there, Ben? In fact it would have been stupid."

"Because they hired you to kill for them?"

"Of course," Henri said.

"But how would that benefit the Alliance?"

"Benjamin," Henri said patiently. "They didn't hire me to do *hits*. I film my work. I make the films for *them*. They pay to *watch*."

Chapter 85

HENRI HAD SAID he killed for money, and now his story was coming together. He had been killing and creating films of these sexual executions for a select audience at a premium price. The stagelike setting for Kim's death made sense now. It had been a cinematic backdrop to his debauchery. But I didn't understand why Henri had drowned Levon and Barbara. What could possibly explain that?

"You were talking about the Peepers. The assignment you took in Hawaii."

"I remember. Well, understand, the Peepers give me a great deal of creative freedom," Henri said. "I picked Kim out from her photos. I used a ploy to get information from her agency. I said I wanted to book her and asked when would she be returning from—where was she shooting?

"I was told the location, and I worked out the rest: which island, her time of arrival, and the hotel. While I was waiting for Kim to arrive, I killed little Rosa. She was a tidbit, an *amuse-bouche*—"

"*Amuse* what?"

"It means an appetizer, and in her case, the Alliance hadn't commissioned the work. I put the film up for auction. Yes, there's a market for such things. I made some extra money, and I made sure the film got back to the Dutchman. Jan especially likes young girls, and I wanted the Peepers to be hungry for my work.

"When Kim arrived in Maui for the shoot, I kept watch on her."

"Were you going under the name of Nils Bjorn?" I asked.

Henri started. Then he frowned.

"How did you know that?"

I'd made a mistake. My mental leap had connected Gina Prazzi to the woman who'd phoned me in Hawaii telling me to check out a guest named Nils Bjorn. This connection had apparently struck home—and Henri didn't like it.

Why would Gina betray Henri, though? What didn't I know about the two of them?

It felt like an important hook into Henri's story, but I gave myself a warning. *For my own safety, I had to be careful not to tick Henri off. Very careful.*

"The police got a tip," I said. "An arms dealer by that name checked out of the Wailea Princess around the time Kim went missing. He was never questioned."

"I'll tell you something, Ben," Henri said. "I *was* Nils Bjorn, but I've destroyed his identity. I'll never use it again. It's worthless to you now."

Henri got up from his seat abruptly. He adjusted the awning to block the lower angle of the sun's rays. I used the time to steady my nerves.

I was swapping out the old audiotape for a new one when Henri said, "Someone is coming."

My heart started tap-dancing in my chest again.

Chapter 86

I SHIELDED my eyes with my hands and looked in the direction of the trail stretching through the desert to the west, saw a dark-colored sedan coming over a hill.

Henri said, "Right now! Take your things, your glass and your chair, and go inside."

I did what I was told, hustled back into the trailer with Henri behind me. He unhooked the chain from the floor, put it under the sink. He handed me my jacket and told me to go into the bathroom.

"If our visitor gets too nosy," Henri said, hiding the wineglasses, "I may have to dispose of him. That means you'll have witnessed a murder, Ben. Not good for you."

I squeezed into the tiny washroom, looked at my face in the mirror before flicking off the light. I had a three-day beard, rumpled shirt. I looked disreputable. I looked like a bum.

The bathroom wall was thin, and I could hear everything through it. There was a knock on the trailer door, which Henri opened. I heard heavy footsteps.

"Please come in, Officer. I'm Brother Michael," Henri said.

A woman's authoritative voice said, "I'm Lieutenant Brooks. Park Service. This campsite is closed, sir. Didn't you see the roadblock and the words 'Do Not Enter' in giant letters?"

"I'm sorry," Henri said. "I wanted to pray without being disturbed. I'm with the Camaldolese monastery. In Big Sur. I'm on retreat."

"I don't care if you're an acrobat with the Cirque du Soleil. You have no business being here."

"*God* led me here," said Henri. "I'm on *His* business. But I didn't mean any harm. I'm sorry."

I could feel the tension outside the door. If the ranger used her radio to call for help, she was a dead woman. Years ago, back in Portland, I'd backed my squad car into a wheelchair, knocked over an old man. Another time, I put a little kid in my gun sights when he'd jumped out from between two cars, pointing a squirt gun at me.

Both times I thought my heart couldn't beat any harder, but honest to God, this was the worst.

If my belt buckle clanked against the metal sink, the ranger would hear it. If she saw me, if she questioned me, Henri might feel he had to kill her, and her death would be on me.

Then he'd kill me.

I prayed not to sneeze. I prayed.

Chapter 87

THE RANGER TOLD HENRI that she understood about desert retreats, but that the campsite wasn't safe.

"If the chopper pilot hadn't seen your trailer, there would be no patrols out this way. What if you ran out of fuel? What if you ran out of water? No one would find you, and you would die," Lieutenant Brooks said. "I'll wait while you pack up your gear."

A radio crackled, and I heard the ranger say, "I got him, Yusef."

I waited for the inevitable gunshot, thought of kicking open the door, trying to knock the gun out of Henri's hand, save the poor woman somehow.

The lieutenant said to her partner, "He's a monk. A hermit. Yeah. He's by himself. No, it's under control."

Henri's voice cut in, "Lieutenant, it's getting late. I can

leave in the morning without difficulty. I'd really appreciate one more night here for my meditation."

There was silence as the park ranger seemed to consider Henri's request. I slowly exhaled, took in another breath. *Lady, do what he says. Get the hell out of here.*

"I can't help you," she said.

"Sure you can. Just one night is all I ask."

"Your gas tank is full?"

"Yes. I filled up before I drove into the park."

"And you have enough water?"

The refrigerator door squealed open.

The ranger said, "Tomorrow morning, you're outta here. We have a deal?"

"Yes, we do," Henri said. "I'm sorry for the trouble."

"Okay. Have a good night, Brother."

"Thank you, Lieutenant. And bless you."

I heard the ranger's car engine start up. A minute later, Henri opened my door.

"Change of plans," he said, as I edged out of the washroom. "I'll cook. We're pulling an all-nighter."

"No problem," I said.

I looked out the window and saw the lights of the patrol car heading back to civilization. Behind me, Henri dropped hamburger patties into the frying pan.

"We've got to cover a lot of ground tonight," he said.

I was thinking that by noon of the next day, I could be in Venice Beach watching the bodybuilders and the thong girls, the skaters and bikers on the winding concrete paths through the beach and along the shore. I thought of the dogs with kerchiefs and sunglasses, the toddlers on their trikes, and that I'd have huevos rancheros with extra salsa at Scotty's with Mandy.

I'd tell her everything.

Henri put a burger and a bottle of ketchup in front of me, said, "Here ya go, Mr. Meat and Potatoes." He started making coffee.

The little voice in my head said, *You're not home yet.*

Chapter 88

THE KIND OF LISTENING you do when interviewing is very different from the casual kind. I had to focus on what Henri was saying, how it fit into the story, decide if I needed elaboration on that subject or if we had to move along.

Fatigue was coming over me like fog, and I fought it off with coffee, keeping my goal in sight. *Get it down and get out of here alive.*

Henri backtracked over the story of his service with the military contractor, Brewster-North. He told me how he'd brought several languages to the table and that he'd learned several more while working for them.

He told me how he'd formed a relationship with his forger in Beirut. And then his shoulders sagged as he detailed his imprisonment, the executions of his friends.

I asked questions, placed Gina Prazzi in the time line. I

asked Henri if Gina knew his real identity, and he told me no. He'd used the name that matched the papers his forger had given him: Henri Benoit from Montreal.

"Have you stayed in contact with Gina?"

"I haven't seen her for years. Not since Rome," he said. "She doesn't fraternize with the help."

We worked forward from his three-month-long romance with Gina to the contract killings he did for the Alliance, a string of murders that went back over four years.

"I mostly killed young women," Henri told me. "I moved around, changed my identity often. You remember how I do that, Ben."

He started ticking off the bodies, the string of young girls in Jakarta, a Sabra in Tel Aviv.

"What a fighter, that Sabra. My God. She almost killed *me*."

I felt the natural arc of the story. I felt excited as I saw how I would organize the draft, almost forgot for a while that this wasn't some kind of movie pitch.

The murders were real.

Henri's gun was loaded even now.

I numbered tapes and changed them, made notes that would remind me to ask follow-up questions as Henri listed his kills; the young prostitutes in Korea and Venezuela and Bangkok.

He explained that he'd always loved film and that making movies for the Alliance had made him an even better killer. The murders became more complex and cinematic.

"Don't you worry that those films are out in the world?"

"I always disguise my face," he told me. "Either I wear a

mask as I did with Kim, or I work on the video with a blur tool. The software that I use makes editing out my face very easy."

He told me that his years with Brewster-North had taught him to leave the weapons and the bodies on the scene (Rosa was the one exception), and that even though there was no record of his fingerprints, he made sure never to leave anything of himself behind. He always wore a condom, taking no chances that the police might take DNA samples from his semen and begin to link his crimes.

Henri told me about killing Julia Winkler, how much he loved her. I stifled a smart-ass comment about what it meant to be loved by Henri. And he told me about the McDanielses, and how he admired them as well. At that point, I wanted to jump up and try to strangle him.

"Why, Henri, why did you have to kill them?" I finally asked.

"It was part of a film sequence I was making for the Peepers, what we called a documentary. Maui was a big payout, Ben. Just a few days' work for much more than you make in a year."

"But the work itself, how did you feel about taking all of those lives? By my count, you've killed thirty people."

"I may have left out a few," Henri said.

Chapter 89

IT WAS AFTER THREE IN THE MORNING when Henri told me what fascinated him most about his work.

"I've become interested in the fleeting moment *between* life and death," he said. I thought about the headless chickens from his childhood, the asphyxiation games he played after killing Molly.

Henri told me more, more than I wanted to know.

"There was a tribe in the Amazon," he continued. "They would tie a noose high under the jaws of their victims, right under their ears. The other end of the rope was secured around the tops of bent saplings.

"When they cut off a victim's head, it was carried upward by the young tree snapping back into place. These Indians believed this was a good death. That their victim's last sensation would be of flying.

"Do you know about a killer who lived in Germany in

the early nineteen hundreds?" Henri asked me. "Peter Kurten, the Vampire of Düsseldorf."

I had never heard of the man.

"He was a plain-looking guy whose first kill was a small girl he found sleeping while he robbed her parents' house. He strangled her, opened her throat with a knife, and got off on the blood spouting from her arteries. This was the start of a career that makes Jack the Ripper look like an amateur."

Henri described how Kurten killed too many people to count, both sexes, men, women, and children, used all kinds of instruments, and at the heart of it all, he was turned on by blood.

"Before Peter Kurten was executed by guillotine," Henri said to me, "he asked the prison psychiatrist—wait. Let me get this right. Okay. Kurten asked if, after his head was chopped off"—Henri put up fingers as quotation marks—'If I could hear the sound of my own blood gushing from the stump of my neck. That would be the pleasure to end all pleasures.'"

"Henri, are you saying the moment between life and death is what makes you want to kill?"

"I think so. About three years ago, I killed a couple in Big Sur. I knotted ropes high up under their jaws," he said, demonstrating with the V between thumb and index finger of his hand. "I tied the other end of the ropes to the blades of a ceiling fan. I cut their heads off with a machete, and the fan spun with their heads attached.

"I think the Peepers knew that I was very special when they saw that film," Henri said. "I raised my fee, and they paid. But I still wonder about those two lovers. I wonder if they felt that they were flying as they died."

Chapter 90

EXHAUSTION DRAGGED ME down as the sun came up. We'd worked straight through the night, and although I heavily sugared my coffee and drank it down to the dregs, my eyelids drooped and the small world of the trailer on the rumpled acres of sand blurred.

I said, "This is important, Henri."

I completely lost what I was going to say—and Henri prompted me by shaking my shoulder. "Finish your sentence, Ben. *What* is important?"

It was the question that would be asked by the reader at the beginning of the book, and it had to be answered at the end. I asked, "Why do you want to write this book?"

Then I put my head down on the small table, just for a minute.

I heard Henri moving around the trailer, thought I saw

him wiping down surfaces. I heard him talking, but I wasn't sure he was talking to me.

When I woke up, the clock on the microwave read ten after eleven.

I called out to Henri, and when he didn't answer I struggled out of my cramped spot behind the table and opened the trailer door.

The truck was gone.

I left the trailer and looked in all directions. The sludge began to clear from the gears in my brain, and I went back inside. My laptop and briefcase were on the kitchen counter. The piles of tapes that I'd carefully labeled in sequence were in neat stacks. My tape recorder was plugged into the outlet—and then I saw the note next to the machine.

Ben: Play this.

I pushed the Play button and heard Henri's voice.

"Good morning, partner. I hope you had a good rest. You needed it, and so I gave you a sedative to help you sleep. You understand. I wanted some time alone.

"Now. You should take the trail to the west, fourteen miles to Twenty-nine Palms Highway. I've left plenty of water and food, and if you wait until sundown, you will make it out of the park by morning.

"Very possibly, Lieutenant Brooks or one of her colleagues may drop by and give you a lift. Be careful what you say, Ben. Let's keep our secrets for now. You're a novelist, remember. So be sure to tell a plausible lie.

"Your car is behind the Luxury Inn where you left it, and

I've put your keys in your jacket pocket with your plane ticket.

"Oh, I almost forgot the most important thing. I called Amanda. I told her you were safe and that you'd be home soon.

"*Ciao,* Ben. Work hard. Work well. I'll be in touch."

And then the tape hissed and the message was over.

The bastard had called Amanda. It was another threat.

Outside the trailer, the desert was cooking in the July inferno, forcing me to wait until sundown before beginning my trek. While I waited, Henri would be erasing his trail, assuming another identity, boarding a plane unhindered.

I no longer had any sense of security, and I wouldn't feel safe again until "Henri Benoit" was in jail or dead. I wanted my life back, and I was determined to get it, whatever it took.

Even if I had to put Henri down myself.

Part Four

BIG GAME HUNTING

Chapter 91

ON MY FIRST DAY back from my desert retreat with Henri, Leonard Zagami called to say he wanted to publish fast so we'd get gonzo press coverage for breaking Henri's first-person story before the Maui murders were solved.

I'd called Aronstein, taken a leave from the *L.A. Times*, turned my living room into a bunker and not just because of the pressure from Zagami. I felt Henri's presence all the time, like he was a boa constrictor with a choke hold on my rib cage, peering over my shoulder as I typed. I wanted nothing more than to get his dirty story written and done, and get him out of my life.

Since my return, I'd been working from six in the morning until late at night, and I found transcribing the interview tapes educational.

Listening to Henri's voice behind a locked door, I heard

inflections and pauses, comments made under his breath, that I'd missed while sitting next to his coiled presence and wondering if I was going to make it out of Joshua Tree alive.

I'd never worked so hard or so steadily, but by the end of the second full week at my laptop, I'd finished the transcription and also the outline for the book.

One important item was missing: the hook for the introduction, the question that would power the narrative to the end, the question Henri hadn't answered. *Why did he want to write this book?*

The reader would want to know, and I couldn't understand it myself. Henri was twisted in his particular way, and that included being an actual survivor. He dodged death like it was Sunday traffic. He was smart, probably a genius, so why would he write a tell-all confession when his own words could lead to his capture and indictment? Was it for money? Recognition? Was his narcissism so overpowering that he'd set a trap for himself?

It was almost six on a Friday evening. I was filing the transcribed audiotapes in a shoe box when I put my hand on the exit tape, the one with Henri's instructions telling me how to get out of Joshua Tree Park.

I hadn't replayed the tape because Henri's message hadn't seemed relevant to the work, but before I boxed it up, I dropped tape number 31 into the recorder and rewound it to the beginning.

I realized instantly that Henri hadn't used a fresh tape for his message. He'd recorded on the tape that was already in the machine.

I heard my drugged and weary voice coming through the speaker, saying, "This is important, Henri."

There was silence. I'd forgotten what I wanted to ask him. Then Henri's voice was saying, "Finish your sentence, Ben. *What* is important?"

"Why . . . do you want to write this book?"

My head had dropped to the table, and I remembered hearing Henri's voice as through a fog.

Now he was coming in loud and clear.

"Good question, Ben. If you're half the writer I think you are, if you're half the cop you used to be, you'll figure out why I want to do this book. I think you'll be surprised."

I was going to be *surprised?* What the hell was that supposed to mean?

Chapter 92

A KEY TURNED in the lock, and bolts thunked open. I started, swiveled in my chair. *Henri?*

But it was only Amanda coming across the threshold, hugging a grocery bag. I leapt up, took the bag, and kissed my girl, who said, "I got the last two Cornish game hens. Yea! Also. Look. Wild rice and haricots verts—"

"You're a peach, you know that?" I said.

"You saw the news?"

"No. What?"

"Those two girls who were found on Barbados. One of them was strangled. The other was *decapitated*."

"What two girls?"

I hadn't turned on the TV in a week. I didn't know what the hell Amanda was talking about.

"The story was all over cable, not to mention the Internet. You need to come up for air, Ben."

I followed her into the kitchen, put the groceries on the counter, and snapped on the under-cabinet TV. I tuned in to MSNBC, where Dan Abrams was talking to the former FBI profiler John Manzi.

Manzi looked grim. He was saying, "You call it 'serial' when there've been three or more killings with an emotional cooling-off period in between. The killer left the murder weapon in a hotel room with Sara Russo's decapitated body. Wendy Emerson was found in a car trunk, bound and strangled. These crimes are very reminiscent of the killings in Hawaii a month ago. Despite the distances involved, I'd say they could be linked. I'd bet on it."

Pictures of the two young women appeared on a split screen as Manzi talked. Russo looked to be in her late teens. Emerson in her twenties. Both young women had big, expectant, life-sized smiles, and Henri had killed them. I was sure of it. I'd bet on it, too.

Amanda edged past me, put the birds in the oven, banged pots around, and ran water on the veggies. I turned up the volume.

Manzi was saying, "It's too soon to know if the killer left any DNA behind, but the absence of a *motive,* leaving the murder weapons *behind,* these form a picture of a very practiced killer. He didn't just get started in Barbados, Dan. It's a question of how many people he's killed, over how long a time, and in how many places."

I said to Mandy over the commercial break, "I've been listening to Henri talk about himself for weeks. I can tell you absolutely, he feels no remorse whatsoever. He's happy with himself. He's *ecstatic*."

I told Mandy that Henri had left me a message telling me that he expected me to figure out why he was doing the book.

"He's challenging me as a writer, and as a cop. Hey, maybe he wants to get *caught*. Does that make any sense to you?"

Mandy had been solid throughout, but she showed me how scared she was when she grabbed my hands hard and fixed me with her eyes.

"*None* of it makes sense to me, Benjy. Not why, not what he wants, not even why he picked you to do this book. All I know is he's a freaking *psycho*. And he knows where we live."

Chapter 93

I WOKE UP in bed, my heart hammering, my T-shirt and shorts drenched with sweat.

In my dream, Henri had taken me on a tour of his killings in Barbados, talked to me while he sawed off Sara Russo's head. He'd held up her head by her hair, saying, "See, this is what I like, the fleeting moment between life and death," and in the way of dreams, Sara became Mandy.

Mandy looked at me in the dream, her blood streaming down Henri's arm, and she said, "Ben. Call Nine-one-one."

I threw my arm over my forehead and dried my brow.

It was an easy nightmare to interpret. I was terrified that Henri would kill Mandy. And I felt guilty about those girls in Barbados, thinking, If I'd gone to the police, they might still be alive.

Was that dream-thinking? Or was it true?

I imagined going to the FBI now, telling them how Henri had put a gun on me, took photos of Amanda, and threatened to kill us both.

I would have to tell them how Henri chained me to a trailer in the desert and detailed the killings of thirty people. But were those confessions? Or bullshit?

I had no proof that anything Henri had told me was true. Just his word.

I imagined the FBI agent eyeing me skeptically, then the networks broadcasting "Henri's" description: a white male, six feet, 160 pounds, midthirties. That would piss Henri off. And then, if he could, he'd kill us.

Did Henri really think I'd let that happen?

I stared at headlights flickering across the ceiling of the bedroom.

I remembered names of restaurants and resorts Henri had visited with Gina Prazzi. There were a number of other aliases and details Henri hadn't thought important but that might, if I could figure them out, unwind his whole ball of string.

Mandy turned over in her sleep, put her arm across my chest, and snuggled close to me. I wondered what *she* was dreaming. I tightened my arms around her, lightly kissed the crown of her head.

"Try not to torment yourself," she said against my chest.

"I didn't mean to wake you."

"That's a joke, right? You almost blew me out of bed with all your heaving and sighing."

"What time is it?"

"It's early. Too early, or late, for us to be up. Benjy, I don't think obsessing is helping."

"Oh. You think I'm obsessing?"

"Get your mind on something else. Take a break."

"Zagami wants—"

"Screw Zagami. I've been thinking, too, and I have an idea of my own. You won't like it."

Chapter 94

I WAS PACING in front of my building with an overnight bag when Mandy roared up on her gently used Harley Sportster, a snappy-looking bike with a red leather saddle.

I climbed on, put my hands around Mandy's small waist, and with her long hair whipping across my face we motored to the 10 and from there to the Pacific Coast Highway, a dazzling stretch of coastal road that seems to go on forever.

To our left and below the road, breakers reared up and curled toward the beach, bringing in the surfers who dotted the waves. It struck me that I had never surfed—*because it was too dangerous.*

I hung on as Mandy switched lanes and gunned the engine. She shouted to me, "Take your shoulders down from your ears."

Huh?

"Relax."

It was hard to do, but I willed myself to unclench my legs and shoulders, and Mandy shouted again, "Now, make like a *dog.*"

She turned her head and stuck out her tongue, pointed her finger at me until I did it, too. The fifty-mile-an-hour wind beat on my tongue, cracking me up, making both of us laugh so hard that our eyes watered.

I was still grinning as we blew through Malibu and crossed the Ventura County line. Minutes later, Mandy pulled the bike over at Neptune's Net, a seafood shack with a parking lot full of motorcycles.

A couple of guys called out, "Hey, Mandy," as I followed her inside. We picked out two crabs from the well, and ten minutes later we picked them up at the take-out window, steamed and cracked on paper plates with small cups of melted butter. We chased the crabs down with Mountain Dew, then climbed aboard the Harley again.

I felt more at home on the bike this time, and finally I got it. Mandy was giving me the gift of glee. The speed and wind were blowing the snarls out of my mind, forcing me to turn myself over to the excitement and freedom of the road.

As we traveled north, the PCH wound down to sea level, taking us through the dazzling towns of Sea Cliff, La Conchita, Rincon, Carpinteria, Summerland, and Montecito. And then Mandy was telling me to hang on as she took the turn off the freeway onto the Olive Mill Road exit to Santa Barbara.

I saw the signs, and then I knew where we were going—a

place we had talked of spending a weekend at, but we had never found the time.

My whole body was shaking when I dismounted the bike in front of the legendary Biltmore Hotel, with its red tiled roofs and palm trees and high view of the sea. I took off my helmet, put my arms around my girl, and said, "Honey, when you say you have an *idea,* you sure don't mess around."

She told me, "I was saving my Christmas bonus for our anniversary, but you know what I thought at four this morning?"

"Tell me."

"No better time than now. No better place than this."

Chapter 95

THE HOTEL LOBBY GLOWED. I'm not one of those guys who studies the "House Beautiful" channel, but I knew luxury and comfort, and Amanda, prancing in place beside me, filled in the details. She pointed out the Mediterranean style, the archways and beamed ceilings, the plump sofas and logs burning in a tiled fireplace. The vast, rolling ocean below.

Then Mandy warned me—and she was serious.

"If you mention what's-his-name, even once, the bill goes on your credit card, not mine. Okay?"

"Deal," I said, pulling her in for a hug.

Our room had a fireplace, and when Mandy started tossing her clothes onto the chair, I pictured us rolling around in the king-size bed for the rest of the afternoon.

She read the look in my eyes, laughed, and said, "Oh, I see. Wait, okay? I've got another idea."

I was becoming a big fan of Mandy's ideas. She stepped into her leopard-print bikini, and I put on my trunks, and we went out to a pool in the center of the main garden. I followed Mandy's lead, diving in, and heard—I couldn't quite believe it—*music* playing underwater.

Back in our room, I untied the strings of Mandy's swimsuit, pushed down the bikini bottoms, and she climbed up on me, her legs around my waist. I walked her into the shower and not too many minutes later we tumbled onto the bed, where goofiness became heart-pounding lovemaking.

Later we napped, Mandy falling asleep while lying on my chest with her knees tucked up along my sides. For the first time in weeks, I slept deeply without my eyes flying open at some bloody nightmare.

At sundown, Mandy slipped into a small black dress and twisted up her hair, making me think of Audrey Hepburn. We took the winding stairs down to the Bella Vista and were shown to a table near the fire. There was marble underfoot, mahogany-paneled walls, a billion-dollar view of whitecaps below, and a glass-paned ceiling showing cobalt twilight over our heads.

I glanced at the menu, put it down when the waiter came over. Mandy ordered for us both.

I was grinning again. Amanda Diaz knew how to take a day out of the dumper and light up memories that could take the two of us into old age.

We started our five-star dinner with sautéed jumbo scallops and continued with scrumptious honey-cilantro-glazed sea bass with mushrooms and snow peas. Then the waiter brought dessert menus and chilled champagne.

I turned the bottle so I could read the label: Dom Pérignon.

"You didn't order this, did you, Mandy? This is about three hundred dollars."

"Wasn't me. We must've got somebody else's bubbly."

I reached for the card the waiter had left on a small silver tray. It read, "The Dom is on me. It's the good stuff. Best regards, H.B."

Henri Benoit.

Fear shot right up my spine. How had that fucker known where we were when I hadn't known where we were going myself?

I got to my feet, knocking over my chair. I pivoted around, a full 360 and then back again in the other direction to be sure. I scanned every face in the room: the old man with soup on his whiskers, the bald tourist with his fork poised over his plate, the honeymooners standing in the entrance-way, and every one of the waitstaff.

Where was he? *Where?*

I stood so that I blocked Mandy with my body, and I felt the scream tearing out of my throat.

"Henri, you bastard. Show yourself."

Chapter 96

AFTER THE SCENE in the dining room, I locked and chained the door to our suite, checked the latches on the windows, closed the drapes. I hadn't brought my gun, a gross mistake I wouldn't make again.

Mandy was pale and shaking as I sat her down next to me on the bed.

"Who knew we were coming here?" I asked her.

"I made the reservation when I went home to pack this morning. That's all."

"You're sure?"

"Except for calling Henri on his private line, you mean?"

"Seriously. You talk to anyone on your way out this morning? Think about it, Mandy. He knew we'd be here."

"I just told you, Ben, really. I didn't tell anyone. I just called in my credit card to the reservation clerk. That's all I did. That's *all*."

"Okay, okay," I said. "I'm sorry."

I had been thorough. I was sure of it. I revisited that night when I'd just returned from New York, and Henri called me at Amanda's apartment minutes after I'd walked in the door. I'd checked Mandy's phones and mine, checked both of our apartments for bugs.

I hadn't noticed anything unusual around us on the highway this afternoon. There was no way anyone could have followed us when we took the off-ramp to Santa Barbara. We had been alone for so many miles that we'd practically owned the road.

Ten minutes ago, after the maitre d' escorted us out of the dining room, he'd told me that the champagne had been phoned in, charged to a credit card by Henri Benoit. That explained nothing. Henri could have called from any point on the globe.

But how had he known where we were?

If Henri hadn't tapped Mandy's phone, and if he hadn't tailed us—

A stunning thought cracked through my mind like a lightning strike. I stood up, and said, "He put a tracking device on your bike."

"Don't even think about leaving me in this room alone," Amanda said. I sat back down beside her, took her hand between both of mine and kissed it. I couldn't leave her in the room, and I couldn't protect her in the parking lot either.

"As soon as it's light tomorrow, I'm dismantling your bike until I find the bug."

"I can't believe what he's doing to us," Mandy said, and then she started to cry.

Chapter 97

WE HELD on to each other under the bedcovers, our eyes wide open, listening to every footstep overhead, every creak in the hallway outside the room, every groan and pitch of the air conditioner. I didn't know if I was being rational or extremely paranoid, but I felt Henri watching us now.

Mandy had me tightly wrapped in her arms when she started crying out, "Oh, my God, oh, my God."

I tried to comfort her, saying, "Honey, stop. This isn't such bad news. We'll find out how he's tracking us."

"Oh, my God—*this*," she said, poking me hard high on my right buttock. "This thing on your hip. I've told you about it. You always say it's nothing."

"That thing? It *is* nothing."

"*Look at it.*"

I threw off the blankets, switched on the lights, walked

to the bathroom mirror with Mandy close behind me. I couldn't *see* it without contorting myself, but I knew what she was talking about: a welt that had been tender for a few days after Henri had clubbed me in my apartment.

I'd thought it was a bruise from the fall, or a bug bite, and after a few days the soreness went away.

Mandy had asked me about the bump a couple of times, and, yes, I'd said it was nothing. I reached around and touched the raised spot, the size of two grains of rice lying end-to-end.

It didn't seem so nothing, not anymore.

I rifled through my toiletry kit, dumped it out on the vanity, and found my razor. I beat it against the marble sink until the shaving head broke into parts.

"You're not going to . . . Ben! You don't want *me* to do it?"

"Don't worry. It'll hurt me more than it hurts you."

"Wow, you're funny."

"I'm fucking terrified," I said.

Mandy took the blade from my hand, poured Listerine over it, and dabbed at the spot on my rump. Then she pinched a fold of skin and made a quick cut.

"I've got it," she said.

She dropped the bloody bit of glass and metal into my hand. It could only be one thing: a GPS tracking device, the kind that are implanted into the necks of dogs. Henri must've injected it into my hide when I was lying unconscious on the floor. I'd been wearing this damned bug for *weeks*.

"Flush it down the toilet," Amanda said. "That'll keep him busy."

"Yeah. *No.* Tear some tape off that roll, would you?"

I pressed the device against my side, and Mandy ripped off a length of adhesive tape with her teeth. I patted the tape across the chip, securing it to my body again.

"What's the point of keeping it?" Mandy asked.

"As long as I'm wearing it, he won't know that I know that he's tracking me."

"And . . . what good is that?"

"It starts the ball rolling in the other direction. We know something he doesn't."

Chapter 98

FRANCE.

Henri stroked Gina Prazzi's flank as his breathing slowed. She had a wonderful peach-shaped ass, perfect rounded haunches with a dimple on each cheek at the small of her back.

He wanted to fuck her again. Very much so. And he would.

"You can untie me now," she said.

He patted her, got up, reached under a chair and into his bag, then went to the camera that was clipped to the heavy folds of the curtains.

"What are you doing? Come back to bed, Henri. Don't be so cruel."

He turned on the floor lamp and smiled into the lens, then went back to the canopied bed, said, "I don't think I caught the part when you were calling out to God. Too bad."

"What are you doing with that video? You're not sending it? You're crazy, Henri, if you think they'll pay."

"Oh, no?"

"I assure you, they will not."

"It's for my private collection, anyway. You should trust me more."

"Untie me, Henri. My arms are tired. I want a new game. I demand it."

"You always think of your own pleasure."

"Suit yourself," she said. "But there will be a price to pay for this."

Henri laughed. "Always a price."

He picked up the remote control from the ornate night table, turned on the television set. He clicked past the hotel welcome screen, found the channel guide, pressed the buttons for the BBC.

First there were sports scores, then a market wrap-up, and then there were the faces of the new girls, Wendy and Sara.

"I absolutely loved Sara," he told Gina, who was trying to loosen the knots binding her wrists to the headboard. "She never begged for her life. She never asked any stupid questions."

"If I had use of my, ah, hands, I could do some nice things for you," Gina said.

"I'll think about it."

Henri clicked off the remote, rolled over, and straddled

Gina's fantastic ass. He put his hands on her shoulders, rubbed his thumbs in circles at the base of her neck. He was getting hard again. Very hard, painfully so.

"This is becoming boring," she said. "Maybe this reunion was a bad idea."

Henri closed his fingers gently around her throat, still just playing a game. He felt her body tense and a film of sweat come over her skin.

Good. He liked her to be afraid. "Still bored?" He squeezed until she coughed, pulled at the restraints, wheezing his name as her lungs fought for air.

He released her, and then, as she gulped for breath, he untied her wrists. Gina shook out her hands and rolled over, still panting, said, "I knew you couldn't do it."

"No. I couldn't do that."

She got out of the bed and flounced toward the bathroom, stopping first to wink at the camera. Henri watched her go, then he got up, reached into his bag again, and walked into the bathroom behind her.

"What do you want now?" she asked, making eye contact with him in the mirror.

"Time's up," he said.

Henri pointed the gun at the back of Gina's neck and fired, watched in the blood-spattered mirror as her eyes got large, then followed her body as she dropped to the floor. He put two more slugs into her back, checked her pulse, wiped down the gun and the silencer, placed the weapon at her side.

After his shower, Henri dressed. Then he downloaded

the video to his laptop, wiped down the rooms, packed his bag, and checked that everything was as it should be.

He stared for a moment at the three diamond wristwatches on the nightstand and remembered the day he met her.

I . . . have time for you.

Together, the watches were worth a hundred thousand euros. Not worth the risk, though. He left them on the table. A nice tip for the maid, no?

Gina had used her credit card, so Henri left the room, closing the door behind him. He walked across the forecourt without incident, got into his rented car, and drove to the airport.

Chapter 99

BY SUNDAY AFTERNOON, I was back in my bunker, back to my book. I had a month's supply of junk food in the cupboard and was bent on finishing the expanded chapter outline for Zagami, who was expecting it in his e-mail box by morning.

At seven p.m., I turned on the tube: *60 Minutes* had just started, and the Barbados murders were headlining the show.

Morley Safer was speaking: "Forensic experts say that when combined with the five Maui murders, the deaths of Wendy Emerson and Sara Russo are part of a pattern of brutal, sadistic killings, with no end in sight.

"Right now, detectives around the world are reexamining unsolved murder cases, looking for anything that can lead to a serial murderer who has left no known witnesses, no living victims, not a trace of himself behind. CBS correspondent Bob Simon talked with some of those detectives."

Film clips came on the screen.

I watched retired cops interviewed in their homes and was struck by their somber expressions and quavering voices. One cop in particular had tears in his eyes as he displayed photos of a murdered twelve-year-old whose killer had never been found.

I turned off the set and screamed into my hands.

Henri was living inside my brain — in the past, the present, and the future. I knew his methods, his victims, and now I was adapting my writing to the cadence of his voice.

Sometimes, and this really scared me — sometimes I thought that I was him.

I uncapped a beer and drank it down in front of the open fridge. Then I wandered back to my laptop. I went online and checked my e-mail, something I hadn't done since leaving with Mandy for the weekend.

I opened a dozen e-mails before I came to one with the subject heading "Is everybody happy?" The e-mail had an attachment.

My fingers froze on the keys. I didn't recognize the sender's address, but I blinked at the heading for a long time before I opened the message: "Ben, I'm still working like a madman. Are you?"

The note was signed "H.B."

I touched the strip of bandage stuck to my left side and felt the small device that was beaming my location to Henri's computer.

Then I downloaded the attachment.

Chapter 100

THE VIDEO OPENED with a burst of light and an extreme close-up of Henri's digitally blurred face. He turned and walked toward a canopied bed in what looked to be a very expensive hotel room. I noted the elaborate furnishings, the traditional European fleur-de-lis pattern that was repeated in the draperies, carpet, and upholstery.

My eyes were drawn to the bed, where I saw a naked woman lying facedown, hands stretched out in front of her, tugging at the cords that tied her wrists to the headboard.

Oh no, here we go, I thought as I watched.

Henri got into bed next to her, and the two of them spoke in offhand tones. I couldn't make out what they were saying until she raised her voice sharply, asking him to untie her.

Something was different this time.

I was struck by the lack of fear in her voice. Was she a very good actor? Or had she just not figured out the climax?

I hit the Pause button, stopping the video.

Henri's ninety-second cut of Kim McDaniels's execution flashed into my mind in sharp detail. I would never forget Kim's postmortem expression, as if she was in pain even though her head had been detached from her body.

I didn't want to add another Henri Benoit production to my mental playlist.

I didn't want to see *this*.

Downstairs, an ordinary Sunday night was unfolding on Traction Avenue. I heard a street guitarist playing "Domino" and tourists applauding, the whoosh of tires on pavement as cars passed under my windows. A few weeks ago, a night like this, I might have gone down, had a couple of beers at Moe's.

I wished I could do it now. But I couldn't walk away.

I pressed the Play button and watched the moving pictures on my computer screen: Henri telling the woman that she cared only about her own pleasure, laughing, saying, "Always a price." He picked up the remote control and turned on the TV.

The hotel welcome screen flashed by, and then an announcer on *BBC World News* gave a sports update, mostly football. Another announcer followed with a summary of various international financial markets, then came the breaking news of the two girls who'd been killed in Barbados.

Now, on my computer screen, Henri shut off the TV. He

straddled the naked woman's body, put his hands around her neck, and I was sure that he was going to choke her—and then he changed his mind.

He untied her wrists, and I exhaled, wiped my eyes with my palms. He was letting her go—but why?

On screen, the woman said to Henri, "I knew you couldn't do it." Her English was accented. She was Italian.

Was this *Gina?*

She got out of the bed and strolled toward the camera, and she winked. She was a pretty brunette in her late thirties, maybe forty. She headed to an adjoining room, probably the bathroom.

Henri got out of the bed, reached down, and pulled a gun from a bag that looked to be a 9-millimeter Ruger with a suppressor extending the muzzle.

He walked behind the woman and out of camera range.

I heard muffled conversation, then the *phfffft* sound of the gun firing through the suppressor. A shadow passed over the threshold. There was a soft, heavy thud, two more muffled shots, then the rush of running water.

Except for the empty bed, that's all I saw or heard until the screen went black.

My hands shook as I played the video again. This time I was looking for any detail that could tell me where Henri had been when he had surely killed this woman.

On my third viewing, I saw something I'd missed before.

I stopped the action when Henri turned on the TV. I enlarged the picture and read the welcome screen with the name of the hotel at the top of the menu.

It had been shot on an angle, and it was damned hard to make out the letters, but I wrote them down and then went out to the Web to see if such a place existed.

It did.

I read that the Château de Mirambeau was in France, in the wine country near Bordeaux. It had been built on the foundations of a medieval fortress founded in the eleventh century, reconstructed in the early 1800s, and turned into an expensive resort. Pictures on the hotel's Web site showed fields of sunflowers, vineyards, and the château itself, an elaborate fairy-tale construction of vaulted stone, capped with turrets surrounding a courtyard and formal gardens.

I searched the Web again, found the football scores and the market closings that I'd seen on the TV in Henri's room.

I realized that this video had been shot on Friday, the same night Amanda had brought home Cornish game hens and I had learned about the deaths of Sara and Wendy.

I put my hand over the bandage against my ribs and felt the banging of my heart. It was all clear to me now.

Two days ago, Henri was in France, about a five-hour drive from Paris. This coming week marked the beginning of September. Henri had told me that he always went to Paris in September.

I had a pretty good idea where he might be.

Chapter 101

I SLAMMED DOWN the lid of my laptop, as if I could actually shut out the images Henri had left to my imagination.

Then I called Amanda, talking rapidly as I threw clothes into a suitcase.

"Henri sent me a video," I told her. "Looks like he killed Gina Prazzi. Maybe he's doing cleanup. Getting rid of people who know him and what he's done. So we have to ask ourselves, Mandy, when the book is finished, what's he going to do to us?"

I told her my plan, and she argued with me, but I got the last word. "I can't just *sit* here. I have to *do* something."

I called a cab, and once we were rolling I ripped the adhesive tape from my rib cage and stuck the tracking device underneath the cab's backseat.

Chapter 102

I CAUGHT a direct flight to Paris—midcabin coach, next to the window. As soon as I put the seatback down, my eyes slammed shut. I missed the movie, the precooked meals, and the cheap champagne, but I got about nine hours of sleep, waking only as the plane started its descent.

My bag shot down the luggage chute like it had missed me, and within twenty minutes of landing I was sitting in the backseat of a taxi.

I spoke to the driver in my broken French, told him where to take me: the Hôtel Singe-Vert, French for "Green Monkey." I'd stayed there before and knew it to be a clean two-and-a-half-star lodging popular with journalists on location in the City of Lights.

I walked through the unmanned lobby door, passed the

entrance to the bar called Jacques' Américain on my left, then crossed into the dark inner lobby with its worn green couches, racks of folded newspapers in all languages, and a large, faded watercolor of African green monkeys behind the front desk.

The concierge's nametag read "Georges." He was flabby, fiftyish, and pissed that he had to break off his phone conversation to deal with me. After Georges ran my credit card and locked my passport in the safe, I took the stairs, found my room on the third floor at the end of a frayed runner at the back of the hotel.

The room was papered with cabbage roses and crowded with century-old furniture, jammed in wall to wall. But the bedding was fresh, and there was a TV and a high-speed Internet connection on the desk. Good enough for me.

I dropped my bag down on the duvet and found a phone book. I'd been in Paris for an hour, and before I did another thing *I had to get a gun.*

Chapter 103

THE FRENCH TAKE handguns seriously. Permits are restricted to police and the military and a few security professionals, who have to lug their guns in cases, carry them in plain sight.

Still, in Paris, as in any big city, you can get a gun if you really want one. I spent the day prowling the Golden Drop, the drug-dealing sinkhole around the Basilica of Sacré-Coeur.

I paid two hundred euros for an old snub-nosed .38, a ladies' pistol with a two-inch barrel and six rounds in the chamber.

Back at the Green Monkey, Georges took my key off the board and pointed with his chin to a small heap on one of the sofas. "You have a guest."

It took me a long moment to take in what I was seeing. I walked over, shook her shoulder, and called her name.

Amanda opened her eyes and stretched as I sat down beside her. She put her arms around my neck and kissed me, but I couldn't even kiss her back. She was supposed to be home, safe in L.A.

"Gee. Pretend you're glad to see me, okay? Paris is for lovers," she said, smiling cautiously.

"Mandy, what in God's name are you thinking?"

"It's a little rash, I know. Look, I have something to tell you, Ben, and it could affect everything."

"Cut to the chase, Mandy. What are you talking about?"

"I wanted to tell you face-to-face—"

"So you just got on a plane? Is it about Henri?"

"No—"

"Then, Mandy, I'm sorry, but you have to go back. No, don't shake your head. You're a liability. Understand?"

"Well, thank you."

Mandy was pouting now, which was rare for her, but I knew that the further I pushed her, the more obstinate she'd get. I could already smell the carpet burning as she dug in her heels.

"Have you eaten?" she asked me.

"I'm not hungry," I said.

"I am. I'm a French chef. And we're in Paris."

"This is *not* a vacation," I said.

A half hour later, Mandy and I were seated at an outdoor café on the Rue des Pyramides. Night had blotted up the sunlight, the air was warm, and we had a clear view of a gilded statue of Saint Joan on her horse where our side street intersected with the Rue de Rivoli.

Mandy's mood had taken an upturn. In fact, she seemed almost high. She ordered in French, put away course after course, describing the preparation and rating the salad, the pâté, and the *fruits de mer*.

I made do with crackers and cheese and I drank strong coffee, my mind working on what I had to do, feeling the time rushing by.

"Just try this," Mandy said, holding out a spoonful of crème brûlée.

"Honestly, Amanda," I said with frank exasperation. "You shouldn't be here. I don't know what else to say to you."

"Just say you love me, Benjy. I'm going to be the mother of your child."

Chapter 104

I STARED at Amanda; thirty-four years old, looking twenty-five, wearing a baby blue cardigan with ruffled collar and cuffs and a perfect Mona Lisa smile. She was astonishingly beautiful, never more so than at this very moment.

"Please say that you're happy," she said.

I took the spoon out of her hand and put it down on her plate. I got out of my chair, placed one hand on each of her cheeks, and kissed her. Then I kissed her again. "You are the craziest girl I ever knew, *très étonnante*."

"You're very amazing, too," she said, beaming.

"Boy, do I love you," I said.

"*Moi aussi. Je t'aime* you to pieces. But are you, Benjy? Are you happy?"

I turned to the waitress, said to her, "This lovely lady and I are going to have a baby."

"It is your first baby?"

"Yes. And I love this woman so much, and I'm so happy about the baby I could fly circles around the *moon*."

The waitress smiled broadly, kissed both my cheeks and Mandy's, then made a general announcement that I didn't quite understand. But she made wing motions with her arms, and people at the next table started laughing and clapping and then others joined in, calling out congratulations and bravos.

I smiled at strangers, bowed to a beatific Amanda, and felt the flush of an unexpected and full-blown joy. Not long ago I was thanking God that I have no children. Now I was lit up brighter than I. M. Pei's glass pyramid at the Louvre.

I could hardly believe it.

Mandy was going to have our child.

Chapter 105

AS QUICKLY AS my expanding love for Mandy sent my heart to the moon, my happiness was eclipsed by an even greater fear for her safety.

As we trekked back to our little hotel, I told Amanda why she had to leave Paris in the morning.

"We'll never be safe as long as Henri is calling the shots. I have to be smarter than he is, and that's saying something, Amanda. Our only hope is for me to get out in front of him. Please trust me about this."

I told Mandy that Henri had described walking with Gina around the Place Vendôme.

I said, "It's like looking for one needle in a hundred hay-stacks, but my gut is telling me that he's here."

"And if he is, what are you going to do about it, Benjy? Are you really going to kill him?"

"You've got a better idea?"

"About a hundred of them."

We took the stairs to our room, and I made Amanda stand back as I drew my dainty Smith and Wesson and opened the door. I checked the closets and the bath, pushed aside the curtains, and looked out into the alley, seeing pop-up monsters everywhere.

When I was sure the room was clear, I said, "I'll be back in an hour. Two hours at most. Sit tight, okay? Watch the tube. Swear to me you won't leave the room."

"Oh please, Benjy, call the police."

"Honey. One more time. They can't protect us. We're not protectable. Not from Henri. Now promise me."

Mandy reluctantly held up the three-fingered Girl Scout salute, then locked the door behind me as I headed out.

I'd done some homework. There were a handful of first-class hotels in Paris. Henri might stay at the Georges V or the Plaza Athénée. But I was betting on my hunch.

It was an easy walk to the Hôtel Ritz on the Place Vendôme.

Chapter 106

HENRI POPPED his knuckles in the backseat of a metered Mercedes taxi heading north from Orly toward the Rue de Rivoli and from there to the Place Vendôme. He was hungry and irritated, and the ridiculous traffic was barely crawling across the Pont Royal on the Rue des Pyramides.

As the taxi idled at a traffic light, Henri shook his head, thinking again about the mistake he'd made, a genuine amateur boner, not knowing that Jan Van der Heuvel would be out of town when he visited Amsterdam earlier that day. Rather than leave immediately, he'd made a decision on the fly, something he rarely did.

He knew that Van der Heuvel had a secretary. He'd met her once, and he knew she'd be locking up Van der Heuvel's office at the end of the day.

So he'd watched and waited for Mieke Helsloot, with her cute little body and her short skirt and lace-up boots, to lock Van der Heuvel's big front door at five on the nose. Then he'd followed her in the intense silence of the canal district, only the sound of church bells and seabirds breaking the stillness.

He followed quietly, only yards behind her, crossing the canal after her, turning down a winding side street. Then he called out, "Hello, excuse me," and she'd turned to face him.

He'd apologized right away, falling in step beside her, saying he'd seen her leaving Mr. Van der Heuvel's office and had been trying to catch up to her for the last couple of blocks.

He'd said, "I'm working with Mr. Van der Heuvel on a confidential project. You remember me, don't you, Mieke? I'm Monsieur Benoit. I met you once in the office," Henri had said.

"Yes," she said doubtfully. "But I don't see how I can help you. Mr. Van der Heuvel will be back tomorrow."

Henri had told her that he'd lost Mr. Van der Heuvel's cell phone number, and that it would really help him if he could explain how he'd gotten the date of their meeting wrong. And Henri had continued the story until Meike Helsloot had stopped at the front door to her flat.

He thought of her now, holding the key in her hand, impatience showing on her face, but in her politeness and willingness to help her employer she'd let him into her flat so that she could make the call for him to her boss.

Henri had thanked her, taken the one upholstered chair

335

in Meike's two-room flat that had been built under a staircase, and waited for the right moment to kill her.

As the girl rinsed out two glasses, Henri had looked around at the sloping bookshelves, the fashion magazines, the mirror over the fireplace that was almost completely covered with photos of Mieke's handsome boyfriend.

Later, when she understood what he was going to do, she'd wailed, *no-no-no,* and begged him, please not to, she hadn't done anything wrong, she would never tell anyone, no, *never.*

"Sorry. It's not about you, Mieke," he'd said. "It's about Mr. Van der Heuvel. He's a very wicked man."

She'd said, "So why do this to me?"

"Well. It's Jan's lucky day, isn't it? He was out of town."

Henri had bound her arms behind her back with one of her own bootlaces and was undoing his belt buckle when she said, "Not that. Please. I'm supposed to get married."

He hadn't raped her. He hadn't been in the mood after doing Gina. So he'd told her to think of something nice. It was important in the last moments of life to have good thoughts.

He looped another bootlace around her throat and tightened it, holding her down with his knee in the small of her back until she stopped breathing. The waxed shoelace was as strong as wire, and it cut through her thin neck and she bled as he killed her.

Afterward, he arranged the pretty girl's body under blankets and patted her cheek.

He was thinking now, he'd been so angry at himself for missing Jan that he hadn't even thought to videotape the kill.

Then again—Jan would get the message.

Henri liked thinking about that.

Chapter 107

STILL SITTING IN THE INTERMINABLE SLOG of traffic, Henri's mind turned back to Gina Prazzi, thinking of her eyes getting huge when he shot her, wondering if she'd really understood what he'd done. It was truly significant. She was the first person he'd killed for his own satisfaction since strangling the girl in the horse trailer more than twenty years ago.

And now he'd killed Mieke for the same reason. It wasn't about money at all.

Something inside him was changing.

It was like a light slipping beneath a door, and he could either open it to its full blinding brightness, or slam the door shut and run.

The horns were blaring now, and he saw that the taxi had finally *crept* to the intersection of Pyramides and Rivoli, and then stopped again. The driver turned off the air-conditioning and opened the windows to save gas.

Disgusted, Henri leaned forward, tapped on the glass.

The driver took a break from his cell phone to tell Henri that the street was jammed because of the French president's motorcade, which was just leaving the Elysée Palace on its way to the National Assembly.

"There's nothing I can do, Monsieur. My hands are tied. Relax."

"How long will it be?"

"Perhaps another fifteen minutes. How should I know?"

Henri was more furious at himself than before. It had been stupid to come to Paris as some kind of ironic post-script to killing Gina. Not only stupid, but self-indulgent, or maybe self-destructive. Was that it? *Do I want to be caught now?* he wondered.

He watched the street through the open window, desperate for the absurd politician's motorcade to come and go, when he heard shouts of laughter coming from a brasserie at the corner.

He looked that way.

A man wearing a blue sports jacket, a pink polo shirt, and khakis, an American of course, made a comic bow to a young woman in a blue sweater. People began clapping, and as Henri looked more closely, the man seemed familiar and then — Henri's mind stopped cold.

In fact, he couldn't believe it. He wanted to ask the driver, *Do you see what I see? Is that Ben Hawkins and Amanda Diaz? Because I think I've lost my mind.*

Then Hawkins wiggled the metal frame chair, turning it, sitting so that he faced the street, and Henri knew without a doubt. *It was Ben.* When he'd last checked, Hawkins and the girl had been in L.A.

Henri's mind flashed back over the weekend to late on Saturday night, after he'd shot Gina. He'd e-mailed the video to Ben, but he hadn't checked the GPS tracker, not then. Not for a couple of days.

Had Ben discovered and discarded the chip?

For a moment, Henri felt something completely new to him. He was *afraid*. Afraid that he was getting sloppy, losing his hard-won discipline, losing his grip. He couldn't let that happen.

Never again.

Henri barked at the driver, saying that he couldn't wait any longer. He pushed a wad of bills into the driver's hand, grabbed his bag and briefcase, and got out of the cab on the street side.

He walked between cars, before doubling back to the sidewalk. Moving quickly, he ducked into an alcove between two storefronts only ten yards or so from the brasserie.

Henri watched, his heart racing, as Ben and Amanda left the restaurant and walked arm in arm, east up Rivoli.

When they had gone far enough ahead, Henri fell in behind them, keeping them in view as they reached the Singe-Vert, a small hotel on Place André Malraux.

Once Amanda and Ben disappeared inside, Henri went into the hotel bar, Jacques' Américain, adjacent to the lobby.

He ordered a Scotch from the bartender, who was actively putting the moves on a horse-faced brunette.

Henri sipped his drink and viewed the lobby through the bar's back mirror. When he saw Ben come downstairs, Henri swiveled in the stool, watched as Ben handed his key to the concierge.

Henri made a mental note of the number under the key hook.

Chapter 108

IT WAS ALREADY half past eight p.m. by the time I reached the Place Vendôme, an enormous square with traffic lanes on four sides and a tall bronze memorial to Napoléon Bonaparte in the center. On the west side of the Place is Rue St.-Honoré, shopping paradise for the wealthy, and across the square was the drop-dead-fantastic French Gothic architecture of the Hôtel Ritz, all honey-colored stone and luminous demilune awnings over the doorways.

I stepped onto the red carpet and through a revolving door into the hotel lobby and stared at the richly colored sofas, chandeliers throwing soft light on the oil paintings, and happy faces of the guests.

I found the house phones in an alcove and asked the operator to ring Henri Benoit. My heartbeats counted off the seconds, and then the operator came back on and told

342

me that Monsieur Benoit was expected but had not checked in. Would I care to leave a message?

I said, "I'll call back. *Merci*."

I had been right. *Right*.

Henri was in Paris. At least he would be very soon. *He was staying at the Ritz.*

As I hung up the phone I had an almost violent surge of emotion as I thought about all the innocent people Henri had killed. I thought about Levon and Barbara and about those suffocating days and nights I'd spent chained in a trailer, sitting face-to-face with a homicidal madman.

And then I thought about Henri threatening to kill Amanda.

I took a seat in a corner where I could watch the door, ducked behind the pages of a discarded copy of the *International Herald Tribune*, thinking this was the same as a stakeout in a squad car, minus the coffee and the bullshit from my partner.

I could sit here forever, because I'd finally gotten ahead of Henri, that freaking psychopath. He didn't know I was here, but I knew he was coming.

Over the next interminable two hours, I imagined Henri coming into the hotel with a suit bag and checking in at the desk, and that whatever disguise he was in, I would recognize him immediately. I would follow him into the elevator and give him the same heart-attack surprise he'd once given me.

I was still unsure what I would do after that.

I thought I could probably restrain him, call the police, have them hold him on suspicion of killing Gina Prazzi.

Or maybe that was too chancy. Maybe I'd put a bullet in his head and turn myself in at the American embassy, deal with it after the fact.

I reviewed option one: The cops would ask me, "Who is Gina Prazzi? How do you know she's dead?" I imagined showing them Henri's film in which Gina's dead body was never seen. If Henri had disposed of the body, he wouldn't even be arrested.

But *I'd* be under suspicion. In fact, I would be suspect number one.

I ran through the second option, saw myself pulling the .38 on Henri, spinning him around, saying, "Hands against the wall, don't move!" I liked the idea a lot.

That's how I was thinking when, among the dozens of people crossing the lobby, I saw two beautiful women and a man pass in front of me, heading toward the front door. The women were young and stylish, English-speaking, laughing and talking over each other, directing their attention to the man sandwiched between them.

Their arms were entwined like school buddies, breaking apart when they reached the revolving door, the man hanging back to let the very attractive women go through first.

The rush I felt was miles ahead of my conscious thought. But I registered the man's bland features, his build, the way he dressed.

He was very blond now, wearing large, black-framed eyeglasses, his posture slightly stooped.

This was exactly how Henri disguised himself. He'd told me that his disguises worked because they were so simple.

He adopted a distinct way of walking or speaking, and then added a few distracting, but memorable visual cues. He *became* his new identity. Whatever identity he'd assumed, this much I knew.

The man with those two women was none other than Henri Benoit.

Chapter 109

I DROPPED the newspaper to the floor and followed the threesome with my eyes as the revolving door dispensed them one at a time into the street.

I headed for the main door, thinking I could see where Henri was going, buy some time to come up with a plan. But before I reached the revolving door, a clump of tourists surged in front of me, staggering and giggling and bunching up inside the blades of the door as I stood by wanting to scream, *"You assholes, get out of my way!"*

By the time I got outside, Henri and the two women were far ahead of me, walking along the arcade that lined the west side of the street.

They were now heading down the Rue de Castiglione and toward the Rue de Rivoli. I just caught a glimpse of them turning left when I reached the corner.

Then I saw the two pretty women standing with their heads together in front of a designer shoe store, and I saw Henri's white-blond hair far up ahead.

As I tried to keep him in sight, he disappeared down into the Tuileries Métro station at the end of the street.

I ran across the stream of traffic, ran down the stairs to the platform, but the station is one of the Métro's busiest, and I couldn't see Henri.

I tried to look everywhere at once, my eyes piercing the clots of travelers weaving through the station.

And there he was, at the far end of the platform. Suddenly he turned toward me, and I froze. For one eternal minute, I felt completely vulnerable, as if I'd been illuminated with a spotlight on a black stage.

He had to see me.

I was in his direct line of sight.

But he didn't react, and I continued to stare at him while my feet behaved as though they were glued to the cement.

Then his image seemed to shift and clarify. Now that I was looking at him straight on, I saw the *length* of his nose, the *height* of his forehead, his *receding* chin.

Was I this crazy?

I'd been so sure—but I was just as sure now that I'd gotten it all wrong. That I was a dumb-ass, a total jerk, a failure as a sleuth. The man I had just followed from the Ritz? He wasn't Henri at all.

Chapter 110

I CLIMBED UP out of the Métro, remembering that I'd told Mandy I'd be back in an hour or so but had now been gone for three.

I walked back to the Hôtel Singe-Vert empty-handed, no chocolates, no flowers, no jewelry. I had nothing to show for my Ritz-to-Métro escapade except one scrap of information that could turn out to be critical.

Henri had booked a room at the Ritz.

The lobby of our small hotel was deserted, although a cloud of cigarette smoke and loud conversation floated out from the bar and into the shabby main room.

The concierge desk was closed.

I went behind the desk and grabbed my key from the hook.

I took the stairs to my room, more than anything wanting to sleep.

I knocked on the door, called Mandy's name, and when she didn't answer, I turned the knob, ready to tell Mandy that she had no right to be girlish and irresponsible anymore. She had to be careful for two.

I opened the door and felt instantly that something was wrong. Mandy wasn't in bed. Was she in the bathroom? Was she okay?

I stepped into the room, calling her name, and the door slammed behind me. I swung around and tried to make sense of the impossible.

A black man was holding Mandy, his left arm crossing her chest, his right hand with a gun to her head. He was wearing latex gloves. Blue ones. I'd seen gloves exactly like those before.

My eyes went to Mandy's face. She was gagged. Her eyes were wild, and she was grunting a wordless scream.

The black man grinned at me, tightened his hold on her, and pointed the gun at me.

"Amanda," the man said. "Look who's home? We've been waiting for a long time, haven't we, sweetheart? But it's been fun, right?"

All the fragments of information came together: the blue gloves, the familiar tone, the pale gray eyes, and the stage makeup. I wasn't mistaken this time. I'd heard hours of his voice piped directly into my ear. It was Henri. But how had he found us here?

My mind spun in a hundred directions, all at once.

I'd gone to Paris out of fear. But now that Henri had come to my door, I wasn't afraid anymore. I was furious, and my

349

veins were pumping a hundred percent adrenaline, lifting-a-car-off-a-baby-carriage kind of adrenaline, the running-into-a-burning-building kind of damn-it-to-hell rush.

I whipped the .38 out of my waistband, pulled back the hammer, yelled, *"Let her go."*

I guess he didn't believe I would fire. Henri smirked at me, said, "Drop your gun, Ben. I just want to talk."

I walked up to the maniac and put the gun's muzzle against his forehead. He grinned, gold tooth winking, part of his latest disguise. I got off one shot at the exact moment that he kneed me in the thigh. I was sent crashing backward into a desk, the wooden legs shattering as I went down.

My first thought—*had I shot Mandy?* But I saw blood flowing from Henri's arm and heard the clatter of his gun sliding across the wooden floor.

He shoved Mandy away from him, hard, and she fell on me. I rolled her off my chest, and as I tried to sit, Henri pinned me—with his foot on my wrist, looking down with contempt.

"Why couldn't you just do your job, Ben? If you'd just done your job, we wouldn't be having this little problem, but now I can't trust you. I only wish I'd brought my camera."

He leaned down, bent my fingers back, and peeled the gun from my hand. Then he aimed it—first at me, and then at Mandy.

"Now, who wants to die first?" Henri said. *"Vous or vous?"*

Chapter 111

EVERYTHING WENT white in front of my eyes. This was it, wasn't it? Amanda and I were going to die. I felt Henri's breath on my face as he screwed the muzzle of the .38 into my right eye. Mandy tried to scream through her gag.

Henri barked at her, *"Shut up."*

She did.

Water filled my eyes then. Maybe it was from the pain, or the fierce regret that I'd never see Amanda again. That she would die too. That our child would never be born.

Henri fired the gun—directly into the carpet next to my ear, deafening me. Then he yanked my head and shouted into my ear.

"Write the fucking *book*, Ben. Go home and do your *job*. I'm going to call you every night in L.A., and if you don't pick up the phone, I *will* find you. You know I'll do it, and I promise you both, *You won't get a second chance.*"

The gun was pulled away my face. Henri grabbed up a duffel bag and a briefcase with his good hand and arm, slammed the door on his way out. I heard his footsteps receding down the stairs.

I turned to Mandy. The gag was a pillowcase pulled across the inside of her mouth and was knotted at the back of her head. I plucked at the knot, my fingers trembling, and when she was free, I took her into my arms and rocked her back and forth, back and forth.

"Are you okay, honey? Did he hurt you?"

She was crying, saying she was fine.

"You're sure?"

"Go," she said. "I know you want to go after him."

I crawled around, feeling under the spindly legs and ruffled skirts of the wall-to-wall collection of antique furniture, saying, "You know I've got to. He'll still be watching us, Mandy."

I found Henri's Ruger under the dresser and wrapped my hand tightly around the grip. I twisted open the blood-slicked doorknob and shouted to Mandy that I'd be back soon.

Leaning heavily on the banister, I walked off the pain in my thigh as I made my way down the stairs, trying to hurry, knowing that I had to kill Henri somehow.

Chapter 112

THE SKY WAS BLACK, but the streetlights and the large and perpetually booked Hôtel du Louvre next door had just about turned night into day. The two hotels were only a few hundred yards from the Tuileries, the huge public garden outside the Louvre.

This week some kind of carnival was going on there: games, big rides, oompah music, the works. Even at this late hour, giddy tourists and folks with kids flowed out onto the sidewalk, adding their raucous laughter to the sharp shocks of fireworks and blaring car horns. It reminded me of a scene from a French movie, maybe one that I'd watched somewhere.

I followed a thin trail of blood out to the street, but it disappeared a few yards from the front door. Henri had done his disappearing act again. Had he gone into the Hôtel du Louvre to hide? Had he lucked out and caught a taxi?

I was staring through the crowds when I heard police sirens coming up the Place André Malraux.

Obviously, shots had been reported. Plus, I'd been seen running around with a gun.

I stuffed Henri's Ruger into a potted planter outside the Hôtel du Louvre. Then I gamely limped into the lobby, sat in an overstuffed chair, and thought about how I would approach the *agents de police*.

Finally, I was going to have to explain Henri and everything else to the cops.

I wondered what the hell I was going to say.

Chapter 113

THE SIRENS GOT louder and louder, my shoulders and neck stiffened, and then the looping wail passed the hotel and continued on toward the Tuileries. When I was sure it was over, I reclaimed Henri's gun, made my way back to the Singe-Verts, and climbed the stairs like an old man. I knocked on the door to my room, said, "Mandy, it's me. I'm alone. You can open the door."

Seconds later, she did. Her face was tear-stained, and there were bruises at the corners of her mouth from the gag. I opened my arms to her, and Mandy fell against me, sobbing like a child who might never be soothed again.

I held her, swayed with her for a long while. Then I undressed us both and helped her into bed. I shut off the overhead light, leaving on only a small boudoir lamp on the night table. I slid under the covers, and took Mandy into my arms. She pressed her face to my chest, tethered herself to my body with her arms and legs.

"Talk to me, honey," I said. "Tell me everything."

"He knocked on the door," she finally said. "He said he had flowers. Is that the most simpleminded trick ever? But I believed him, Ben."

"He said they were from me?"

"I think so. Yeah, he did."

"I wonder — how did he know we were here? What tipped him? I don't get it."

"When I unlocked the door, he kicked it open and grabbed me."

"I wish I'd killed him, Mandy."

"I didn't know who he was. A black man. He wrenched my arms behind my back. I couldn't move. He said...oh, this makes me *sick*," she said, crying again.

"What did he say?"

"'I love you, Amanda.'"

I was listening to Mandy and hearing echoes at the same time. Henri had told me that he'd *loved* Gina. He'd *loved* Julia. How long would Henri have waited to prove his love to Mandy by raping her and strangling her with those blue gloves on his hands?

I whispered, "I'm so sorry. I'm so sorry."

"I'm the jerk who came here, Benjy. Oh, God, how long was he here? Three hours? *I'm* sorry. I didn't understand until now what those three days with him must have been like for you."

She started crying again, and I hushed her, told her over and over that everything would be all right.

"Don't take this the wrong way," she said, her voice ragged and strained. "But what makes you so sure?"

I got out of bed, opened my laptop, and booked two morning flights back to the States.

Chapter 114

IT WAS WELL after midnight, and I was still pacing the room. I took some Tylenol, got back under the covers with Amanda, but I couldn't sleep. I couldn't even shut my eyes for more than a few seconds.

The TV was small and old, but I turned it on and found CNN.

I watched the headline news, bolted upright when the talking head said, "Police have no suspects in the murder of Gina Prazzi, heiress to the Prazzi shipping fortune. She was found murdered in a room at the exclusive French resort Château de Mirambeau."

When Gina Prazzi's face came on the screen, I felt as though I knew her intimately. I'd watched her pass in front of the camera in the hotel room, not knowing that her life was about to end.

I said, "Mandy, Mandy," shook her arm. But she turned away, settled even more deeply into the feather bed and sleep.

I watched the police captain brief the press on TV, his speech translated and recapped for those just tuning in. Ms. Prazzi had checked into the Château de Mirambeau alone. The housekeepers believed that two people stayed in the room, but no other guest was seen. The police were not releasing any further information about the murder at this time.

That was enough for me. I knew the full story, but what I hadn't known was that Gina Prazzi was a *real name*, not an alias.

What other lies had Henri told me? For what possible reason? Why had he lied—*in order to tell me the truth?*

I stared at the TV screen as the anchor said, "In the Netherlands, a young woman was found murdered this morning in Amsterdam. What brings this tragedy to the attention of international criminalists is that elements of this girl's death are similar to elements of the murders of the two young women in Barbados, and also to the famous American swimsuit models who were murdered this spring in Hawaii."

I dialed up the volume as the faces came on the screen: Sara Russo, Wendy Emerson, Kim McDaniels, and Julia Winkler, and now another face, a young woman whose name was Mieke Helsloot.

The announcer said, "Ms. Helsloot, twenty years old, was the secretary to the well-known architect Jan Van der Heuvel of Amsterdam, who was at a meeting in Copenhagen at the time of the murder. Mr. Van der Heuvel was interviewed at his hotel minutes ago."

Jesus Christ. I knew his name.

The picture cut away to Van der Heuvel leaving his hotel in Copenhagen, suitcase in hand, journalists crowding around him at the bottom of a rounded staircase. He was in his early forties, had gray hair and angular features. He looked genuinely shocked and *scared.*

"I have only just now learned of this terrible tragedy," he said into the clutch of microphones. "I am shocked and devastated. Mieke Helsloot was a proper, decent young lady, and I have no idea why anyone would harm her. It is a terrible day. Mieke was to be married."

Henri had told me that Jan Van der Heuvel was an *alias* for one of the members of the Alliance, the man Henri called "the Dutchman." Van der Heuvel was the third wheel who'd joined up with Henri and Gina during their romp through the French Riviera.

And now, soon after Henri had killed Gina Prazzi, Van der Heuvel's secretary had also been murdered.

If I hadn't once been a cop, I might have dismissed these two killings as a coincidence. The women were different types. They were killed hundreds of miles apart. But what I saw were two more flags on a grid, a part of a pattern.

Henri had loved Gina Prazzi, and he killed her. He'd hated Jan Van der Heuvel. Maybe he'd wanted to kill him, too, so, just thinking it out...what if Henri hadn't known that Van der Heuvel was in Denmark that day?

What if he'd decided to kill his secretary instead?

Chapter 115

I WOKE UP to sunlight seeping in through a small window. Amanda was lying on her side, facing away from me, her long, dark hair fanned out over the pillow. And in a flash, I was enraged as I remembered Henri in blackface, his gun pointed at Amanda's head, her eyes wild with fear.

Right then, I didn't care why Henri had killed anyone, what he was planning to do next, why the book was so important to him, or why he seemed to be spinning out of control.

Only one thing was important to me. I had to keep Mandy safe. And the baby, too.

I grabbed for my watch, saw that it was almost seven thirty. I shook Mandy's shoulder gently, and her eyes flew open. She gasped, then saw my face and sagged back into the bedding.

"I thought for a moment—"

"That it was a dream."

"Yeah."

I put my head very gently on her belly, and she stroked my hair.

"Is that the baby?" I asked.

"You dummy. I'm hungry."

I pretended she was speaking for the baby. I made a little megaphone with my hands, called out, "Hellloooo in there, Foozle. This is Dad," as though the tiny clump of our combined DNA could hear me.

Mandy cracked up, and I was glad she could laugh, but I cried in the shower, where she couldn't see me. If only I'd killed Henri when I had him in my gun sight. If only I had done that. Then it would all be over now.

I kept Mandy close to me as I paid the bill at the front desk and then hailed a cab and told the driver to take us to Charles de Gaulle airport.

Mandy said, "How can we go back to L.A.?"

"We can't."

She turned her head and stared at me. "So what are we doing?"

I told Mandy what I'd decided, gave her a short list of names and numbers on the back of my business card, and told her that she'd be met when the plane landed. She was listening, not fighting with me, when I told her that she couldn't phone me, or send me e-mail, nothing. That she had to rest and eat good food. "If you get bored, think about the dress you want to wear."

"You know I don't wear dresses."

"Maybe you'll make an exception."

I took a ballpoint pen out of my computer case and drew a ring on Mandy's left ring finger with lines radiating out from a big sparkly diamond in the center.

"Amanda Diaz, I love every bit of you. Will you marry me?"

"Ben."

"You and Foozle."

There were happy tears rolling down our cheeks now. She threw her arms around me, said, "Yes, yes, yes," and swore she wouldn't wash off the ring I'd drawn until she had a real one.

I bought breakfast for us at the airport, chocolate croissants and café au lait, and when it was nearly time to board, I walked with her as far as I could go. Then I wrapped my arms around her, and she sobbed against my chest until I was crying again, too. Could anything be scarier than this? The thought of losing someone you love so much? I didn't think so.

I kissed Mandy's poor bruised mouth again and again. If love counted for anything, she would be safe. Our baby would be safe. And I would see them both soon.

But the opposing thought went through me like a lance. *I might never see Amanda again. This could be the end for us.*

I dried my eyes with the palms of my hands, then watched Mandy go through the checkpoint. She looked back, waved, threw kisses, then turned away.

When I couldn't see her any longer, I left the airport, took a cab to the Gare du Nord, and boarded a high-speed train to Amsterdam.

Chapter 116

FOUR HOURS AFTER I boarded the train in Paris, I disembarked in the Centraal Station in Amsterdam, where I used a public phone to call Jan Van der Heuvel. I had contacted him before I left Paris about our getting together as soon as possible. He asked me again what made this meeting so urgent, and this time I told him, "Henri Benoit sent me a video I think you should see."

There was a long silence, then Van der Heuvel gave me directions to a bridge that crossed the Keizersgracht Canal only a few blocks from the train station.

I found Van der Heuvel standing by a lamppost, looking into the water below. I recognized him from the news clip that had been shot of him in Copenhagen, the journos asking him to comment on Mieke Helsloot's murder.

Today he was wearing a smart gray gabardine suit, a

white dress shirt, and a charcoal-colored tie with a silken sheen. The part in his hair was as crisp as if it had been drawn with a knife, and it highlighted his angular features.

I introduced myself, saying that I was a writer from Los Angeles.

"How do you know Henri?" he asked after a long pause.

"I'm writing his life story. His autobiography. Henri commissioned it."

"You met with him?"

"I did, yes."

"All of this surprises me. He told you my name?"

"In publishing, this type of book is called a 'tell-all.' Henri told me everything."

Van der Heuvel looked extremely uncomfortable out on the street. He appraised my appearance, seemed to weigh whether or not to take this meeting further, then said, "I can spare a few minutes. My office is right over there. Come."

I walked with him across the bridge to a handsome five-story building in what appeared to be an upscale residential area. He opened the front door, indicated that I should go first, and I took the four well-lit flights of stairs to the top floor. My hopes rose as I climbed.

Van der Heuvel was as twisted as a snake. As part of the Alliance, he was as guilty of multiple murders as if he'd killed people with his own hands. But as despicable as he was, I wanted his cooperation, and so I had to control my anger, keep it hidden from him.

If Van der Heuvel could lead me to Henri Benoit, I would get another chance to bring Henri down.

This time, I wouldn't blow it.

Van der Heuvel took me through his design studio, a vast uncluttered space, bright with blond wood and glass and streaming sunlight. He offered me an uncomfortable-looking chair across from him at a long drawing table near the tall windows.

"It is hilarious that Henri is telling you his life story," Van der Heuvel said. "I can only imagine the lies he would say."

"Tell me how funny you find this," I said. I booted up my laptop, turned it around, and pushed the Play button so that Van der Heuvel could see the last minutes of Gina Prazzi's life.

I didn't think he had seen the video before, but as it ran, his expression never changed. When it was over, Van der Heuvel said, "What is funny is...I think he loved her."

I stopped the video, and Van der Heuvel looked into my eyes.

I said, "Before I was a writer, I was a cop. I think Henri is doing *mop-up*. He's killing the people who know who he is. Help me find him, Mr. Van der Heuvel. I'm your best chance for survival."

Chapter 117

VAN DER HEUVEL'S back was to the tall windows. His long shadow fell across the blond table, and his face was haloed by the afternoon light.

He took a pack of cigarettes from his drawer, offered me one, then lit one for himself. He said, "If I knew how to find him, there would no longer be a problem. But Henri has a genius for disappearance. I don't know where he is. I have never known."

"Let's work on this together," I said. "Kick around some ideas. There must be something you know that can lead me to him. I know about his imprisonment in Iraq, but Brewster-North is a private company, closed tight, like a vault. I know about Henri's forger in Beirut, but without the man's name—"

"Oh, this is too much," Van der Heuvel said, laughing, a

terrible laugh because there was actual humor in it. He found me amusing. "He is psychopathic. Don't you understand this man at all? He's delusional. He's narcissistic, and most of all he lies. Henri was never in Iraq. He has no forger other than himself. Understand something, Mr. Hawkins. Henri is *glorifying* himself to you, inventing a better life story. You're like a small dog being pulled along—"

"Hey!" I said, slapping the table, jumping to my feet. "Don't screw with me. I came here to find Henri. I don't care about you or Horst Werner or Raphael dos Santos or the rest of you sick, pathetic motherfuckers. If you can't help me, I have no choice but to go to the police and give them everything."

Van der Heuvel laughed again and told me to calm down, take a seat. I was rocked to my core. Had Van der Heuvel just answered the question of why Henri wanted to write the book? To glorify his life story?

"The Dutchman" opened his laptop, said, "I got an e-mail from Henri two days ago. The first one he ever sent to me directly. He wanted to sell me a video. I think I just saw it for free. You say you have no interest in us?"

"I don't care about you at all. I just want Henri. He's threatened my life and my family."

"Maybe this will help your detective work."

Van der Heuvel ran his fingers over the keyboard of his laptop as he talked, saying, "Henri Benoit, as he calls himself, was a juvenile *monster*. Thirty years ago, when he was six years old, he strangled his infant sister in her crib."

The shock showed on my face as Van der Heuvel nodded,

smiling, tapping ashes into a tray, assuring me that this was true.

"Cute little boy. Fat cheeks. Big eyes. He murdered a baby. He was diagnosed with psychopathic personality disorder, very rare that a child would have all the hallmarks. He was sent to a psychiatric facility, the Clinic du Lac in Geneva."

"This is documented?"

"Yes, indeed. I did the research when I first met him. According to the chief psychiatrist, a Dr. Carl Obst, the child learned a lot during his twelve years in the crazy house. How to mimic people, of course. He picked up several languages and learned a trade. He became a printer."

Was Van der Heuvel telling me the truth? If so, it explained how Henri could become anyone, forge documents, slip through the cracks at will.

"After he was released at age eighteen, our boy got busy with casual murders and robberies. He stole a Ferrari, anyway. Whatever else, I don't know. But when he met Gina four years ago, he didn't have to dine on scraps anymore."

Van der Heuvel told me that Gina "fancied Henri," that he opened up to her, told her how he liked his sex and that he had committed acts of extreme violence. And he said he wanted to make a lot of money.

"It was Gina's idea to have Henri provide entertainment for our little group and Horst went along with this plan for our sex monkey."

"This is where you came in."

"Ah. Yes. Gina introduced us."

"Henri said you sat in a corner and watched."

Van der Heuvel looked at me as though I was an exotic bug and he hadn't decided whether to smash me or put me under glass.

"Another lie, Hawkins. He took it up the ass and squealed like a girl. But this is what you should know because it is the truth. We didn't make Henri who he is. We only fed him."

Chapter **118**

VAN DER HEUVEL'S fingers flew across the keyboard again. He said, "And now, a quick look, for your eyes only. I'll show you how the young man developed."

Delight brightened his face as he turned the screen toward me.

A collection of single frames taken from videos of women who'd been tied up, tortured, decapitated, flickered across the computer screen.

I could hardly absorb what I was seeing as Van der Heuvel flashed through the pictures, smoking his cigarette, providing blithe commentary for a slide show of absolute and, until now, unimaginable horror.

I felt light-headed. I was starting to feel that Van der Heuvel and Henri were the same person. I hated them equally. I wanted to kill Van der Heuvel, the worthless shit, and I thought I could even get away with it.

But I needed him to lead me to Henri.

"At first I didn't know that the murders were real," he was saying, "but when Henri began to cut off heads, then, of course, I knew.... In the last year, he began writing his own scripts. Getting a little too drunk with attention. Getting too greedy.

"He was dangerous. And he knew me and Gina, so there was no easy way to end it."

Van der Heuvel exhaled a plume of smoke and went on.

"Last week, Gina planned to either pay Henri off or make him disappear. Obviously, she misjudged him. She never told me how she contacted him, so once again, this is the truth, Mr. Hawkins, I have no idea where Henri is. None at all."

"Horst Werner signs Henri's paychecks, doesn't he?" I said. "Tell me how to find Werner."

Van der Heuvel stubbed out his cigarette. His delight was gone. He spoke to me with dead seriousness, emphasizing every word.

"Mr. Hawkins, Horst Werner is the last person you ever want to meet. In your case in particular. He will not like Henri's book. Take my meaning. Don't let it out of your hands. Scrub your computer. Burn your tapes. Never mention the Alliance or its members to anyone. This advice is worth your life."

It was too late to scrub my hard drive. I'd sent my transcripts of the Henri interviews and the outline of the book to

Zagami in New York. The transcripts had been photocopied and passed around to editors and Raven-Wofford's outside law firm. The names of the Alliance members were all over the manuscript. I had planned to change the names, as I'd promised Henri, in the final draft.

I bulled ahead. "If Werner helps me, I'll help him."

"You have the brain of a brick, Hawkins. Listen to what I'm telling you. Listen. Horst Werner is a powerful man with long arms and steel fists. He can find you wherever you are. Do you hear me, Hawkins? Don't be afraid of Henri, our little windup toy.

"Be afraid of Horst Werner."

Chapter 119

VAN DER HEUVEL abruptly called our meeting to an end, dismissed me, saying that he had a flight to catch.

My skull felt like a pressure cooker about to blow. The threat against me had been doubled, a war on two fronts: If I didn't write the book, *Henri* would kill me. If I did write the book, *Werner* would kill me.

I still had to find Henri, and now I had to stop Van der Heuvel from telling Horst Werner about Henri's book, and about me.

I dug Henri's Ruger out of my computer case and aimed it at the Dutchman. My voice was hoarse from the stress of unexpressed fear and fury when I said, "You remember I said I didn't care about you and the Alliance? I've changed my mind. I care a lot."

Van der Heuvel looked at me with scorn.

"Mr. Hawkins, if you shoot me, you will be in a prison for the rest of your life. Henri will still be alive and living in luxury somewhere in the world."

"Take off your coat," I said, hefting the gun in my hand. "And everything else."

"What is the point of *this,* Hawkins?"

"I like to watch," I said. "Now shut up. Take off all your clothes. The shirt, the shoes, the pants, every stitch you have on."

"You are really a fool," he said, obeying me. "What have you got on me? Some pornography on my computer? This is Amsterdam. We are not prudes like your citizens of the United States. You can't tie me to any of it. Did you see me in any of those videos? I don't think so."

I stood with the gun clasped in both my hands, leveled at Van der Heuvel, and when he was naked, I told him to grab the wall. Then I whacked him on the back of his head with the gun butt, the same treatment Henri had given me.

Leaving him unconscious on the floor, I lifted Van der Heuvel's tie from the pile of clothes on the chair and used it to secure his wrists tightly behind his back.

His computer was connected to the Internet, and I worked fast, attaching the Henri Benoit videos to e-mails that I addressed to myself. *What else?*

There was a box of marking pens on his desk, and I dropped one of them into my coat pocket.

Then I walked through Van der Heuvel's immaculate, full-floor flat. The man was house-proud. He had beautiful things. Expensive books. Drawings. Photographs. His closet was like a clothes museum. It was sickening that a man this base, this vile, could have such a carefree and luxurious life.

I went to Van der Heuvel's magazine-quality kitchen and turned on the gas burners on his stove.

I set dish towels and two-hundred-dollar ties on fire, and as flames reached for the ceiling, the overhead sprinkler system opened.

An alarm rang out in the stairwell, and I was sure another alarm was ringing in a firehouse nearby.

As water surged across the fine wooden floors, I returned to the main room, packed away the computers, slinging both mine and Van der Heuvel's over my shoulder.

Then I slapped Van der Heuvel's face, yelled his name, jerked him to his feet. "Up! Get up. Now!" I yelled.

I ignored his questions as I marched him down the stairs to the street. Smoke billowed from the windows and, as I'd hoped, a thick crowd of witnesses had congregated around the house: men and women in business attire, old people and children on bicycles that the city provided free to residents.

I sat Van der Heuvel down on the curb and uncapped the marking pen. I wrote on his forehead, "Murderer."

He called out to people in the crowd, his voice shrill. He was pleading, but the only word I could understand was "police." Cell phones came out and numbers were punched.

Soon sirens screamed, and as they came closer I wanted to howl along with them. But I kept Henri's gun trained on Van der Heuvel and waited for the police to arrive.

When they finally did, I set down the Ruger on the sidewalk, and I pointed at Van der Heuvel's forehead.

Chapter 120

SWITZERLAND.

Two cops were in the front seat, and I sat in the back of a car speeding toward Wengen, a toylike Alpine town in the shadow of the Eiger. Despite the ban on cars in this idyllic ski resort, our armored vehicle twisted around the narrow and icy roads. I clenched the armrest, leaned forward, and stared straight ahead. I wasn't afraid that the car would sail over a guardrail. I was afraid that we wouldn't get to Horst Werner in time.

Van der Heuvel's computer had yielded his contact list, and in addition to the complete playlist of Henri Benoit's videos, I'd turned over my transcripts of Henri's confessions in the trailer. I'd explained to the police the connection between Henri Benoit, serial killer for hire, and the people who paid him.

The cops were elated.

Henri's trail of victims, dozens of horrific killings in Europe and America and Asia, had been linked only since the recent murders of the two young women in Barbados. Now the Swiss police were optimistic that with the right kind of pressure, Horst Werner would give Henri up.

As we sped toward Werner's villa, law enforcement agents were moving in on members of the Alliance in countries around the world. These should have been triumphant hours for me, but I was in a state of raw panic.

I'd made calls to friends, but there were no phones where Amanda was staying. I didn't know if it would be hours or days before I would know if she was safe. And although Van der Heuvel had referred to Henri as a toy, I had more evidence than before of his ruthlessness, his resourcefulness, his lust for revenge. And I finally understood why Henri had drafted me to write his book. He wanted the Alliance, his puppeteers, to be caught so that he could be free of them, to change his identity again and lead his own life.

The car I was riding in braked, wheels shimmying on ice and gravel, the heavy vehicle sliding to a stop at the foot of a stone wall. The wall fronted a fortresslike compound built into the side of a hill.

Car doors opened and slammed, radios chattered. Armored commando units flanked us, dozens of men in flak jackets who were armed with automatic weapons, grenade launchers, and high-tech equipment I couldn't even name.

Fifty yards away, across a snowy field, glass shattered. A window had been knocked out in a corner room of the villa.

Bullets flew, and grenades boomed as they exploded inside the target area.

Under covering fire, a dozen agents charged the villa, and I heard the rumble of snow cracking loose from the steep grade behind Horst's stronghold. There was shouting in German, more small-arms fire, and I visualized Horst Werner's dead body coming out on a stretcher, the final act of this takedown.

With Horst Werner dead, how would we find Henri?

The massive front door opened. The men who were leaning against the wall aimed their weapons.

And then I saw him.

Horst Werner, the terror who Van der Heuvel had described as a man with long arms and steel fists, "the last man you'd ever want to meet," came out of his house of stone. He was barrel-chested, with a goatee and gold wire-framed glasses, and he wore a blue overcoat. Even with his hands folded on top of his head, he had a confident "military" bearing.

This was the twisted man behind it all, the master voyeur, the murderer's murderer, the Wizard of some hellacious, perverted Oz.

He was alive, and he was under arrest.

Chapter 121

HORST WERNER WAS BUNDLED into an armored car, and Swiss cops piled in behind him. I went with two Interpol investigators in another. An hour after the takedown, we arrived at the police station in Bern, and the questioning of Horst Werner began.

I watched anxiously from a small observation chamber with a window onto the interrogation room.

As Werner waited for his lawyer to arrive, his face streamed with sweat. I knew that the heat had been turned up, that the front legs of Werner's chair were shorter than the back, and that Captain Voelker, who was questioning him, was not getting much information.

A young officer stood behind my chair and interpreted for me. "Herr Werner says, 'I do not know Henri Benoit. I haven't killed anyone! I watch, but I do nothing.'"

Captain Voelker left the interrogation room briefly and returned holding what looked like a CD. Voelker spoke to Werner, and my interpreter told me that this disc had been found inside a DVD player, along with a cache of other discs in Werner's library. Werner's face stiffened as Voelker inserted the disc into a player.

What video was this? The Gina Prazzi murder? Maybe some other killing by Henri?

I angled my chair so that I could see the monitor, and I took a deep breath.

A man's bowed head came on the screen. I could see him from the crown of his skull to the middle of his T-shirt. When he lifted his swollen and bloodied face, he turned away from the camera, away from me.

From the one brief glimpse, the man looked to be in his thirties and had no distinguishing features.

An interrogation was clearly in progress. I felt the most extreme tension as I watched. Off camera, a voice said, "Onnn-reee, say the words."

My heart jumped. Was it him? Had Henri been caught?

The bloodied prisoner said to his questioner, "I'm not Henri. My name is Antoine Pascal. You've got the wrong man."

"It's not hard to say, is it, Henri?" asked the voice from the wings. "Just say the words, and maybe we will let you go."

"I tell you, *I'm not Henri.* My identification is in my pocket. Get my wallet."

The interrogator finally came into view. He looked to be in his twenties, dark-haired, had a spiderweb tattooed on his neck and the inked netting continued to his left cheek. He adjusted the camera lens so that there was a wide shot of the bare, windowless room, a cellar lit by a single bulb. The subject was hog-tied to a chair.

The tattooed man said, "Okay, 'Antoine.' We've seen your ID, and we admire how you can become someone else. But I am getting tired of the game. Say it or don't say it. I give you to the count of three."

The tattooed man held a long, serrated knife in his hand, and he slapped it against his thigh as he counted. Then he said, "Time is up. I think this is what you've always wanted, Henri. To know that moment between life and death. Correct?"

The voice I'd heard from the hostage was familiar. So was the look in his pale gray eyes. It *was* Henri. I knew it now.

Suddenly I was filled with horror as I realized what was going to happen. I wanted to shout out to Henri, express some emotion that I didn't understand myself.

I had been prepared to kill him, but I was not capable of *this*. I couldn't just watch.

Henri spit at the lens, and the tattooed man grabbed a hank of his brown hair. He pulled his neck taut. "Say the words!" he yelled.

Then he made four powerful sawing strokes at the back of Henri's neck with the knife, separating the screaming man's head from his shoulders.

Blood spurted and poured everywhere. On Henri. On his killer. On the camera lens.

"Onnnn-reee. *Henri*. Can you hear me?" asked the executioner. He brought the severed head on a level with the camera.

I backed away from the glass, but I couldn't stop watching the video. It seemed to me that Henri was making eye contact with me through the monitor, through the glass. His eyes were still open—and then he *blinked*. He actually did that—*blinked*.

The executioner bent to the camera, his chin dripping sweat and blood, smiling with satisfaction, as he said, *"Is everybody happy?"*

Chapter 122

GORGE ROSE IN MY THROAT, and I was trembling horribly, perspiring heavily. I suppose I was relieved that Henri was dead, but at the same time my blood was screaming through my arteries. I reeled from the sickening, indelible images that had been freshly branded on my brain.

Inside the silent interrogation room, Horst Werner's unfeeling expression hadn't changed, but then he looked up and smiled sweetly as the door opened, and a man in a dark suit came in, put a hand on his shoulder.

My interpreter confirmed what I'd guessed; Werner's lawyer had arrived.

The conversation between the lawyer and Captain Voelker was a short, staccato volley that boiled down to one unalterable fact: the police didn't have enough to hold Werner at this time.

I watched in shock as Werner strolled from the interrogation room with his lawyer, a free man.

A moment later, Captain Voelker joined me in the observation room, told me emphatically that it wasn't over yet. Warrants for Werner's bank and phone records had been obtained. Alliance members around the world would be squeezed, he said. It was just a matter of time before they had Werner locked up again. Interpol and the FBI were on the case.

I walked out of the police station on unsteady legs, but into clean air and daylight. A limo was waiting to drive me to the airport. I told the driver to hurry. He started the engine and raised the glass divider. But still, the car took off and maintained only a moderate speed.

Inside my mind, Van der Heuvel was saying, *"Be afraid of Horst Werner"* — and I was. Werner would find out about my transcripts of Henri's confession. It was admissible evidence against him and the Peepers. I had replaced Henri as the Witness, the one who could bring Werner and the rest of them down on multiple murder charges.

My brain sped across continents. I slapped at the divider, shouted to the driver, *"Go faster. Drive faster."*

I had to get to Amanda, by plane, by helicopter, by pack mule. I had to get to her first. We had to draw the walls around us and stay hidden, I didn't know for how long, and I didn't care.

I knew what Horst Werner would do if he found us.

I knew.

And I couldn't stop myself from wondering one other thing. Was Henri really dead?

What had I just watched back there at the station?

That *blink* of his eye—was it a wink? Was the film some kind of video trick he'd played?

"Drive faster."

Epilogue

By Benjamin Hawkins

A letter to my readers.

When this book came out, the sales far exceeded my publisher's expectations, but it had never occurred to me that it would be in thousands of bookstores around the world—and that I would be living in a shack on the side of a mountain in a country not my own.

Some would say, "Be careful what you wish for because you may get it." And I would answer, "I got what I wished for in a way I could not have imagined."

I am with Amanda, my love, and she has adapted easily to the breathtaking beauty and solitude of our new life together. She is bilingual, and has taught me to speak another language, and to cook. From the start, we planted a vegetable garden and took weekly hikes down the mountain to a charming village for bread and cheese and supplies.

Amanda and I were married in this village, in a small church made by devout hands, blessed by a priest and a congregation of people who have taken Amanda and me into their hearts. The Foozle will be baptized here when he comes into the world, and I can hardly wait for him to be born. Our son.

But what is his birthright? What promises can I make him?

The first time I saw the off-road vehicle climbing the rut that winds up from the valley, I armed my bride and lined up guns on the table near the window.

The car was a private carrier that my publisher had hired to bring me mail and news of the world. After I searched the driver and let him go, I read everything Zagami sent me. I learned that the Peepers had been rounded up, that every one of them will go to trial for murder, and for conspiracy to commit murder, and for lesser crimes that will keep them in prisons for as long as they live.

Some days, my mind fastens on Horst Werner, his long arms and steel fists, and as his trial drags on, I think, *At least I know where he is.*

And then I think about Henri.

Sometimes I run the images of Henri's death through my mind like a length of film through the sprockets of an old-time film projector. I watch his horrific execution and convince myself that he really is dead.

At other times, I'm just as sure that he has fooled everyone. That he is living his life under an assumed name — as I am. And, one day, he will find us.

I thank my loyal readers for your letters, your concern, and your prayers for our safety. Life is good here. Sometimes I am very happy, but I can't quite dismiss my fear of the psychopathic monster I knew too well—and I cannot ever forget the McDaniels family, Levon, Barbara, and Kim.

Acknowledgments

The authors are grateful to these fine professionals for giving generously of their time and expertise: Dr. Humphrey Germaniuk, Capt. Richard Conklin, Clint Van Zandt, Dr. David Smith, Dr. Maria Paige, and Allison Adato.

We also thank our excellent researchers: Rebecca DiLiberto, Ellie Shurtleff, Kai McBride, Sage Hyman, Alan Graison, Nick Dragash, and Lynn Colomello.

Special thanks to Michael Hampton, Jim and Dorian Morley, Sue and Ben Emdin, and to Mary Jordan, who makes it all possible.

THE WORLD ALL AROUND YOU.
LIFE AS YOU KNOW IT.
EVERYTHING YOU LOVE.
IT ALL CHANGES — NOW.

This is the story I was born to tell.
Read on, while you still can.
—JAMES PATTERSON

COMING IN DECEMBER 2009

Prologue

WISTY

IT'S OVERWHELMING. A city's worth of angry faces staring at me like I'm a wicked criminal—which, I promise you, *I'm not*. The stadium is filled to capacity—*past* capacity. People are standing in the aisles, the stairwells, on the concrete ramparts, and a few extra thousand are camped out on the playing field. There are no football teams here today. They wouldn't be able to get out of the locker-room tunnels if they tried.

This total abomination is being broadcast on TV and on the Internet too. All the useless magazines are here, and the useless newspapers. Yep, I see cameramen in elevated roosts at intervals around the stadium.

There's even one of those remote-controlled cameras that runs around on wires above the field. There it is—hovering just in front of the stage, bobbing slightly in the breeze.

So, there are undoubtedly millions more eyes watching

than I can see. But it's the ones here in the stadium that are breaking my heart. To be confronted with tens, maybe even hundreds of thousands of curious, uncaring, or at least indifferent, faces...talk about *frightening*.

And there are no moist eyes, never mind tears.

No words of protest.

No stomping feet.

No fists raised in solidarity.

No inkling that anybody's even thinking of surging forward, breaking through the security cordon, and carrying my family to safety.

Clearly, this is not a good day for us Allgoods.

In fact, as the countdown ticker flashes on the giant video screens at either end of the stadium, it's looking like this will be our *last* day.

It's a point driven home by the very tall, bald man up in the tower they've erected midfield—he looks like a cross between a Supreme Court chief justice and Ming the Merciless. I know who he is. I've actually met him. He's The One Who Is The One.

Directly behind his Oneness is a huge N.O. banner—*the New Order*.

And then the crowd begins to chant, almost sing, "The One Who Is The One! The One Who Is The One!"

Imperiously, The One raises his hand, and his hooded lackeys on the stage push us forward, at least as far as the ropes around our necks will allow.

I see my brother, Whit, handsome and brave, looking down at the platform mechanism. Calculating if there's any way to jam it, some way to keep it from unlatching and dropping us to our neck-snapping deaths. Wondering if there's some last-minute way out of this.

I see my mother crying quietly. Not for herself, of course, but for Whit and me.

I see my father, his tall frame stooped with resignation, but smiling at me and my brother — trying to keep our spirits up, reminding us that there's no point in being miserable in our last moments on this planet.

But I'm getting ahead of myself. I'm supposed to be providing an *introduction* here, not the details of our public *execution*.

So let's go back a bit....

One

WHIT

SOMETIMES YOU WAKE up and the world is just plain different.

The noise of a circling helicopter is what made me open my eyes. A cold, blue-white light forced its way through the blinds and flooded the living room. Almost like it was day.

But it wasn't.

I peered at the clock on the DVD player through blurry eyes: 2:10 a.m.

I became aware of a steady *drub, drub, drub*—like the sound of a heavy heartbeat. Throbbing. Pressing in. Getting closer.

What's going on?

I staggered to the window, forcing my body back to life after two hours passed out on the sofa, and peeked through the slats.

And then I stepped back and rubbed my eyes. Hard.

Because there's no way I had seen what I'd seen. And there was no way I had heard what I'd heard.

Was it really the steady, relentless footfall of hundreds of soldiers? Marching on my street in perfect unison?

My street wasn't close enough to the center of town to be on any holiday parade routes, much less to have armed men in combat fatigues coursing down it in the dead of night.

I shook my head and bounced up and down a few times kind of like I do in my warm-ups. *Wake up, Whit.* I slapped myself a couple of times for good measure. And then I looked again.

There they were. Soldiers marching down our street. Hundreds of them as clear as day, made visible by a half-dozen truck-mounted spotlights.

Just one thought was running laps inside my head: *This can't be happening. This can't be happening. This can't be happening.*

Then I remembered the elections, the new government, the ravings of my parents about the trouble the country was in, the special broadcasts on TV, the political petitions my classmates were circulating online, the heated debates between teachers at school. None of it meant anything to me until that second.

And before I could piece it all together, the vanguard of the formation stopped in front of my house.

Almost faster than I could comprehend, two armed squads detached themselves from the phalanx and sprinted across the lawn like commandos, one running around the back of the house, the other taking position in front.

I jumped back from the window. I could tell they weren't here to protect me and my family. I had to warn Mom, Dad, Wisty—

But just as I started to yell, the front door was knocked off its hinges.

TWO

WISTY

IT'S QUITE HIDEOUS to get kidnapped in the dead of night, right inside your own home. It went something like this.

I awoke to the chaotic crashing of overturning furniture, quickly followed by the sounds of shattering glass, possibly some of Mom's china.

Oh God, Whit, I thought, shaking my head sleepily. My older brother had grown four inches and gained thirty pounds of muscle in the past year. Which made him the biggest and fastest quarterback around, and, I must say, the most intimidating player on our regional high school's undefeated football team.

Off the playing field, though, Whit could be about as clumsy as your average bear—if your average bear were hopped-up on a case of Red Bull and full of himself because he could bench-press 275 and every girl in school thought he was the hunk of all hunks.

I rolled over and pulled my pillow around my head. Even

before the drinking started, Whit couldn't walk through our house without knocking something over. Total bull-in-the-china-shop syndrome.

But that wasn't the real problem tonight, I knew.

Because three months ago, his girlfriend, Celia, had literally *vanished* without a trace. And by now everyone was thinking she probably would never come back. Her parents were totally messed up about it, and so was Whit. To be honest, so was I. Celia was—*is*—very pretty, smart, not conceited at all. She's this totally cool girl, even though she has money. Celia's father owns the luxury car dealership in town, and her mom is a former beauty queen. I couldn't believe something like that would happen to someone like Celia.

I heard my parents' bedroom door open and snuggled back down into my cozy, flannel-sheeted bed.

Next came Dad's booming voice, and he was as angry as I've ever heard him.

"This can't be happening! You have no right to be here. Leave our house *now!*"

I bolted upright, wide awake. Next came more crashing sounds, and I thought I heard someone moan in pain. Had Whit fallen and cracked his head? Had my dad been hurt?

Jeez, Louise, I thought, scrambling out of bed. "I'm coming, Dad! Are you all right? Dad?"

And then the nightmare to start a lifetime of nightmares truly began.

I gasped as my bedroom door crashed open. Two hulking men in dark gray uniforms burst into my room, glaring at me as if I were a fugitive terrorist cell operative.

"It's her! Wisteria Allgood!" one said, and a light bright enough to illuminate an airplane hangar obliterated the darkness.

I tried to shield my eyes as my heart kicked into over-drive. "Who are *you?!*" I asked. "What are you doing in *my freaking bedroom?*"

Witch & Wizard.
In stores December 2009.

About the Authors

JAMES PATTERSON is one of the bestselling writers of all time, with more than 170 million books sold worldwide. He is the author of the top-selling detective series of the past twenty years—the Alex Cross novels, including *Kiss the Girls* and *Along Came a Spider,* both of which were made into hit movies. Mr. Patterson also writes the bestselling Women's Murder Club novels, set in San Francisco, and the new series of #1 *New York Times* bestsellers featuring Detective Michael Bennett of the NYPD. He won an Edgar Award, the mystery world's highest honor, for his first novel. He lives in Florida.

James Patterson's lifelong passion for books and reading led him to launch a new Web site, ReadKiddoRead.com, which helps parents, grandparents, teachers, and librarians find the very best children's books for their kids.

MAXINE PAETRO is a novelist and journalist. She lives with her husband in New York.

Books by James Patterson

FEATURING ALEX CROSS

Cross Country

Double Cross

Cross

Mary, Mary

London Bridges

The Big Bad Wolf

Four Blind Mice

Violets Are Blue

Roses Are Red

Pop Goes the Weasel

Cat & Mouse

Jack & Jill

Kiss the Girls

Along Came a Spider

THE WOMEN'S MURDER CLUB

The 8th Confession (with Maxine Paetro)

7th Heaven (with Maxine Paetro)

The 6th Target (with Maxine Paetro)

The 5th Horseman (with Maxine Paetro)

4th of July (with Maxine Paetro)

3rd Degree (with Andrew Gross)

2nd Chance (with Andrew Gross)

1st to Die

FEATURING MICHAEL BENNETT

Run for Your Life (with Michael Ledwidge)

Step on a Crack (with Michael Ledwidge)

THE JAMES PATTERSON PAGETURNERS

Daniel X: Watch the Skies

MAX: A Maximum Ride Novel

The Dangerous Days of Daniel X

The Final Warning: A Maximum Ride Novel

Maximum Ride: Saving the World and Other Extreme Sports

Maximum Ride: School's Out — Forever

Maximum Ride: The Angel Experiment

OTHER BOOKS

For previews of upcoming books by James Patterson and more information about the author, visit www.JamesPatterson.com.